My Highlander

The Highlanders

Book 8

Terry Spear

My Highlander

Copyright © 2017 Terry Spear

Cover by Cora Graphics

Discover more about Terry Spear at:

http://www.terryspear.com/

ISBN-13: 978-1-63311-029-8

DEDICATION

To Michelle Haumberger. Thanks for loving my books for years and years. Hope you love this Highlander, and he sweeps you off your feet! May you dream good dreams of Highlanders of old.

ACKNOWLEDGMENTS

Thanks so much to Dottie Jones, Sandi Carstensen, and Donna Fournier for helping me make this book so much better. No matter how many reads and how many eyes look at these, it's so easy to miss typos and such. I so appreciate them for helping to catch the bloopers. And thanks, Donna, for always being there when I need to bounce stuff...lots and lots and lots of stuff...off you!

Also, many thanks to Cora Bignardi for the beautiful cover. And to all my readers who encourage me to keep on writing from world to world!! YOU are my inspiration.

NOTE FROM AUTHOR

Scotland is magical and some of my ancestors came from there and from England, Ireland, Wales, Germany, and France, and we learned that our MacNeill line had Viking roots. Just like it is anywhere in the world, people move, marry, have children who represent not only their mother's heritage, but their father's, a combination of all those who came before them. Even back in the times of old. I hope that you enjoy The Highlanders series!

CHAPTER 1

Quinn eyed his older brother with contempt. If Cormac wanted to steal a chief's daughter from the Hebrides Islands to wed her, then Cormac should be the one to do it. Quinn halfway suspected his brother thought this time he wouldn't survive. That Cormac didn't want the woman, as much as he wanted Quinn to face the very real chance of dying at the hands of the woman's kin. Quinn was surprised Cormac hadn't sent him to fight a battle to the east where he'd sent many of his men in support of a clan he was allied with. Why not let Quinn chance getting killed in *that* battle? Or even set it up so that he did?

For two months, his brother had sent him on missions where he was ambushed, and Quinn swore Cormac had planned it. This time, the sorry lot accompanying Quinn were belligerent, all five of them mercenaries, not his own kin. They were more likely to turn tail and run, than fight for his brother's cause, leaving Quinn to face stealing the lass away on his own. None of the men had family and Quinn suspected his brother felt no one would miss them should they fail to return to the clan. That was the way Cormac dealt with men he'd rather be rid of. Send them on a task with little chance of survival.

"You will do this for me, aye?" his brother asked, his blond brows raised in question. "Fenella has no other way to leave her family to join me, if you dinna fetch her. And I've told her I was sending you to rescue her. Her kin are a disagreeable lot and dinna want her wed to me, but we will well suit and they'll see that in time."

"Aye." Though Quinn thought his brother wanted to wed a lass to make an alliance with another clan, not an enemy of one, so this was a surprise to him. Unless Quinn wished to leave their lands for good, he had little recourse but to do as his brother commanded. Where would he go otherwise? What would he do?

He supposed he could join Malcolm MacNeill's clan for a while, see if he could help to fight his battles instead. They had become friends once, while they were allied with his da and fought several battles together. When Quinn's da was killed in one of those battles, Cormac had taken over and accused Malcolm of not providing as many men as he had promised, which was the reason Quinn's da had died.

Truth was, with more men or not enough, Quinn had to remind himself that their da could still have been cut down like he was in the field that day. Maybe Malcolm wouldn't welcome Quinn into his clan after the accusation Cormac had made against him.

Even though Cormac seemed to despise Quinn, the

warriors he fought with, and the lassies he teased, appreciated him. Which, Quinn felt, irked his brother even more. Cormac was well thought of enough to lead the clan, though not as well liked. Still, Quinn didn't understand the animosity his brother felt for him.

"You dinna looked pleased with the task," Cormac chided. "Should I send someone else to get the task done?"

As if his brother would send anyone else to steal the lass away from her kin. Quinn stood taller, prouder, and frowned at his brother. "I will leave as soon as I can."

"See that you do. I canna wait to bed the lass. Be careful that you dinna get yourself killed in the process. I wouldna be able to live with myself."

Then why send Quinn into a situation where he could very well die? His brother loved to twist the truth.

Quinn gave him a quick incline of his head, and Cormac turned his attention to one of his men. "Tell the men that I want to go on a hunt."

That was Quinn's cue to leave, and he hastened out of the great hall where his brother loved to rule with an iron fist.

Quinn's good friends, Lorne and Liam, hurried to join him. "I asked the chief if we could sail with you, but he said he had more important business for us to take care of," Liam said.

"More important than securing his bride?" Quinn arched a brow at his friend.

Liam glanced around. Seeing no one within earshot, he said, "He means to kill you this time."

"I'm certain he tried the other times too," Quinn said

dryly.

"That goes without saying."

"I'm hard to kill. He should have learned that by now."
Quinn meant it as a jest, even though it seemed to be true.
Liam's mood was as dark as his black hair and brown
eyes. He didn't even crack a smile like he usually did when
Quinn tried to make light of a dangerous situation. Instead,
Liam's brooding expression darkened further.

"Keep on his good side, or you'll be assigned such tasks
in the future," Quinn warned. Unlike the way Quinn felt
about his brother, ever since their da had died and his
brother had taken over the clan, Quinn's friends were like
real family to him.

"I have half a mind to stow away on the birlinn to aid
you."

"That would be a grave mistake, my friend. Before
long, I will return with the lassie in hand."

"And then your brother will come up with another
mission to have you killed."

"I can only focus on one assignment at a time. Take
care, Liam, Lorne. I will return soon."

"If those five lazy louts accompanying you end up
returning without you, they're dead men," Liam said.

"Aye, I will help Liam," Lorne said.

"What if they return with the lady, and I'm the only
casualty?" Quinn continued to walk to his chamber to pack.

"We will wait until the time is right, then wring the
truth out of them. Then we will kill them. Your death will be
avenged," Liam said

Quinn slapped him on the back. "You are both good

and loyal friends. I will return. Too many lasses will miss me if I dinna."

Lorne rubbed his chin in thought. "Mayhap you should stay away for a time."

Quinn smiled. "I will see you both upon my return." But Quinn knew not to take this mission lightly. The gods would have to favor him if he were to return home in one piece.

Once Quinn packed and headed to the harbor, he thought maybe a storm, which was off in the distance, would bypass them. It looked to be heading out to sea. He and the other men boarded the birlinn. The sturdy oak vessel was outfitted with a single mast, the square sail made of thick, threaded wool, small squares sewn together, and the ropes made of heather or moss-fir. The long-ships could be sailed or rowed. This one had a dozen oars and three men per oar. The ships were often used to carry troops to battle, cattle, and people and other items for transport, though Quinn had never known them to use one to steal a bride before.

He prayed the weather would hold out, and it seemed the captain wasn't worried about it. Since he was used to navigating in these waters, he should know.

The first part of the journey, the sea was rough, the sky filled with clouds, but not overly dark. It worsened the closer they got to the island, the clouds suddenly darkening, and he knew they were in for rain. But it was much worse, the wind creating massive waves, the rain pouring down in a deluge, the sky nearly black as night. Lightning flashed overhead, and thunder boomed and crackled with a vengeance. The wind whipped the sea into a frenzy. Quinn was certain they wouldn't make it. Not with the way the ship creaked and groaned under the assault. Or from the panicked looks on the sailors' faces.

With a thunderous boom, the single mast snapped in two and fell toward the deck. The sailors, Quinn, and the mercenaries dove out of its path.

Cries of terror sounded as two sailors were crushed under the weight of the mast. The broken mast and voluminous sail slammed into the sea and dragged through the water like a soggy anchor.

Everyone was trying to keep from being washed overboard. Even so, the five mercenaries conferred briefly with one another and then headed straight for Quinn. Two of them brandished their swords, letting him know their intent.

The rain and wind whipped everything in its path, and they were all drenched, the air cold and blustery. If they'd just wait, they'd probably all end up in watery graves, no need to fight. But it appeared they had a mission—and killing him couldn't wait. Maybe they worried that they might die, and he'd still survive. If they did nothing else with their miserable lives, they were going to end his.

Not planning to give them the chance, he withdrew his sword and grabbed some of the rigging flailing in the high winds to keep from falling while the ship rocked in the high seas. The sailors shouted, trying to do what they could to keep the ship from breaking up, or themselves from being washed overboard.

"My brother paid you to kill me, aye?" Quinn needn't have asked. He knew the truth.

"Everyone says you canna die," Griswold shouted in the high winds, the surliest of the five. If anyone looked cross-wise at him, he was ready to slit throats. "We plan to prove how wrong they are."

"'Tis true I canna die. You know it to be so." Not that Quinn was so conceited to believe such, but if it made any of the five fear him, he would do or say whatever he could to improve his odds. He knew he couldn't fight all five of the brigands at once and hope to win.

The ship rolled heavily to the leeward side and two of the mercenaries collided with each other and snatched at the railing. Another fell and landed hard on the deck, sliding in seawater. The other two grabbed the railing. Once the ship rocked back, Griswold and Ivar lunged at him, swinging their swords before another wave slammed into the ship.

Holding onto the wet rigging, Quinn kicked out with his feet and slammed his boots into Griswold's stomach, knocking him back. With the water washing over the deck and the rocking and rolling of the ship, Griswold lost his footing and fell back on his arse.

Quinn immediately swung his sword at Ivar and the two swords clashed with resounding clanks.

One of the other men had gotten to his feet and rushed at Quinn with a *sgian dubh* in his clenched fist. Quinn swung around and cut him from his shoulder to his hip and the man dropped his weapon, clutching his belly and screaming like a wee lassie. Another of the mercenaries tried to advance on Quinn. The next wave crashed over the side of the ship and washed him and the wounded man overboard.

Ivar came at Quinn again, Griswold having a time getting to his feet between dealing with the wet slippery deck and the rolling ship.

The other mercenary was holding onto the railing, waiting for Ivar to finish Quinn off, but the man didn't have hold of any rigging like Quinn did, and his arms were flailing as he tried to keep his balance and dash in to fight Quinn again.

Then Ivar rushed forward, swinging his sword. Quinn leaped out of the way and came around and struck Ivar's sword again, this time so hard, the man lost it. He lunged for his sword, and Griswold came in for the kill. But then his gaze shifted to the rigging above Quinn, and he assumed the man hoped to cut it loose, so Quinn wouldn't have the advantage. He swung forward and struck at Griswold, whose only recourse was to defend himself and fall back, slipping, falling on his arse again, and sliding across the deck.

Quinn turned to see where Ivar had gone and witnessed the biggest wave cresting that he'd ever seen. It slammed into the ship and the birlinn cracked in two. This was the end.

Not that Quinn was giving up. He'd only begun to fight.

He let go of the rigging as men yelled and fell into the boiling sea.

The next wave washed Quinn overboard. He struck crates and barrels hard before he hit the cold water. He gasped, got a mouthful of seawater, and spit it out. Trying to keep his head above water, he couldn't avoid the ship's wreckage as splintered wood struck him in the head, shoulder, and ribs. In the high waves and pouring rain, with lightning stabbing the restless sea, he swam toward the island, maybe a mile away. He prayed he wasn't making a mistake and was heading in the right direction.

***

"Avelina! Come quickly. An injured man, mayhap even dead, is sprawled out on the shore. Shipwrecked during the storm, from the looks of it. Pieces of splintered wood are scattered about the sand," said Fenella, Avelina's cousin and the chief's daughter, as she ran up the stairs to Avelina's chamber to fetch her.

Dashing into the stairwell, Avelina started to join her down the stairs, but stopped. "Wait. I must get my sword."

"He might have died."

"You didna check him to be certain?" Avelina cast a look over her shoulder as her cousin followed her up the stairs, her blond hair lighter than Avelina's. *Her* hair was more reddish in color. But they both had blue, blue eyes and they looked very much like sisters.

"Nay. I came straight away to get you."

"Och, he may be dead then, and we will have to bury him." They had trouble enough with the storm that had damaged several farms and the western wall protecting the keep. There was barely anyone able to do the work. The few men who were left behind were responsible for defending the keep and fishing for food when they needed it.

"Better that than having to fight the devil on our lands. Though mayhap he can rebuild some of the farmers' damaged crofts after the storm tore them down. With none of the able-bodied men able to do the work now, we have enough chores to manage."

"A fighting devil?" Avelina grabbed her sword from her chamber and hurried down the circular stairs in the tower to the great hall and headed for the door.

Fenella eyed Avelina's sword, created just for her so that she could wield the much shorter sword in self-defense. "Could be. He had a *sgian dubh* in his boot and a sword belted at his waist. I dinna think you will be a match for him, should he come to and want to fight you, or worse."

"What would be worse than wanting to fight me?" Avelina shook her head at her cousin. "He's wounded, so you say. And besides, I have killed three marauders on my own."

"*Mostly*, on your own," Fenella reminded her.

Avelina did not need the reminder. She was glad that her da had approved her learning to fight with a sword to protect the women and children who could not protect themselves, if brigands attacked and she was needed, even if it was as a last resort. She knew she wasn't as strong as the men, even the ones she had mostly killed. "Except for the one. I took him down all on my own." Though she was well aware she had the advantage that time or she wouldn't have managed. Standing high above him on the stairs where he couldn't swing at her, she'd been so angry that he'd tried to kill a bairn that she'd had more strength than she ever thought she could call on.

Still, no matter how much she practiced, she didn't have the weight or massive muscles, and long reach of their great swords. But she was fleet of foot, and she knew every bit of the keep, the grounds, and the outlying farms. She always used what she could to her advantage like her da and others had taught her. "You are sure he is not a sailor then? Or a fisherman?"

"A warrior, by the looks of him. Muscled, strong, tall, wounded. Not an archer, unless he lost his bow and quiver of arrows. But he wouldna be carrying a sword too then, I wouldna think."

"That doesna bode well. Unless he is dead."

They made their way across a creek and rushed over several rocky knolls covered in heather and bracken and finally reached the cliffs and the path that wound down to the shore. They'd never found a man alive before, who'd been washed up on their shores after a storm. It *would* have to be when most of their men were gone, off to support a war between clans on the mainland of Scotland. Three of the men left behind were off hunting. Only seven were left to defend the keep at all costs, and she wasn't about to bother them when she was certain she would have this well in hand.

Especially since it would be a miracle if this man had survived. But he could be the worst sort of trouble too.

"What do we do with him if he's alive? We canna put him in the dungeon."

Avelina glanced at her cousin, who was her age. They'd always been close growing up. Her father served Fenella's father, Avelina's uncle, as his second-in-command. The two men were brothers and best of friends. "We dinna have a dungeon."

"Aye, which is why we canna put him in one. What are

we going to do with him, if he's alive?" Fenella asked.

"I should've brought Wolf."

"To kill the injured man?" Fenella's eyes widened with surprise. "Shouldna we make sure he's no' going to be trouble first? He could repair our farmers' crofts, mayhap," she reminded Avelina, "and we need some muscle to help build the west wall that was damaged in the storm. It will take a lot more men than we have right now."

"You said he is injured." Avelina was beginning to worry that the man was waiting to cut them down with his sword, if he was as armed and dangerous looking as Fenella believed, and he wasn't badly injured or dead.

"He is. He was lying still in the sand, his head and arm bleeding. The tide had gone out, but if we dinna move him, it will carry him back out."

"If he is dead, the tide can take him out, and the fish can eat him, which would save us from having to bury him." Avelina didn't mean it, of course. She could just imagine the body being drawn out and rolled back in with each new tide. What a horrible sight and smell that would be.

When they finally reached the shore, there was no sign of any man. Fenella looked right, then left.

"Where is he? Farther down the beach?" Avelina asked, believing her cousin had been mistaken as to where he had ended up exactly.

"He was right there." Fenella motioned to a group of rocks. "Right next to those rocks. And his head was bleeding. I didna imagine it. He was right there." Fenella pointed again toward the rocks.

"Maybe he's a selkie and swam off again." When

Avelina was a child, her mother had told her the stories of selkies who removed their seal skins, becoming human, and luring a woman or man with their beauty. Some believed the stories were true. Some did not. When Avelina had bairns of her own, she would tell her children about them and let them decide for themselves. She didn't believe in selkies, but it didn't mean they weren't real.

"He wasna naked. Almost though. A selkie would be naked as a new-born bairn." Fenella sounded quite sure of it, and she did believe in them.

"Nearly naked?" Avelina had tended to men's wounds since she was a young lass, and she was used to seeing men nearly naked, but she'd known them forever. Tending to a naked stranger was an entirely different matter, especially if he was a danger to them.

"Aye. His plaid was draped over a leg, his shirt ripped to shreds."

Avelina stopped to look at her.

"He is well-muscled. I told you so. Mayhap he's beyond those rocks." Fenella motioned to another group of rocks, waiting for Avelina to move beyond them, her sword at the ready.

Not that Avelina could fight a warrior and win the battle, if he was healthy and ready to kill her. "If he is beyond them, he had to have... wait. There are tracks." She pointed to the crawl marks that the water hadn't washed away. "He crawled beyond the edge of the rocks. And if he has any clothes at all, he isna a selkie. Come on." Instead of following his trail in the white sand, she climbed to the top of the rocks to give her an advantage. When she crested them, she saw a man lying on the other side of them on the damp sand, his eyes closed, his brown hair streaked by the sun, lying in straggles across his cheek.

Fenella was right. He was nearly naked, a muscled warrior, a wet plaid draped over his leg and his most private parts, his long shirt tattered, his sword still sheathed at his waist. A gash across his forehead and right arm were bleeding.

Splintered wood had washed up on shore near him, the only remnants left of the ship he must have sailed on. Sometimes, another storm or the shifting tide would carry more of a ship's goods to the shore for weeks afterward, so they might be able to salvage something from the shipwreck. She just hoped they didn't find any more bodies, dead or alive.

Avelina turned to her cousin. "Return at once to the keep to retrieve some of my brother's clothes for him and rags, so I can stop the bleeding."

"And leave you alone with him?" Fenella sounded horrified.

Avelina considered the man. "You can take his sword and *sgian dubh,* and then he willna be armed. Just try not to be seen with them. Send Wolf to me. He'll reach me a lot faster than you will, and he will be additional protection if I should need it."

Fenella hesitated, studied the prone man, took a deep breath, and let it out, then nodded. "I will make haste."

When Fenella scrambled down the rocks to return to the keep, Avelina climbed down to where the man was lying and poked at his shoulder with the toe of her shoe, but he didn't move. She watched as his chest rose and fell, assuring herself that he was still living, his breathing steady, not labored. A rough stubble covered his square jaw. He was bewitchingly braw, unconscious, and looked disarmingly safe, but she knew not to be taken in by the deception. She would do well to keep her distance until Wolf was standing at her side, ready to tear the man to shreds if he showed any indication he wished to harm her.

Yet, she couldn't help herself and crouched closer to brush her hand over his sun-warmed muscles speckled with bits of white sand. She swore his breathing sped up a bit. She quickly rose to her feet, stepped back, and stared down at the man, observing him for any other sign of movement. Was he pretending to be dead? Or a selkie who had cast his seal skin into the briny sea, luring a maiden to fall in love with him? He couldn't be. Not when he was partially clothed and was revealing so much of his glorious self.

CHAPTER 2

Quinn knew he was in a bad way when he made it to the sandy beach, his head and arm paining him, both burning and stinging at the same time, his ribs aching, but he'd been lucky to even make it to shore. He hoped the remaining four men who had accompanied him hadn't survived. Even if they might have been an aid to each other in hostile territory, they no doubt would still be trying to kill him. He didn't believe they'd behave any differently if he met up with them on the island when they'd tried to murder him on the ship during the height of the storm. He hadn't been sure if the storm had meant his salvation, or his demise, but since he was still alive, he'd say it was his salvation, despite the tight fix he could be in now.

Then he heard two women coming, confused about where he'd disappeared to. The fact they'd come alone while looking for him, and not sent men who might have killed him, said a lot about their situation. They didn't have any men close by to take care of the matter. No one in their right mind would send lasses to do a man's job. Not when the one woman knew full well he was armed and could be dangerous.

The women, cousins, from what they'd said, must have thought him mortally wounded since they hadn't lowered their voices while searching for him, alerting him they were growing closer. Despite the crashing of the waves against the beach and the seabirds calling out high above, he'd heard them well enough. He just hoped the other men with him hadn't survived and couldn't cause them trouble. He'd been certain the ship had been close to the island where they needed to land before waves crashing into them broke the ship in two and it quickly filled with water, the men's shouting silenced forever. But now Quinn didn't have a way to take the woman back to his brother either.

Fenella. She was the woman who had returned to get Avelina's brother's clothes for Quinn.

And Avelina? The lass who'd run her soft hand over his heated skin. He wished she'd do it again, for longer and over more of his body that wasn't battered.

She seemed to be the one in charge, or at least of the two women, which confused him if Fenella was supposed to be the chief's daughter. Quinn had planned to guard his sword and *sgian dubh* with his life—especially considering he would most likely have to fight what remained of his brother's own mercenaries to the death, if any of them had survived. He had believed the men would be smart enough to wait until they had the woman in hand and were returning to their lands. He was known to be a fierce warrior and it would have been to their advantage had they used him to assist them in escorting the woman home. He had misjudged them.

When Quinn had felt Avelina's warm hand on his chest, he realized he must have drifted into unconsciousness before she touched him, and now the other woman was hurrying off with his weapons, because his sword and sheath were no longer belted at his waist. He could have easily taken Avelina hostage, but then what would he do? He couldn't take her anywhere, or fight her people to keep her.

He wanted to open his eyes and see what the lass looked like, and wondered about her cousin's appearance too and what his brother was getting himself into—if Quinn managed to take her home to him. But he was even having second thoughts about that. Still, if Fenella wanted to leave her kin to live with his brother, he would do it for her, not for his brother. He hoped she wasn't making a mistake in wanting to be Cormac's wife, though Quinn reminded himself that his difficulties with his brother didn't mean Cormac couldn't make the lass happy.

Admittedly, Quinn did enjoy proving to Cormac that, try as he might, he couldn't easily kill him. Even though at the moment, Quinn was feeling bruised and beaten, and that it wouldn't take too much to finish the job. He couldn't just murder his brother outright either. Without a good enough reason, he knew many of his clansmen, having declared their loyalty to their chief, would turn on him, and Quinn would be dead anyway. For now, he didn't have much of a choice. Hire out as a mercenary for some other clan, if Malcolm MacNeill wouldn't take him in? He suspected his brother would still try to have him killed. What was worse was, as much as he'd tried to come up with a plausible reason, he didn't know why his brother wanted him dead.

Cloth swept over his uninjured shoulder as Avelina moved around on the sand near his body, and the tender sweep of the fabric felt foreign to the rest of the way he was feeling. He'd relocated to this side of the rocks, hoping to crawl further away from the remnants of the ship, but he hadn't made it very far. And he knew he had to move beyond where the tide was sure to reach. He envisioned having made it safely to the beach, and then drowning in high tide.

Her hands brushed his skin where part of his shirt hung in tatters over his chest. And he practically sighed. Every time she touched him, she made other parts of his body stir, while he was trying to keep from thinking about how he was enjoying her touch. Her touching him was undoing him. What if she saw his staff rising with eagerness when he was supposed to be half dead?

A strip of his shirt gave way with a rip. He envisioned her tying his wrists together, to protect herself. Instead, she carefully tied the strip of wool around his head, her touch gentle, probably so she wouldn't wake him.

Once she was done, she moved around him again, her warm hands brushing his skin, tormenting him in an exquisite way, and then she tore off another strip of cloth with a rip. Either she was impatient and couldn't wait for her cousin to return with her brother's clothes and rags, or she worried he was bleeding too much. He wondered how her brother would feel about her offering his clothing to a complete stranger who planned to whisk his cousin away to another clan to wed a man her family didn't want her to wed. Her brother would want to kill Quinn. He must not be on the island right now.

Avelina tied the cloth around the wound on Quinn's arm, just as gently as she did for his head wound.

He should let her know he was awake, but he was afraid she would fear him too much, and for now, he wanted her to be at ease. As difficult as it had been to crawl as far as he had, his head splitting in two, he wasn't sure he could even sit up again.

Then again, if she knew he had come to take her cousin to his brother, Avelina might be ecstatic with the news. If she would be happy that her cousin would wed the man she wanted to. Quinn was about to open his eyes and speak when he heard something that sounded like a huge dog galloping across the sand, too big to be a normal dog, too small to be a horse—most likely a wolfhound that took down wolves. Ironic that she should call him Wolf.

"Wolf, where is Fenella?" Avelina sighed. "On her way, I suspect. You are so fleet of foot, you must have known I needed you here at once, and came as soon as she gave the order." Avelina's words were soft, hushed, trying not to wake Quinn, he thought. The dog started to sniff him all over, pushing aside his plaid, uncovering his manhood. He'd had his fair share of hunting dogs poke their noses at his crotch, but this time, he didn't know the dog, and he'd exposed him to the woman, who could be ready to faint.

God's wounds, Quinn sorely wanted to cover his staff and protect himself from the dog.

"Wolf," Avelina said, her voice harsh, but hushed as she scolded him, and then gingerly, the plaid brushed across his staff, the wool shifting back in place.

Either she'd been looking away when the dog poked around at him, or she'd waited to get a good eyeful before she covered him back up because he was exposed for entirely too long before she even scolded the dog.

He heard her climb the rocks and turn to the dog. "Stay, Wolf. Guard him. If he moves, you know what to do."

The dog sat next to Quinn's head and did as the woman commanded. He thought she might be departing the area to help her cousin. Quinn waited and didn't open his eyes. What if Avelina was opposed to her cousin leaving the island and marrying his brother? He needed to speak to Fenella privately about the matter.

He still hadn't heard Avelina climbing down the rocks on the other side.

She let out her breath, and he thought her back was to him, so he chanced a peek. Petite, standing on top of the rocks, her gown billowing in the breeze, a plaid wrapped around her shoulders, she watched toward the direction from which she and the other woman must have come. Wisps of braided red gold hair fluttered about her shoulders. Was she green-eyed? Blue-eyed? He wished he could see.

But now what worried him most was that the waves were beginning to roll in, inching closer as the tide was coming in. He looked over at the dog to see if it was a wolfhound like he suspected, and his jaw hung agape.

The dog was a large gray wolf with white markings, black and gray face, a white muzzle and chest, and a saddle of gray and black. A *wolf*!

Wolf was panting, watching the lass, but when Quinn caught his eye, he pulled in his tongue and studied Quinn. Thankfully, Quinn had a way with beasts of all kinds. At least he thought the wolf would protect him as much as he'd protect the lass. Though Quinn suspected if he did anything to frighten the woman, the wolf would take her side over his.

"You're awake," Avelina said, sounding both shocked and annoyed.

His heart thundering, he quickly shifted his gaze to the woman, her beautiful blue eyes narrowed at him, and he said the first thing that came to mind. "He's a wolf."

"Aye, and he will kill you if I give the command."

"I'm surprised your da would allow you to have a wolf for a pet."

"I raised him from a pup. We are close. If you try to lay a hand on me, he'll take it right off. Dinna you forget that."

"I willna." Not that he wouldn't want to kiss her beautiful, pursed lips, or pull her into a warm embrace, feeling all of her winsome curves now on display as the wind tightened the fabric around them.

"Who are you?" she asked.

"My name is Quinn. The ship I was on was lost at sea."

"I am Avelina, and you are now my prisoner."

"Prisoner."

She shrugged. "Wolf will be watching every move you

make. You couldna take a step from here before he'd take you down. If you cause any trouble, we'll put you in the dungeon. Dinna test my resolve. And if you think you're going to escape the island, where do you think you'd go? Swim to the mainland? You'd never make it."

He raised a brow. He expected someone in charge to say that, if he didn't outright kill Quinn. But a beautiful woman? He would be her prisoner any day. Then he came to his senses, somewhat, recalling her cousin was supposed to wed his brother.

"What were you doing in the area?" Avelina asked.

"I was on my way to pick up my brother's bride, but the storm hit us and tore the ship carrying me to shreds, as well you know. Do they always put you in charge of prisoners?"

"Someday, I'll be married, and I'll be in charge when my husband is away." Avelina quickly added, "Which is why our chief has me take care of minor issues like this."

He wondered if Fenella felt the same way. Once she was married to Cormac, he wouldn't have her seeing to wounded strangers on their shores. Avelina looked back in the direction Fenella had gone and he eyed the short sword sheathed at her belt.

"Surely one of the men would be better equipped to guard me." He suspected they were all away, fighting for some clan's cause and only a few men were left behind. They might not even know what the women were up to.

She ignored him, continuing to watch for her cousin. The next wave wetted his head, and he struggled to sit. He had to move beyond the rocks before the tide came in any further.

The wolf woofed, and she turned to see what the matter was.

Quinn's head splintered once he'd barely lifted it off the beach, and he dropped his head back on the sand.

"We must move you." She scrambled down the rocks to reach him, the wolf wagging his bushy tail.

He wondered who "we" was.

"Come on. You are a braw warrior, aye? You must sit up, and I'll help you the best I can. But remember, Wolf will attack you if you do anything that makes him feel he must protect me."

"I'm in no shape to do anything to you or him or anyone," Quinn ground out.

"Good." She smiled at him, then helped him to sit, but as soon as he did, he felt the blood rush from his face, and she made him sit forward so he didn't collapse on the beach again. "Dinna you pass out on me."

"As if I want to."

"Then dinna." She studied him, her warm hand on his naked back still, keeping him from collapsing again. "Can you crawl up on the rocks? I'll aid you."

"Aye." He wasn't sure he could. Not that he wouldn't try, but every movement pained his head and he felt as though he would pass out every time he tried to do anything.

The wolf was right next to him as if he wanted to help.

Quinn grabbed the first of the rocks and began to pull himself up, the tide washing over his legs now.

"Do hurry," she said, then stepped into the water and

grabbed his plaid. She was back on the rocks again, encouraging him. "You're almost there. Just a little bit farther."

He knew he'd have to go a lot farther, the barnacles on the rocks indicating the water would cover them at high tide and it swept around the rocks on the other side. He'd have to get to the beach and continue until he reached the hill covered in wildflower-filled, machair grasses beyond that.

"Can you move a little faster?"

If you could carry me, he wanted to say. God's knees, he was trying.

He finally reached the top of the rocks and must have collapsed from the sheer pain shrieking through his skull, because the next thing he remembered was the woman pulling on his uninjured arm, trying to get him to move. He opened his eyes and saw her beautiful blue—*worried*— eyes, looking down at him. He heard the seawater splashing halfway up the rocks, the spray covering him in droplets of briny water.

"Leave me. I'll join you soon." Which was a lie, but he didn't want her to be swept out to sea. He suspected the waves were not as rough here normally, but the storm had churned them up, and he worried that she and the wolf might have difficulty making it safely to the hill.

"And let my prisoner drown? When I have so much work for you to do?"

As if he could do anything in the condition he was in. When the men returned, they'd probably kill him. Especially if they learned he had come to steal Fenella away. "Leave me."

"Not on your life. Come on. Get up." She tugged at him again, and the wolf, appearing to want to help, yanked at his plaid still hanging from his belt, pulling it clean away from his body.

He was fair naked; his shredded shirt, boots, and belt was all that remained.

"You are a warrior. Be a warrior. You can collapse on the hill where the tide willna take your body out to sea for the fishes to feed on. But you may no' lay here."

He wanted to ask her if her cousin would have taken this long to return, or if she'd had trouble along the way. Maybe found another injured man. Maybe even one of the mercenaries he hoped had died.

He finally got to his knees, and she helped him to stand. "We havena much time." She wrapped her arm around his waist, the wolf standing on the hill with the plaid still hanging from his mouth. "We must hurry. As soon as the tide slips out, we must run across that stretch of beach to the hill. Run. Not walk, or the tide's liable to sweep us off our feet and pull us out to sea."

"Aye." If his head wasn't splintering in two, he would have swept the lass up in his arms and raced her across the receding tide. In his current condition, he would be lucky if he could walk and not collapse again.

"Now," she said, and dragged him off the rocks and into the receding water.

He hated that he had to use her strength to get him to where they needed to go.

She tried to drag him quickly, her voice urgent. "Hurry.

We are no' going to make it."

He was hurrying as fast as he was able, every step sending pain into his upper body and his head and arm. He suspected he'd bruised his ribs also, hoping none were fractured. He was in agony, his breathing shallow, and he could barely do anything but keep his focus on taking one step after another through the water.

"It's coming in. Now." She tugged at him, but no matter how much she tried to drag him, he couldn't go any faster. His mind kept blackening. "No!" she screamed at him.

Water lapped at his neck, and he realized he'd collapsed and the water was covering his body. She was holding his head out of the water, the wave soaking her clothes, which would make it even more difficult for her to move. Her blue eyes were filled with tears, and he'd done that to her. She'd been so vigilant about saving him, she could be in harm's way herself, and he couldn't allow that. He mustered every bit of strength he could, and attempted to stand as the tide washed out and nearly dragged them with it. The seawater was now halfway up their legs, or higher on hers because she was shorter than him.

When she helped him to stand, she trudged through the water toward the hill, trying to keep him on his feet and moving forward. "I would carry you, lass, across the ocean itself, if I could." He had to tell her that, to ensure she knew he wasn't a ruffian who would let a lass perish for him, if he wasn't suffering from so many injuries.

She looked up at him. "I believe you would."

"I would." He gritted his teeth against the pain

stabbing his ribs and to keep his senses about him. They were getting closer. They could do this.

The tide rushed in and nearly knocked them off their feet again, only this time, somehow, he managed to keep Avelina from falling, and she clung to him, looking shocked that the roles had been reversed, but he groaned in pain as her soft body pressed against his injured ribs.

"Hurry. We must hurry." She began tugging at him again, as if she were afraid the pain she'd inflicted on him had caused him further injury and would make him collapse again.

Truth was that he couldn't get the image of her pressing against him out of his mind. Not a lassie who wanted to share his bed with him, but one who was trying her darnedest to rescue him, even if she was taking him as her prisoner.

To his annoyance, he had to lean on her strength again, but when the tide pulled out, he fought staying on his feet and holding her up too. He knew as petite as she was, she could easily be swept off her feet and pulled under. "Do you know how to swim?" Though even if she did, she could easily drown if she was pulled under and couldn't get to her feet fast enough.

"Aye, but this isna a time to go swimming. Not after a violent storm has passed through here. The waves attest to that. Save your breath." She sounded like she needed to save her own, her words labored. "Can you move no faster?"

"We are nearly there." Halfway at least, but that was better than where they were minutes ago.

"We are no' nearly far enough. Hurry." She half clung to him as the water pulled at her, half dragging him. She was having just as much trouble moving now as he was.

On the hill, Wolf sat watching them, eagerly waiting for them to join him, the plaid at his feet.

A wave slammed into him and Avelina, and both fell. They were submerged, and he quickly found Avelina, and pulled her out of the water. She was sputtering, coughing, trying to catch her breath. The water began to recede, and he managed to get to his feet and lifted her to hers. The wave had pushed them closer to the hill, but was threatening to pull them under and out to sea again. He struggled to keep moving forward, the water at his thighs and at her hips.

Another wave hit them, but this time he was able to move forward with it, dragging her with him, and he was close enough to the hill before the water receded that he managed to collapse on it, pulling her down with him. "We...made...it." Barely. The water still bathed his legs, but his head and body were above the water. "Thank you."

She snorted, but she couldn't move either for a moment, and lay on top of him, her skirts covering his bare skin. Their wet bodies warmed each other. He needed Wolf to bring his plaid, so he could cover himself properly, but neither Avelina or he moved, just remained there to catch their breaths. She was shivering, and he wrapped his arms around her and tried to hold her tighter to warm her further, but his ribs hurt. He groaned a little.

"Your ribs..."

"You're cold," was all he could get out.

She glanced up at Wolf. "Bring the plaid, Wolf."

The wolf came down the hill and greeted her, without the plaid. "Go fetch the plaid, Wolf."

Wolves had a mind of their own. Quinn didn't believe she could have trained him like she might have trained a dog to fetch.

"We're going to have to work on that," she said. "Wait here, Quinn. I'll get your plaid." She carefully moved off Quinn and headed up the hill, then grabbed the plaid and hurried back down to him. "Can you crawl up the hill? Or walk? You need to get out of the water."

"Aye. Just let me rest a moment more."

"Nay, you're too cold. You must move out of the water. Get up." She helped him to sit, and then struggled to help him to stand.

He groaned in agony. Every bit of him hurt. Though he admired her persistence.

"A cave is nearby. You can stay in that until you recover more. I'll bring you food."

He wanted to ask her why she was "hiding" him away from her people. He figured they would kill him if they knew he was here and why. For some reason, she wanted to keep him alive.

Somehow, he climbed the hill with her assistance, and she helped wrap his wet plaid around him. Then she again aided him until they reached a small cave. The floor was sandy and a couple of holes in the cave walls let in some light. The walls were covered in moss and moisture. At least the cave protected him from the blustery wind and rain, if they had any further storms. "I have to return home, and I'll come back with food, a clean, dry blanket, and shirt. Yours is wet and torn, and your plaid is sopping."

"And *your* clothes are wet."

"I'm not injured like you. I'll change clothes when I return to the keep."

He wondered if anyone would notice that she was drenched and make her explain why.

She helped him to sit on the floor of the cave. "I'll start a fire for you at the mouth of the cave to provide some heat and help dry your things. Wolf will stay here and pro... guard you."

Protect, was what he was sure she was going to say.

"Thank you."

"You willna thank me when I put you to work. I will return as soon as I can." She started a fire, and then she ordered Wolf to stay. "Guard the prisoner."

She started off for the keep.

To Quinn's surprise Wolf did stay. Except he didn't remain outside the cave guarding Quinn.

"Come here, Wolf," Quinn said, needing the wolf's warmth if the animal was agreeable.

Wolf loped into the cave and Quinn patted the ground next to him. "Sit."

The wolf sat down next to him and watched out the cave entrance for his mistress. Before long, the wolf was lying next to Quinn, keeping him warmer than he would have been without the animal sharing his body heat. The fire helped to take the chill out of the air too. He still worried about Fenella and why she had never returned. He hoped she hadn't run into trouble and that Avelina wouldn't run into the same trouble.

She should have taken Wolf with her to protect herself! And he should have insisted! Which showed how he wasn't thinking clearly at all, as he collapsed against the sandy ground.

CHAPTER 3

Avelina couldn't believe that Fenella hadn't returned by now. Wolf was fast, but Fenella should have brought her brother's clothes long before this, unless she'd run into trouble with one of their men. Or if she'd encountered another injured man from the ship that Quinn had been on.

She couldn't believe how injured he was, or how he'd rescued her when she'd been pulled under the water. She was grateful that he had, but she reminded herself that she wouldn't have been in the trouble she'd been in if it hadn't been for trying to rescue him in the first place. She had to remember he was the enemy, unless proven otherwise, and he could cause all kinds of trouble for her people. But she hoped when he mended, he could be a help to them.

She hadn't even asked what woman he was supposed to be taking to his brother. Was she on one of the other islands? He couldn't have meant anyone from here.

Fenella? *No.* Avelina shook her head. Not her cousin.

She would have known if her uncle had arranged a marriage for her cousin.

When she reached the keep, she saw three men in the inner bailey, her people standing around them, giving them water and bandaging their injuries. She frowned. More of the men from the ship?

Then she saw Fenella and hurried to join her.

"Oh, och, what happened to you?" Fenella asked, taking hold of Avelina's hand and hurrying her into the keep. "You are sopping wet."

"What happened to you? You were supposed to bring clothes for the man on the beach. Are those more of the men who were shipwrecked?"

"Aye, but there is something odd about them. They asked if any other men had washed up. Some of our men found them a long way from where the other was. One of my da's guards wouldna let me leave once they began finding these men on the beach. I sent Wolf to you right away, but I didna know what else to do. I tried to send one of our lads, but they wouldna let him go either."

Avelina hurried into her chamber and began to strip off her wet clothes.

"How is he? And where is he?"

"I had to move him from the tide water."

"That is why you're all wet."

"Aye, and with great effort, I moved him to Yorun's Cave. Wolf is guarding him. But he still needs warm, dry clothes. We took a dunking when I tried to move him. He's badly injured. Did you mention him to his friends?"

"I didna. One of the men said to his companions that

Quinn never dies and if he managed to survive the shipwreck, they had to kill him before he caused them any trouble. Did you learn what the half dead man's name was?"

"Quinn. And he isna in any shape to protect himself from these men if they are brigands, and he isna. What did you do with his sword and *sgian dubh*?"

"I put them in your chamber, underneath your bed. You're no' giving them back to him, are you?"

"Nay." Though Avelina should if he was going to be able to defend himself against the other men, if he was the same Quinn they spoke of. He couldn't defend himself right away though. He would need to heal first.

"What are you going to do?"

"I need to take him healing herbs, clothes, and to bandage his wounds. But we must keep him secret from the other men until we learn the truth. Did the men say who they were?"

"They work for Cormac and they are Ivar and Griswold, but I didna hear the other man's name."

"Quinn said he was supposed to fetch a bride for his brother. Surely, if his brother sent him on the mission, he must be the one in the right, and the other men—"

"In the wrong. Unless he intended to steal his brother's bride," Fenella said.

"Aye." Avelina went through the bundle Fenella had gathered for her—her brother's shirt, boots, a plaid, loaf of brown bread, cheese, and a flask of wine. "You have done well, Cousin."

"I'm sorry I couldna get the items to you. You dinna

think anyone will be angered that you have given him your brother's clothes?"

"He can no longer wear them," Avelina said sadly, still missing her brother who had died during the conflict last year.

"Is Quinn badly injured?"

"Aye, and cold and wet. I started a fire at the mouth of the cave where we have played before, and Wolf is guarding him."

"Did he tell you the name of the woman he had come for?"

"Nay. I was too busy trying to get him out of the reach of the incoming tide and up the hill. I will ask when I return. But he did say the woman wished to leave her kin."

"If her kin doesna wish it and they catch him, he will be a dead man."

"I agree. Tell no one about him. If our men bring him to the inner bailey, these men could attempt to kill him. What if they are the ones who are in the wrong?"

"True. He is braw, is he no'?"

"Aye." Avelina belted her sword around her waist, and stuck her *sgian dubh* in one boot, Quinn's in the other. She wasn't sure she should arm him, but after learning what she had from Fenella, she was afraid to chance him being unarmed, in case more of these men had survived the shipwreck and intended to kill him. "Once he has healed a bit, mayhap the widow Judith could take him in, and he could repair her byre and her croft. I will speak to her of it. I must get on my way and move him before anyone searching the beach thinks to look for a man in the cave nearby."

"Godspeed, Avelina. Take care and I will wait here and learn what I can concerning the other three men."

"Aye. Good idea." Then Avelina left the keep and moved with purpose toward the gate, wanting to run, but not wanting to catch anyone's attention. She glanced in the direction of the three strangers', all seated on the ground where two men were guarding them.

A black-haired and bearded man smiled at her, and she switched her attention to the other two men—a redheaded man, sprouting fresh whiskers, and a man with dark brown hair and beard. All were bedraggled, their clothes tattered and damp, their hair still wet, the redhead wearing a bloodied cloth around his head, the black-haired man with his arm bandaged and bloody cuts on his face, the last of the men having a bandage wrapped around his chest.

The brown-haired man winked at her. Fenella hurried after her, and they walked together toward the gate.

"I didna think you could leave," Avelina said to her cousin.

"I canna. But I wanted to come out and learn more about these men. The black-haired man is Griswold, Ivar is the redhead. The other man is the one I didna catch the name of," Fenella said, her words hushed for Avelina's ears only. "Och, Hamish is observing us. The other guards are watching to see what he will do, since he's in charge. He will stop me for sure, but he might no' let you leave either."

"Then you need to convince him to allow me to leave."

"As if I could do that."

When they reached Hamish, Avelina was going to just smile and continue on her way, but he raised his hand to stop her.

"Where do you think you're off to, lass?" Hamish said to Avelina, though he cast a look in Fenella's direction as if reminding her she wasn't going anywhere.

Avelina wanted to tell him that it was nothing of importance to him, but she knew he was only doing his job and concerned for her welfare. "One of the women in the outlying farms needs my help. I will return before supper."

"More of these men who were on the ship might be out there," Hamish said, motioning to the three men. "Some of our men are searching for any more of them along the beach. Your da wouldna like it if you were out there and ran into any more of these men."

"Thank you. I dinna intend to go to the shoreline." Avelina wasn't lying. She would be at the cave that was above the shore. "Just to see the widow Judith." She had planned to today before Fenella had warned her about the half-dead warrior on the beach. She would still do so, on her return trip.

Hamish glanced at her bundle. She didn't want to have to explain why she was taking her brother's clothes with her if Hamish asked her to reveal all she had inside her own spare plaid. Her da had wanted her to save them in case they had some great need for them. As far as she was concerned, she did. But she was certain her da wouldn't feel the same way.

"All right, be quick about it then, lass. Dinna stray toward the shore where the shipwreck occurred. Stay inland."

"Aye. I will." She wouldn't be able to return quickly.

She had to move Quinn to another location, and once she had him settled, she had to see Judith. Both would take time. Judith was lonely and loved the company. Getting away from her was always a challenge, though Avelina enjoyed visiting her and making sure she was getting along all right. Yet, Avelina could use that to her advantage. Everyone knew how Judith was.

Fenella was wringing her hands and nodded to her. Then Avelina hurried off, her heart beating spastically as she eyed another guard who was standing near the gates, watching her in return. She was certain she looked guilty, rather than appearing to just go about her business like on any other day.

"Where are you off to, Avelina?" Dar asked. He had to have seen her speaking with Hamish and had to know the head of the guards had approved her leaving, or he would have stopped her from going any further with her bundle.

"To gather more herbs and see to one of the women who lives on an outlying farm." Avelina added the part about gathering herbs in case anyone worried she was returning too late. "I must hurry so that I may return before the meal."

"You are armed."

"Always, and Wolf is waiting for me. I will be safe enough." She did worry that Quinn might be real trouble. Or maybe the other men were. Maybe all of them were. At least the men guarding the castle were in charge of *these* men.

"Dinna tarry then."

"Aye." Relieved when the guard let her pass, she

hurried through the gates and down the path through rocks and bracken. From there, she made her way to the meadows of gorse and heather. Once she was well out of sight of the castle, she turned in the direction of the cave, and began to run, worried now that the men searching for more shipwreck victims would find Quinn. What if they took him to the inner bailey and the other men killed him? She needed to move him to another location, far away from the beach.

Nearly out of breath, she finally reached the outcropping of rocks and saw the dark cave. The fire had gone out, and Wolf wasn't sitting at the entrance like she'd ordered. Her heartbeat quickened, and her palms grew sweaty. What if Quinn had believed she would bring her kin to arrest him, either by her own will, or that she'd been forced to, and he'd run off? Or while she'd been gone, her men had found him? But where was Wolf?

She drew close to the dark cave and saw light streaming into it from up above. Quinn was lying on his back, Wolf sleeping against him, sharing their warmth with each other. She couldn't be any more surprised to see Wolf's actions. She'd never observed him reacting to a stranger like that, maybe realizing she was trying to help Quinn, and knowing he was injured.

Wolf raised his head, watching her, his eyes glowing a bit in the darkness, his tail wagging. She frowned at Quinn, hoping he was still alive. She drew close enough to hear his breathing, and relieved, she placed her hand on his chest with a gentle touch, not wanting to alarm him, but having to know if he was cool or hot to the touch. He didn't stir, but she felt his heart beating and his skin was cool, not cold, thankfully.

She began to remove Quinn's boots so that she could dress him in dry clothes, and he stirred. "Quinn? 'Tis me, Avelina. I've come with dry clothes and rags to bind your wounds. But I must also move you farther from here."

"Avelina," Quinn said, a hand to his chest, his voice dry and raspy, his eyes half-lidded.

"Aye." She brought out a flask of ale and helped him to sit, then pressed the flask to his lips. "Drink." He needed to rest, but they couldn't afford for him to stay here now that they'd found the other men.

He drank a few sips of the ale, and she closed the flask and set it aside.

"Some of our men are combing the beach for shipwreck survivors. I must move you to another location." She placed her brother's plaid over his lap, then pulled the damp one off him—trying not to look at his nakedness any more than she had to. Not that she wasn't fascinated to see his manhood, but the poor man was shivering, and she was trying to ensure he didn't get sick.

She removed his shredded shirt and the other bandages she'd made out of his shirt that were now wet with salty water. She applied a paste of herbs to his wounds, and then bound his ribs, his arm, and his head with clean, dry cloths. "Tell me about the men you traveled with and where you were bound." She helped him pull on her brother's shirt.

"My brother sent me to bring a woman home to be his bride. She wishes to be, but her family doesna, according to my brother, Cormac. He sent five men with me, not of the clan. They are armed mercenaries who tried to kill me on the ship during the height of the storm before the ship sank. I managed to kill one of the men before the ship broke up. I hope the others drowned in the sea."

"So that means four are left."

"Unless they drowned."

"Ivar, Griswold, and…?"

Quinn's brown eyes widened. "They live?"

"They were picked up on the shore and taken to the keep. My cousin, Fenella, overheard them saying they needed to kill a man who wouldna die, by the name of Quinn. You, aye? Why would they want to kill you?" She helped him into her brother's spare boots, and then worked with him to replace his wet plaid with her brother's dry one.

"You would have to ask my brother that question."

"Your brother wishes you dead?" Avelina couldn't imagine anything more horrible.

"Aye, but I dinna know the reason. He has tried to have me killed—unsuccessfully—four times before."

Avelina pondered the whole situation further. "Sending you to steal a woman away from her kin to wed your bother could have meant your death anyway."

"Aye, I'm a good swordsman. Killing me meant one less person to successfully rescue the lady and escort her to my brother. I dinna understand why the men wouldn't have waited until we had her on the ship and bound for home."

Avelina didn't know what to think. She wanted to believe Quinn, but she couldn't. Not when she didn't know anything about him. "We must move. If my men find you, they'll take you to the keep and if your brother's men can find a way, they'll kill you, even though they've been disarmed." She bundled everything up. "You must get to your feet. Can you?"

"Aye."

But he leaned heavily on her as she helped him to his feet. She wasn't sure he was going to do much better than when they were on the shore. At least the tide wouldn't be pulling their feet out from under them, or half drowning them. "Okay, hold onto the cave wall for a moment, and I'll tie the bundle to my belt." After she did that, she pulled the flask leather strap over her neck. She would feed him later once they were settled. Unless eating a little would give him some strength for now. "Do you need to eat right this minute?"

"Nay, let us move. I'll do better than before, I promise. Thank you again for aiding me."

"Does Cormac believe you want his bride-to-be?" she asked, trying to come up with a reason the brothers would be at odds.

"Nay. I dinna know the lass. And I would have naught to offer her. Especially if my brother manages to kill me one of these days."

"Why do you stay?"

"Everyone else likes me." Quinn smiled down at her, but he shifted his weight so he wasn't leaning on her as much.

"Except for your brother and his mercenaries, so it seems." She felt Quinn swaying. "I'll help you. But if you think you can do this on your own and you fall, I might no' be able to get you back on your feet."

Wolf was running ahead of them, sniffing the air, looking back to make sure they were following him, and dashing off again.

Quinn leaned on her a little bit more, but he was still trying to support himself more. "Where are we going?"

"To an abandoned croft on a stream. Some say 'tis haunted and selkies visit there and snatch people away."

He groaned and she paused. "Are you okay?"

"Aye. I dinna think anything is broken, maybe...cracked a rib or two. Hopefully, just bruised."

"I'm sorry."

"I will live."

But how long would he live if his brother kept trying to have him killed? "Who is the woman you were sent to fetch?" she asked.

Quinn didn't answer her, and she looked up at him to see if he was getting ready to pass out, yet he hadn't shifted his weight any. He looked like he hated to speak about it. "I canna lie to you, after all that you've done for me. You may no' wish to aid me any longer, and I will understand. Cormac said that Fenella is the lady who wishes to wed him."

Avelina jerked away from Quinn so fast, he teetered on his feet, looking like he was barely able to stand on his own, but she was so outraged, she couldn't do anything but scowl at him. "He lies. Or you lie."

"I have naught to gain by telling you the truth. When the rest of your kin learn my business here, they're sure to kill me outright."

She had to admit he was right. "She doesna love some brigand by the name of Cormac," Avelina said, scowling. She knew her cousin well, and she would have told her if she loved someone and hoped he'd steal her away.

Quinn wavered a little and Avelina was afraid he'd fall. She should let him. She should call for the men searching for Quinn or any other men who were cast upon the beach. She should let the men who said they'd kill him finish the job. Cormac must have heard of her cousin's beauty and wanted her for his wife, not for any other reason.

"You will tell Hamish, the man left in charge, what you, your brother, and his men's wicked plans were."

"Fenella longed to be with Cormac, according to him."

"'Tis a lie!"

"Is it?" Quinn raised a brow.

With every fiber of her being, Avelina thought so. But what if Fenella *had* met Cormac during some clan meeting, fallen in love, and *wanted* to be with him? What if she'd been afraid to confide in Avelina, fearing she would have told Fenella's father?

Avelina glowered at Quinn. "You are sure you dinna want to steal Fenella away, and that's why your brother's men wished you dead?"

"Nay, Avelina. 'Tis as I've said. I've never met the lass before. I know naught about her. If I wished to steal anyone away..." He didn't finish what he was going to say, his hand going to his chest, and Avelina quickly moved to support him.

"I should call for our men to come and take you away." She helped him to move a few more steps. "I know that

Fenella doesna want to wed some man by the name of Cormac, but I will ask her just the same. Just to be sure. Would you still plan to steal her away if it wasna her idea and you had the opportunity?" Avelina doubted that he could now, but she wanted to know his feelings anyway.

"Nay. Then I would believe my brother orchestrated this whole mission, so I wouldn't survive this time."

"If 'tis as you say, even if Fenella had wanted to marry him, I would convince her otherwise."

"She is happy here?"

"Aye, of course."

"And her da doesna plan to marry her to a man she despises?"

"No' that we are aware of."

"Is this place you are taking me very far?" He was barely walking, his breathing labored.

"Aye. If you are a great warrior, you can make it." She knew he had to be hurting, but she didn't want him giving up, and she would say anything that she could to encourage him. "You will have to prove you are worthy of staying with us. If a widow will take you in, I will take you to her croft on the morrow. But she has to be willing. She needs help with repairs to her byre and the roof of her croft. You will repair them, *if* you know how to do more than just fighting and stealing lasses from their homes. That is, if my people dinna learn what you were up to, and kill you outright."

CHAPTER 4

Quinn wondered what Avelina would do when she returned to her keep. He suspected she'd tell Fenella first what his mission was and learn if what Cormac had said was true, or if he had lied. Quinn had considered lying to her to protect himself, but he was certain the truth would come out and it was better that it happened now, with her, when she seemed to be more sympathetic. Her people would not treat him as kindly, of that he was sure. And he couldn't blame them. Though stealing a bride was a time-honored tradition if the man got away with it. If he didn't...

"I canna believe you planned to steal Fenella away," Avelina grumbled under his weight.

He was trying his darnedest not to use her strength, and draw on more of his own. His ribs and head pained him something fierce, and he hoped they would reach the haunted croft sooner than later. "Because she wished it, according to my brother. Believe me, had I had the opportunity to speak with your cousin and learn that she didna, *if* she didna, I would never have taken her from your island."

"But you do what your brother wishes, even when he attempts to murder you...repeatedly." Avelina was still angry with him, but he didn't blame her.

"Not something like this, once I'd learned the truth."

"Has Cormac ever lied to you about something like this?"

"When I went into a village to right a wrong at my brother's request the last time, and I discovered the men had been warned I was on my way, and they were ready for me. I still got the best of them, but I had to fight twice as hard to do it. And there have been other occasions."

"How do you know your brother had anything to do with it?"

"I've been ambushed four times in the last two months. And he was always the one who sent me. Not to mention the last man I had to kill said my brother warned him I was coming."

"Could he have been lying?"

"Because of the other cases, I doubt it."

Avelina frowned up at him. "Have you thought of killing your brother for the wrong he has done you?"

Quinn sighed and considered her words for a moment before he spoke.

She looked up at him. "You have."

"He saved my life when I was young. I owe him my life. I wouldna be here today if he hadna."

She snorted. "Then you wouldna have been here trying

to steal my cousin away. And could very well have died in the shipwreck. And if my kinsmen got hold of you..."

"Aye. As to your question, aye, I have considered it." Quinn had to keep pausing to catch his breath, and he would have done better not talking while they made their way over the uneven ground. But he had to convince the lass he wasn't in the wrong on this. "Who wouldna, whose blood relation keeps trying to have you murdered? But I know this would be folly on my part. I would have to live with what I had done—and I would be a wanted man. My brother is careful to make it appear that he had naught to do with the trouble I had that could easily have resulted in my death."

"Does no one know of his treachery? Surely, someone—those who tried to kill you—would know and the word would get out."

"Many assume the worst of my brother. The men who attacked us are no more. A couple of the men who had been with me during the ambushes, Liam and Lorne, know also. Still, it would be our word against the chief. Lorne and Liam both insisted on accompanying me this time even, sure my brother intended to have his mercenaries kill me. I thought they would wait until we had Fenella on the ship first."

"You were one fighting against five." Avelina shook her head.

"Four now. Unless one of the other men didna make it to shore alive." He desperately wanted to ask her if they were nearly to the croft, but he didn't want to sound like he could barely make it, even though he was taking steps like a wee bairn would.

"We are nearly there," she finally said.

He tried not to breathe in a sigh of relief that she would notice, but she smiled up at him, and he figured she'd heard him.

Then he saw the stone croft, the roof partly missing, the rest moss-covered, like the stones. The byre was in shambles, much like the ship he'd been on, and he felt like *he* was in as bad a shape as the stone croft's roof.

"Dinna run out of here screaming in the middle of the night should you see something you hadna expected. You could fall in a bog, off a cliff, or end up in the ocean again, even though we are a long way from there now."

"The banshees or the dead dinna scare me. We only have to worry about the living." Which, in his case, meant both her kin *and* his brother's own men. Quinn was trying to come up with a plan where he could turn this around so that he had a chance of surviving. It didn't look good.

She released her hold on him and hurried into the croft. "I'll leave what's left of your clothes in here, the flask of wine, and the food. I must see to the widow I mentioned before to you to ask if she can take you in. I must go before my people worry about me not returning for the meal as I promised. I will return on the morrow when I can get away. Rest, and I will see you when I can."

"Be safe, Avelina, and thank you."

"Take care of yourself. If you are caught here with my brother's things, it willna go well for either of us. Just dinna get caught. This place is far enough away from any others that if you burn peat at the hearth, no one should notice. If anyone did, they'd be assured the ghosts have returned. I must go." She offered him brown bread and fish.

He broke apart the bread and offered her a piece. She frowned and shook her head. "You'll need your strength. You'll have to work to earn your food as soon as you're healed."

He didn't state the obvious. That he hadn't seen any men, any women, children, nobody, as if he and she were the only two people here. And Fenella, but he couldn't let her know he knew about her too or Avelina would realize he hadn't been unconscious the whole time she and her cousin had been with him on the shore.

But she kept him away from her people for some reason. Why? Because she was left in charge of the women and children? Maybe elderly men past their prime? And she was afraid Quinn would try to take over? What of the other shipwreck survivors? The mercenaries? She had mentioned Hamish, the man left in charge. For his sake, Quinn hoped he had enough men at the keep to ensure the mercenaries didn't cause them any trouble.

"I have work to do. See that you eat everything, and I'll visit with you…later. Wolf, stay, guard the man." She considered Quinn for a minute more, took in a deep breath, then left the croft.

He watched her go as she walked up the slope, her hips swaying suggestively, though only because she couldn't help it as she navigated around the gorse, and disappeared beyond the hill.

"Here, boy, have a bite," Quinn said to the wolf. He'd never dealt with a halfway tamed wolf before, but he figured a well-fed wolf was better than one that was hungry.

Wolf glanced in the direction his mistress had gone. When he saw she was out of sight, he hurried over to get a chunk of bread and excitedly wolfed it down, then looked eager for more.

Quinn petted the wolf's head and gave him part of the fish, then secured the rest for the morrow. He'd learned long ago not to trust that he'd have an easy time getting food the next day. Rationing had saved his life many a time. "If your mistress brings enough tomorrow for us to eat, I will share more. You know, this is our secret. If she learns we're best of friends, we're both liable to be in trouble."

Wolf looked up at him with beautiful amber eyes, the sunlight streaming through the holes in the roof, glinting off them. Wolf licked his chops.

"Sorry, there's no more for you, or me, this eve. You wouldna know where there's a boat to get off this island, would you?"

Wolf sat down next to the hearth.

"We're going to have to work at your growling at me. Just for show. That way Avelina doesn't know that you're keeping me company and not guarding me."

In one respect, Quinn wished she'd taken the wolf with her for protection. But he was glad to have the company. The wolf could possibly warn him if anyone showed up unexpectedly. Quinn glanced up at the roof. He could repair it mayhap on the morrow after he'd had the night to rest. He debated on making a fire and decided he'd start one so that he could warm up until he could fall asleep. He made the fire. Then he untied the bundle and found his sheathed *sgian dubh*. He smiled, unsure whether she had left it on purpose to afford him some protection, or by accident, but he was glad to have his *sgian dubh* back. He would have loved having his sword returned too, but maybe she would bring it tomorrow.

He wanted to do more for himself, so she wouldn't have to return and risk getting caught.

Before it was dark, Quinn made a bed of her extra plaid, and left his drying by the fire. He wrapped himself in her brother's plaid. Wolf curled up next to him. Quinn suspected he didn't get a "pack" mate to sleep with normally. The wolf seemed to like the arrangement.

"You warn me if we have any unwelcome visitors, aye?" Quinn said to Wolf.

The wolf pulled his panting tongue into his mouth and stared at Quinn for a moment, then laid his head on his chest.

Pain shot up Quinn's ribs, and he groaned. But he didn't make Wolf move his head, figuring the pain would be worse moving around and hoped it would subside soon. He appreciated the wolf's companionship and warmth.

***

Avelina hoped she wasn't making the worst mistake of her life by aiding Quinn. She could tell the others where he was, if she should change her mind and feel he was as much a brigand as the other men, but her people would know she hid him away for a while and wouldn't like that she had. She would lose their trust. Her cousin might even be implicated since they had been together earlier, and Fenella had been trying to leave the castle grounds, carrying the bundle, before Avelina finished the task.

When Avelina reached widow Judith's home, the elderly woman was cooking fish inside.

"Come in, come in, and join me."

"I have to return to the castle soon. They'll send out search parties if I dinna. But I must ask you, can you take care of an injured stranger, who was shipwrecked on our shores, if I bring him to you?"

Judith's gray eyes widened. She licked her lips. "How badly injured?"

"Bruised or cracked ribs. His head and arm were bleeding, and he was having a devil of a time walking."

"Where is he now?"

"Somewhere safe. But we canna tell anyone about him. Could you care for him? And in return, when he's feeling better, he'll repair your croft and byre?"

"Oh, aye, of course."

"Good. Eat your food, Judith. I just wanted to come by to see how you were faring."

"And learn if I would take in a rogue, aye?" Judith smiled a little, her eyes lit up with humor and intrigue.

"Aye, but I'd planned to visit you earlier, before we found the man."

Judith frowned. "We? Who else knows about him?"

"Fenella." Avelina told her about the other men, about their mission, Cormac, all of it.

"Och, lass."

Avelina had to tell her everything, but she was afraid now that Judith would think Quinn would be too much trouble.

"He could repair—"

Judith waved her hand, silencing her. "I will take him in, care for him, and protect him. I will enjoy the company."

"Do you mind if Wolf stays with the two of you? I want him to guard Quinn."

"To protect him, or to keep him from leaving?"

"To keep him from leaving. Though I dinna know where he would go if he thought to steal a fishing boat. I doubt he would be able to manage the coracle by himself because of his injuries."

"Tell me what Fenella says about this Cormac before you bring Quinn here, will you?"

"Aye. I must leave now. Take care, and if all goes as planned, I will return sometime tomorrow and then fetch Quinn and bring him to stay with you."

"Take care, and I'll see you on the morrow."

That was the fastest Avelina had ever gotten away from Judith, but she could tell the older woman was delighted to have someone stay with her for a time. Avelina just hoped she wouldn't be in trouble for it too, should anyone learn of it.

Avelina ran as fast as she could back to the keep, but slowed down the closer she got to the castle. Then she saw some of the men returning.

"Where have you been, lass?" one of the men asked, frowning at her. He'd been on a hunt earlier, before news of the shipwreck had changed the men's focus.

"Seeing to Judith, and she is well. Did you find any more bodies?"

"Some."

Avelina took a deep breath, hoping that one of them was the other mercenary who had tried to kill Quinn. "Are they all sailors, or are some of them like the men captured and waiting in our outer bailey?"

"I have no idea. They'll bury them in the morning, but we'll have the men at the castle identify them first."

"Good idea. Do you think you have found all of the men from the ship?"

"Hard to say. If one wasna injured badly, he might have made it inland a way. We'll resume our search in the morning. The others are probably lost at sea. 'Tis getting to be too late this eve to look any further. I am surprised Hamish allowed you beyond the castle gates, once we learned of the sunken vessel."

"He knew I was staying away from the sea. I had my sword and *sgian dubh*, and know how to use them. If any of the men had survived, they would be injured like the ones already found."

"Aye. Unless one was lucky."

When they reached the keep, Fenella hurried out to greet Avelina. She cast her a warning look not to appear overanxious, and Fenella quickly smiled, but didn't throw her arms around her in a grateful hug, like she appeared to want to do.

"I'm so glad you made it home in time for the meal."

"Judith is well," Avelina said. "I will tell you all the rest later. They found more bodies on the shore."

"Oh, no."

Avelina was dying to ask Fenella about her supposed

love interest in Cormac, but she was afraid she might be overheard when they entered the great hall for the feast. Still, she couldn't wait and warned her cousin first, "Dinna overreact when I tell you some news."

Fenella frowned at her. "What is wrong now?"

Avelina whispered to her, "Do you know a man by the name of Cormac?"

Fenella's eyes widened. "Nay. Should I?"

Avelina let out her breath with relief. She was glad her cousin hadn't planned to leave here without her da's permission. "I will tell you all about it later. Come, let us eat."

They took their seats at the head table. The great hall seemed so empty now that most of the men were gone.

"You canna say that and keep me in suspense. Tell me what? Just whisper it to me," Fenella said.

Against her better judgment, Avelina did.

Immediately, Fenella's face reddened and outraged, she said, "Steal me?"

"Lower your voice, Cousin. Others will take notice. He thought you wished it."

"I dinna wish to be stolen away from my kin to wed some, some brigand."

"Aye, I gathered as much when you told me you didna know the man."

Fuming, Fenella poked at her fish soup. "Now that this Quinn knows the truth, does he still plan to steal me away to hand over to his brother?"

"Nay. He would be foolish to even think of such a thing. He had to know the truth though, that wedding his brother wasna your wish."

"It isna. Do you believe him?"

"Aye. He knew he'd be in more trouble if he told me, than if he kept quiet about it. He could have said he was bound for another place and the storm sidetracked them. Once I tell him that was never your intention, he willna attempt to take you anywhere, but the rest of the men? Mayhap. Did you learn anything more about them?"

"When I tried to get close to overhear anything the men might say, Hamish shooed me away, but he used my name and the men's eyes widened. They cast each other glances. Now that I know that they were actually planning to land on our island, and well, the rest, I'm sure they were glad to learn who I was. Shouldna we tell Hamish what they had intended to do?"

"What if he doesna believe us? If the men say and do naught to incriminate themselves, our men may believe we are crazy."

Fenella finished her soup. "Then we need to somehow trick them into giving themselves away. Unless, we bring Quinn here, and he tells the truth."

"It would be his word against the three men. Dinna you go near them until I return on the morrow."

"You were gone forever. Hamish was getting ready to send men looking for you, though he was concerned with the others searching the beach, and the rest watching the prisoners and guarding from the wall walk, he didna want to leave too few men here. The prisoners will be staying with the men in the barracks this eve." Fenella tore off a piece of bread. "What if this Cormac realizes his men aren't returning, and he sends more to fetch me?"

"Mayhap it was only a ruse. That he thought he could get rid of Quinn, once we discovered his purpose in coming here. And Cormac never intended to have you taken from your family."

"He set him up to be killed then."

"Like before, if Quinn is correct in his assumptions."

Fenella chewed on her bread, appearing deep in thought. Avelina glanced around the great hall, but noticed they must have fed the prisoners elsewhere as they weren't here. She was thankful for that. She could imagine Fenella having difficulty eating if she had to see the men in here. Hamish was watching Avelina, and she worried he might know that she hadn't been perfectly honest with him about just seeing Judith. If the other guard told him, he would think she'd also been gathering herbs. But she hadn't. She'd carried some with her just in case she had to show them to any of the guards. Hopefully, they wouldn't realize they were dried and not freshly cut, if anyone asked her about them now.

After the meal was done, she and Fenella left the great hall to go to Avelina's chamber so she could pack more items for Quinn when she met him on the morrow, including bread and cheese from the meal she'd slipped into a spare pouch of Fenella's on her lap. Fenella, likewise, had added some more food to the pouch under the table. Avelina hoped the hounds wouldn't think they were casting them leftovers and grab the bag of food.

Hamish moved toward them and Avelina slipped the pouch to Fenella. "Go to your chamber. I'll meet up with you there."

Fenella looked ill-at-ease that she was carrying the pouch filled with food from the supper, or that she would leave Avelina alone when Hamish was sure to question her about where she'd gone. Reluctantly, Fenella moved away from there, and Avelina was glad she had gotten it right and that Hamish hadn't intended to speak to Fenella instead.

"How is Judith?" Hamish asked.

Avelina wanted to sigh in relief, but she still didn't trust that Hamish was only concerned about Judith's health. "She is well, but I'm returning on the morrow to help her out."

"Where is Wolf?"

Avelina didn't think anyone noticed when he was with her or not. She hadn't expected anyone to question her about him. "Guarding. He'll remain beyond the castle walls this eve and will alert us if he sees any strangers about."

"You dinna believe he will howl to be let in to join you?" Hamish and others had objected to her raising the wolf from a pup, but when Avelina's mother had died from a fever, she'd been inconsolable.

"He will mind me and stay out there guarding, like I told him to do." When her da had brought her the wolf pup from the mainland, she'd been overjoyed, and everyone believed her da would eventually take the wolf from her and return it to the wild, but she was his pack. Wolf was her family, just as much as her da, her uncle, and her cousin were. And she knew if they released him elsewhere, someone would kill him.

"Did you find the herbs that you went in search of?" Hamish asked.

"Aye. Thank you for worrying about me." Before Hamish could question her further, Avelina asked him, "Where were the men headed who were shipwrecked on our island?"

"Home, they said. They were blown off course by the storm."

"Do you believe them?"

Hamish narrowed his eyes a little as he considered her.

She shrugged as if she had only mentioned it as an afterthought. "Why keep them prisoner, if you believe they wish us no harm?"

His eyes narrowed further. "You are no' intrigued with one of the men, are you?" Now he sounded all growly.

"Nay, of course no'. Whatever made you think such an outlandish notion? You must be jesting. I only mentioned it because you seem concerned about their intentions, and I wondered if we should be also. All of us, I mean. Did they say where they came from?"

"They work for a chief named Cormac on the mainland."

At least they had told her people the truth about that. She frowned. "Has Cormac ever been here to see my uncle?"

"In one of the skirmishes we sent forces to aid those who have alliances with us, aye."

"You have met him?"

"Aye." Hamish was still looking at her as if he knew something more was up because of all her questions. "You have naught you wish to tell me, do you, lass?"

"You dinna think Cormac would want to take Fenella as

a bride to make an alliance between our clans, do you?" Though her uncle had said nothing of the sort, and if there had been some such agreement, he would have told Fenella, she would think. But maybe Hamish knew more.

Hamish folded his arms. "You believe these men had come here intentionally, but were shipwrecked before they could make it to shore, and what? Take Fenella from here to wed Cormac? Why would you come up with such a notion?"

Avelina felt her face heat from embarrassment. She wasn't good at this secretive business. But she was afraid not to say something in case these men got loose and somehow managed to grab her cousin.

"I know it is foolish to suggest such a thing, but I overheard them saying that they had come for Fenella. You spoke to her in front of them, using her name when you did, she said, and she felt uncomfortable afterward because of the way they shared glances. I tried to overhear any conversation they were having among themselves and that's when I heard them mention her name. I could be wrong, and I hope that I am, but I worried that if I'm right..." She shrugged again, figuring Hamish would deal with the men as he saw fit.

She knew he'd question them severely, but if they'd planned to steal Fenella away against her will, and they'd attempted to murder Quinn, this was on their heads, not hers.

"You are certain that's what they said?"

"Aye. If you had someone attempt to overhear their conversation, mayhap they'd give themselves away."

"I must speak with Fenella."

Och, Avelina could imagine her cousin falling to pieces without knowing what Avelina had told Hamish first. "I'll send her down."

"I'll be waiting."

Relieved beyond measure that Avelina could speak to Fenella beforehand, she hurried off to Fenella's chamber. When she finally reached it, she knocked. "'Tis me, Avelina."

Fenella hurried to cross the floor and opened the door for her. "You're as white as a ghost. What did Hamish say?"

"I'm afraid 'tis what *I* said that is the problem." Avelina quickly gave her a rundown on what she told him. "He wants you to speak with him."

"I didn't hear anything from the two mercenaries, except for two of the men's names."

"And that when they heard your name mentioned, they exchanged glances. That's all you have to say. I made up the other part to implicate them, not you."

Fenella wrung her hands. "I canna believe you said that to Hamish."

"I decided we had to stop them if they still intended to steal you away."

"They'll torture them."

"They tried to murder Quinn for no reason. He was trying to fight off five of them on the ship during the storm. One man against five?"

"We only have his word for it."

"You told me that they said they had to kill him. You heard that too."

"True. But that part I canna mention to Hamish, unless you want to reveal the truth about Quinn."

"Nay. I dinna know what to do about him. For now, he should be safe enough at the haunted croft. Hopefully, he'll be fine at Judith's croft when I move him. I canna make excuses to see him every day until his injuries have mended, or Hamish and the others will grow suspicious. And he needs someone to help look after him until then. Beyond that, I dinna know. Come, Hamish is waiting for you to speak with him."

"Dinna fault me if I make a mistake in what I say."

They left her chamber.

"Just dinna mention Quinn or that these men intend to murder him." Avelina frowned at her as they descended the stairs. "Quit looking so nervous and wringing your hands."

They finally reached the main hall and found Hamish with three more of the guards waiting for them. Avelina was afraid Fenella was going to melt into the rushes on the floor.

When they joined the men, Fenella repeated what she had told Avelina she'd overheard, leaving Quinn out of it.

The men were frowning at them, looking menacing, and Avelina knew they would get the truth out of the men. She just hoped they didn't say Quinn was the cause of them being there, and not Cormac. She realized afterward, they might not use Cormac's name, but Quinn's, as a way to hurt him should anyone discover him alive. She was wondering now if there was any way she could aid him to leave the island, if nothing more than moving him to one of the other islands. One that was uninhabited. At least until he could heal from his injuries.

CHAPTER 5

Wolf stirred, raising his head, and Quinn was instantly alert, listening. It was too dark for anyone to be roaming through the area at this time of night. Unless it was just a ghost wandering around.

Wolf listened for a long time, so did Quinn, but all he heard were the sounds of bugs, a frog, and the wind. Then he fell fast asleep and only woke when he realized Wolf had left. He wondered if he'd gone looking for Avelina. Quinn hoped she'd gotten home all right last night after seeing to the widowed woman.

Quinn had a terrible time getting to his feet, his head, arm, and ribs still throbbing with pain. He felt sticky and caked in salt from the swim in the sea. He needed to wash in the nearby river, or the inland loch he'd seen when they'd made their way here. He was grateful to Avelina for mentioning all the landmarks on their way to the croft. He ate the rest of the bread, fish, and cheese that he had left over from last eve. Just in case any of Avelina's people came to the abandoned croft while he was gone, he took the bundle of his clothes with him.

The air was cool and damp this morning as he slowly made his way to the loch, hoping he could swim a little and didn't drown himself. He was a good swimmer, but he still hurt all over. He would be glad when he was feeling more like himself.

When he reached the loch, he stripped off his belt, boots, plaid, and shirt, then took his own plaid and walked slowly into the water. Once he was waist deep, he washed his plaid in the water, then returned it to the shore, laying it out to dry. Then he returned to the water and when he was in deep enough, he dove in and began to slowly dog paddle. As sore as he was, he didn't feel as bad as when he'd been walking here.

He swam for a little bit, feeling cleaner, and loosening his muscles up. He was about to head back into shore, when he saw movement in the brush. Heart pounding, he eyed the bushes. Wolf's head popped up, and Quinn took a relieved breath. Then Quinn swam toward shore. He reached the shallower area and began to walk out, glad to see Wolf. But then Wolf turned his head, listening to something only he could hear.

If some of Avelina's kin had shown up, he couldn't fight them. Not if he wanted to live. Nor did he want to kill any of her people if Cormac had lied to him about Fenella wanting to marry him.

He tried to reach the shirt first, thinking the person approaching might be Avelina, and he didn't want to alarm her with his state of undress. He grabbed the shirt off the ground. He was yanking it over his head and down, when he saw Avelina, her mouth agape, her cheeks pink with embarrassment.

"I worried when I couldna find you at the croft." She looked down at his wet plaid spread out on the grasses.

"I washed and removed the brine from my plaid." He began wrapping her brother's plaid around him, groaning with the movement.

"You worried someone would find my things at the croft." She hurried forth when he sat down to pull on her brother's spare boots. Crouching, she brushed off the dirt from his feet before she helped him with one of the boots. "'Tis haunted. No one comes near it." She looked up at him. "Did...did you have any visitors?"

"Nay, though I worried at one point because Wolf lifted his head, waking me. He must have heard something. Just a critter that hunts at night, I'm certain."

Quinn glanced around for the wolf, but he'd run off again, exploring, doing wolfish things.

"I may have done the wrong thing and said what I ought not to," she warned Quinn.

As worried as she appeared, he was afraid she'd told her people the reason the other men were there—to abscond with Fenella. He knew they'd torture them for all the details, and the men would quickly tell them about him.

"You have to do whatever you feel is right. Even if it means telling your people about me."

She shook her head. "I didna, but it doesna mean they willna discover you, and if they do, you will suffer the fate of the other men. I told Hamish, the man left in charge while the others are off fighting, why the mercenaries were there. Fenella knows naught about this Cormac. Mayhap your brother sent you so that you'd die in an attempt to steal her away. Mayhap he thought, if you managed to do so, he could return her and turn you over to her da, so he could deal with you. Whatever the reason, she doesna know him and never agreed to wed him. She was horrified to learn of your brother's plan. Hamish did say that your brother has met him before, which might be why he even knows about my cousin. She is beautiful."

"*You* are beautiful."

Avelina blushed again.

"What of the other men?" Quinn asked.

"They will be tortured until they tell the truth."

He assumed as much.

"I fear I made a mistake. What if they say you were the one who put them up to it? They dinna know that you're alive, but if they think you are hard to kill, they may believe you could still live and put the blame on you. You wanted to steal Fenella away. You wanted to make her your wife. Then Cormac would appear innocent of any wrongdoing, once again."

He couldn't let his brother get away with it this time. Attempting to murder him was one thing. Blaming Quinn for stealing a woman so she could be his bride was quite another.

"I'm sorry," she said softly.

"You need no' be, Avelina. You are caught between. None of this is your doing."

"How are you feeling this morn?"

"Better. Much better."

"Och, tell me the truth. As much as you were groaning when you were dressing, I dinna believe you are feeling much better."

He smiled at her. "Just seeing you here makes me feel much better."

She frowned at him. "I could have just gotten you killed. If they find you, they will torture you just the same. It matters no' if you are innocent, and that your brother is the guilty party. I've thought about borrowing a boat to take you over to one of the uninhabited islands. But you would have to fend for yourself once you are there. I'm no' sure you could survive. I couldna see you for days. I could gather as much as I can to help you make it through until I could return to see you again, but I might get caught doing so. If I could manage, I would send Wolf with you. He can fish, though he might no' share with you."

"If we get caught, I wouldna want you to be in trouble for assisting me."

Ignoring what he said, Avelina added, "I told Judith I was bringing you to her croft, and she was eager to see you. But I'm afraid that once the other men are made to speak, and if they mention you and your ability to stay alive, our men will rally to search for you. They will see you as the man in charge, no matter if they say Cormac told you to do it. You were the one responsible for these men when you made your way here to fulfill your brother's request. It would be your word against theirs that they tried to murder you."

"To keep you from getting into trouble over this, I should steal the coracle. Then your people will know I did it, if they should catch me, and that you didna aid me."

"Nay. I must return the boat. They would search all the islands otherwise, looking for it, if anyone found it to be missing."

"You dinna think they will search them anyway, looking for me in case I made it to one of them?"

"Nay. They are located much too far from where the ship sank. The currents and waves would have beached you on our shores." She took a breath and appeared to be considering their alternatives. "All right, we will do this. I'll collect extra supplies from Judith and replenish hers as soon as I can. I'll gather as much as I'm able to from the keep, and bring the boat up the river near here. It leads back to the sea on the leeward side of the island, and that will put us at the closest point to reach the next island. But you should go to the island beyond that, just to be sure no one would find you. 'Tis early, and if we are to do this today, I will need to hurry back and fetch what I can."

"What can I do to help?" Quinn knew this could be a disaster for both of them. But if she were caught, he hoped they would consider that she was just a woman, who thought to save an injured man. Nothing more.

"Gather your things." She gave him a new bundle of items. "Stay at the croft for a couple of hours and then head directly in that direction." She pointed the way. "You will come to a river. If you walk along it that way"—she again motioned in the direction she meant—"you will meet me somewhere along the river, and we'll head out to sea."

"In the same direction I'll be walking to join up with you?"

"Aye."

"Then I'll walk as far as I can go until I see you. You willna have to paddle as far in the wrong direction."

"You wait, first. It will take me time to borrow a coracle and gather more food and such. We have very few men right now, while the majority are off fighting. Even so, some will surely be out looking for more survivors, and I dinna want you to get caught roaming about."

"Aye, thank you, Avelina. Someday, I hope to repay you."

"Just keep yourself safe until we can decide what to do with you later." She stood and helped him up, and he was trying his darnedest not to groan, but he couldn't help it.

"You are no' much better," she accused.

He took her frowning face in his hands and kissed her forehead. "Seeing you makes me feel much better."

And then he kissed her mouth, knowing he shouldn't. But what if he didn't make it out of this alive? What if he wasn't ever able to see her again? He couldn't quit thinking about her lovely mouth, her devastatingly soulful blue eyes, her red-gold curls, and her soft, womanly curves, but most of all? The way she genuinely cared about his welfare, despite that he'd intended to steal her cousin away before he was shipwrecked on her island.

She leaned against him lightly, and he wanted to pull her tight against his body, to feel her soft body, but just the slightest bit of pressure against his ribs hurt. Yet his mouth on hers stole his attention, the warm, sweet taste of her, and his body reacted, his staff stirring to life. He was afraid she'd pull away, but the vixen stayed where she was, kissing him back, and she had to feel his growing arousal.

She finally broke free of his kiss, as if she recalled her mission. "I...I must get the coracle. I must hurry." Tears glistened in her eyes, her hand holding his.

"You dinna have to do this for me—"

"Nay, do as I say. I will return as soon as I can."

"Be safe," he said, and she pulled away, wishing him to do the same.

She hurried off, but when Wolf followed her, she turned to him. "Stay and guard the prisoner."

Quinn smiled, and Wolf stood still while she continued on her way. Wolf's tail relaxed, his ears perked. Quinn knew Wolf wanted to follow her in the worst way, and he wished *he* could see her safely off also, but he was certain that would be the death of him.

He gathered his wet plaid and the other items, including the new bundle she'd brought him. He wished he could at least see Judith and help her with anything he could before he had to leave here, but he didn't know his way to her croft. Would Wolf?

Avelina suddenly let out a blood-curdling scream. Enraged and worried for her safety, Quinn dropped the bundles and tore off to reach her.

CHAPTER 6

The grizzly-faced, blond-haired man grabbed Avelina around the waist, his hand clapped over her mouth, and he whispered in her ear, "Dinna make another squeak, lass, or it will be your last one."

Avelina didn't doubt he meant to do her harm. He had his arm around her arms, pinning her to his damp body, smelling of the sea, and she couldn't reach her sword or *sgian dubh*. She was afraid Quinn would try to save her and get himself killed. The same with Wolf as she saw both of them racing toward her. Yet they gave her a sense of hope, and she was grateful to see them, despite worrying about their safety.

Quinn's face was dark with rage, and she thought as angry as he looked, the man holding her should have released her and fled. She had hoped he was just one of the sailors, but he was wearing a sword, and he'd leaped out of the brush at her when she'd tried to pass. She'd been so concerned about reaching Judith's croft and doing what she could for Quinn, she hadn't been watching for any signs that someone else from the ship could be lurking about.

"My, my, what they say is true. Quinn has the Gods watching over him." He glanced down at her. "And...you?"

Wolf was nearly to them, and the brigand pulled out his sword.

"No, Wolf, stop!" she shrieked.

"Wolf!" Quinn commanded, and the wolf stopped and looked back at Quinn, as if expecting him to do something about this. "Let the woman go, and fight me, you bastard."

The man sneered at him. "You are unarmed?"

"And he's been badly injured," Avelina said, hoping the man would let her go, thinking Quinn couldn't fight him, and he would be an easy kill. She hadn't seen Quinn put the *sgian dubh* in his boot. She hoped he, at least, had that weapon on him. Now she regretted that she hadn't returned his sword to him. She wished she could toss her own shorter sword to him, so he'd have a fighting chance. Though this man, who seemed uninjured and was carrying a much larger sword, would be hard to beat.

"They say the lasses always love him. You too? Do you know what he planned to do? Steal Fenella away to be his bride."

"Good. The woman is a menace and sharp of tongue. He can have her. Let me go, and the two of you can be on your way," Avelina said, her voice angry.

"Do you hear that Quinn? We can both be on our way, and the lass willna tell her kin about us. I think no'." The man moved his sword to cut her. Suddenly, he was falling backwards and her with him. When she felt his grip loosen on her, she quickly rolled away and stared at the dead man, his mouth gaping, his eyes staring heavenward, Quinn's *sgian dubh* centered in the middle of the man's forehead.

"Is…is that one of the men who tried to kill you before?" She looked up to see Quinn crouching down next to her before he grabbed her up in his arms and carried her a few feet away from the dead man. She hadn't even heard Quinn moving toward her, she'd been so shocked when the man fell dead to the ground.

Wolf was smelling the man.

She was shaking so badly, Quinn tightened his hold on her and groaned.

"I'm so sorry." She wrapped her arms around him, unable to quit shaking.

"Nay, lass, dinna be."

She didn't want him to let her go, though she knew she had to leave. "I…I must go."

"I will bury him as soon as you are gone."

"That is the last of them?"

"Aye. Unless the other three, who are still in the hands of your kin, are still alive." Quinn set her on her feet.

She wrapped her arms around Quinn and kissed him again. "Thank you, for saving my life. He would have killed me."

He kissed her warmly back. Like a man who wanted much more, and she knew she shouldn't, but every bit of her ached for him.

"You must go, now, lass. I'll take care of him."

"Aye."

But he kissed her again in the same heartwarming, and then lust-filled, way and she wished this was the man of her dreams, not someone her kin would want to string up. She quickly said her goodbyes again, told Wolf to stay with Quinn, and hurried off, her whole body shaky from the near-death encounter. She wished they could just leave this man's body on the beach for her men to find, but how would they explain the bloody knife wound to his head?

***

After Quinn weighted the brigand's body down with stones, he dumped him in a bog, hoping no one would come across him, ever. He hoped Avelina felt better soon, hating that the man had accosted her like he had. He sheathed the dead man's sword at his belt.

Quinn still had it in mind to help Judith out, and said to the wolf, "Wolf, take me to see Judith."

The wolf just looked at him.

"Where is Judith?" He suspected the wolf had been with Avelina when she went to see Judith and would know the way. If he understood the command to take him somewhere and connected his command with Judith's location, Wolf could take him there.

The wolf looked back in the direction that Avelina had gone. Quinn bundled everything together, then said to Wolf again, "Take me to Judith's croft."

He hoped this wasn't a mistake, but Avelina had promised Judith he'd help her with some repairs, and that would give him something to do while he waited for her to return for him. He wasn't good with waiting to do something, but he wasn't sure the wolf would take him where he needed to go.

He loped off and Quinn tried to keep him in sight, but the wolf soon disappeared. Not wanting to call out to him in the event anyone in the area might hear, Quinn tried to follow the narrow path cutting through the gorse, and hoped he was going the right way.

It seemed to take him forever, though he was attempting to move as quickly as he could, but every step and breath he took, the pain shot through every injured part of him. He finally saw a curl of smoke and prayed it was coming from Judith's croft.

He saw an older woman, her gray hair braided down her back, fetching water from the river. He didn't want to scare her, but there was no way to alert her that he was there without alarming her. Wolf was nowhere to be seen, so he worried this woman wasn't the right one.

Then he saw Wolf poke his head out of the woman's croft, and Quinn smiled a little. Wolf hurried out of the croft to greet him, and the woman turned to see where he was going. Just like Quinn was afraid would happen, she gave a little, startled squeak.

"Avelina sent me, if you are Judith, and Wolf didna lead me astray. Here, let me fetch the water for you."

"You are injured! Avelina told me she was taking you away from here, not bringing you here."

"I came to help you fix what needs"—he stared at the byre in shambles—"fixing."

"Och." She dismissed him with a wave of her hand. "You were to come here to heal, but she says you may be in worse trouble than before."

Quinn hurried to reach the woman and take the bucket from her, then with much effort, he waded into the water and crouched down to fill it.

Even though she was shaking her head, frowning at him, he saw a glimmer of a smile on her lips. He wished he could stay and help her for a time while he mended. But he feared it wouldn't be safe for either of them.

He carried the bucket of water into the croft.

"She told me you planned to steal Fenella away." Judith tsked.

"Because she wanted to be taken to my brother, so my brother said."

"Your brother isna worthy of your loyalty."

"Aye." After this, Quinn wouldn't return to his clan. He hoped Malcolm MacNeill would allow him to join his men. Somehow, he had to make it back to the mainland. Still, if he lived through this final treachery, he would have loved to prove to his brother that he'd failed in another attempt to have him murdered.

"Have you eaten?"

"I have, thank you." Quinn left the croft and began moving stones to create a more secure byre.

She watched him for a moment and sighed heavily. "This wasna our intent. You should rest. You'll have to fend for yourself when you reach the island. You need your strength. I will make do until the men return from battle."

"I will help to get it started. It will give your animals some protection from future storms until then."

She cooked oats for him anyway, and when he had made some progress, she gave him the bowl. "Now, sit, and rest. Avelina will be fair sore with me when she learns what you have done."

Quinn thanked her and began to eat the oats.

"You were to meet her at the river. Rather than cut back through to the abandoned croft, you can take a path in that direction and be closer." Judith motioned in the direction he would need to go.

"I dinna believe she would have had time to make all her preparations, borrow her coracle, and make it this far. I'll continue to work for a while longer."

"You will rest."

After he finished the oats and washed the bowl, he returned to work on the byre. She left the croft, shaking her head, and took hold of his uninjured arm and dragged him back into the croft. She was a wiry, older woman, but she had a lot of strength too. "I've made a pallet for you by the fire, and your plaid is nearly dry. Lie down. The work will get done, but I dinna want to see how angry Avelina will be if she returns to find you worse off than before."

She reminded him of his great aunt, and he appreciated her kindness. With a groan, he settled onto the pallet by the fire and thought about Avelina, worried about her, concerned she'd be caught before she could make any headway, and would be in the worst sort of trouble.

***

Avelina hurried back to the keep as quickly as she could, excited about helping the stranger, and terrified that her own people would be angry with her over her deceitfulness. When she reached the outer bailey, everyone was going about their chores—some feeding the horses and mucking out the stable, a blacksmith sharpening swords, a woman retrieving grain from the granary, another collecting eggs from the hens in the hutch, another milking cows—and Avelina wondered where the prisoners were and if they were still alive.

She couldn't think about that now and moved quickly through the outer bailey to the inner one, past the well where a couple of women were gathering water. She greeted them in passing, not stopping, hurried into the keep, and up the stairs to her chamber. Fenella must have been watching her out of one of the windows because she quickly joined her at her chamber.

"What news?" Fenella asked.

"I need to gather what things I can and borrow a coracle and take him to one of the uninhabited islands."

"You would never make it back in time for supper." Fenella frowned. "Would he even be able to survive? Not only is he injured, but there's no shelter there." She shook her head. "How do you think you're going to borrow one of the coracles without getting caught?"

"I will do this. I have to." Avelina was hurrying to wrap her bedroll she used for traveling.

"He'll need food."

"Aye. A fishing net, mayhap. He'll have to fend for himself. I'm leaving Wolf with him."

"Willna everyone miss Wolf?"

"He goes off on his own sometimes for days. Mayhap in a few days, I can check on Quinn and return with Wolf."

Fenella folded her arms. "You are sure you can navigate all the way there and back again?"

"Aye." Avelina would have to, if she was going to try and save Quinn.

"I dinna know. That's an awfully long way. Did you tell Judith that he willna be staying with her?"

"Aye. I will have to return to her place on the morrow to give her more food. I took some of hers to give to Quinn."

"I've got more." Fenella rushed to leave Avelina's chamber.

Avelina was glad her cousin was willing to aid her, despite that Quinn had planned to steal her away. When Avelina was done gathering what she thought he could use—her bedroll, a thread and needle, her spare plaid, and a bowl—she met Fenella, who also had a bundle, in the stairwell.

"I'll help you carry this through the keep. We'll have to go the back way. Did…he see any ghosts?" Fenella asked.

"Nay." Avelina had been so worried when she'd reached the abandoned croft to speak with Quinn, and he and Wolf had been nowhere in sight. She'd been afraid her men had caught Quinn and hauled him off, and she'd missed seeing them. She also had worried that Quinn had left of his own accord, anxious that someone might find him. When she asked Wolf where Quinn was, he had led her straight to the loch and to a very naked Quinn.

She hadn't expected to see him dripping wet and all his manly parts exposed. *Again.*

He was beautiful. Despite his wounds, he couldn't have been any brawer than he was. She'd never seen such a beautiful man in her life.

When he'd seen her gawking at him, she'd felt her face flame with heat. Aye, she'd seen his staff before—several times—when he was injured on the beach and trying to make it to higher ground, but he'd been unconscious or too busy trying to reach safety. It wasn't the same when the man knew she had seen him in all his glorious skin.

Even now, she felt her face flush with mortification.

And then there was the kiss. She loved how gentle he was with kissing her, how she had excited that part of him that even in pain showed how intrigued he was with her. She reminded herself that her mother had said that any man who touched a woman would become so aroused, and to see it for what it was—not an act of undying love for the lass, but pure and simple, animalistic lust.

"You dinna need to go with me all the way," Avelina warned her cousin. She didn't want her to get into trouble like she knew she would be if she got caught.

They left the keep and Avelina directed her cousin toward the postern gate concealed in the castle curtain wall, which allowed them to come and go unnoticed.

"Nay. You will need me to help move the coracle into the water, and I'll assist you in loading everything into it. Are you sure he is worth saving? You will be risking your life once again."

"Aye. We must hurry."

Fenella sighed. "Whose coracle will we be borrowing?"

"Lendon's. He's off to battle and willna be home for who knows how long. No one will be using his coracle, and no one should miss it. *For now.* If no one sees me paddling in it. Though I have borrowed it before to fish for Wolf when

Lendon was away because he said I could. In this rough water, I'm sure no one would want me out fishing."

They went out through the postern gate and entered the tunnel that led away from the castle. A few of the women had greeted them as they went about their chores, but to them, Fenella and Avelina appeared to be doing work too, so they didn't seem to draw undue attention.

They made their way to one of the crofts closest to the river that led to the sea. Fenella glanced at the waves crashing on the beach. "The waves are still higher from the storm."

"We will make it." Avelina was determined to see this through. They set their bundles down and pulled the coracle out of Lendon's byre where he stored his boat and fishing nets.

Fenella studied the bull-skin covered craft. "Too bad you couldna just let Quinn borrow it himself, and then he could use it for fishing too."

"I would have to borrow another to search for him later, to ensure he was getting enough to eat."

"You just want to go with him." Fenella said the words in a jesting way, but she was studying Avelina to see her reaction.

"He is very braw," Avelina said, not about to make up some tale about how she didn't care what happened to him, because it was too late to pretend such a thing.

Fenella's eyes widened. "What happened between the two of you? Even now, your cheeks are flaming red."

"Fenella, we must hurry." Avelina threw her bundles into the craft and Fenella loaded hers.

They began to carry the craft, but Fenella was trying to take it to the ocean and Avelina was moving toward the river. "To the river. I will pick him up near the abandoned croft, and we will paddle to the ocean."

"Aye." They carried the craft toward the river this time in a unified effort, but Fenella wouldn't leave off on her query. "Tell me what happened between the two of you."

"Fenella." They needed to save their breath to carry the craft.

"I can imagine quite a lot, unless you wish to tell me what really did happen."

Avelina groaned. "Naught more happened than he kissed me to thank me for saving his life."

"He kissed you!" Fenella didn't say anything for a blessed few feet, but Avelina knew it wouldn't last. "What kind of kiss?"

The most pleasurable kind. "To thank me, naught more. I'm sure he would have given anyone such a kiss."

"No' if a man had aided him." Fenella turned to look at Avelina. "Your cheeks are as red as before."

Avelina smiled.

"Och, you will tell me when you return then. I want all the details."

They both quit talking while they saved their breaths, not wanting to alert anyone as to what they were doing, as they made their way over the uneven ground. Though one man could carry the boat, with all the stuff inside it, they needed two women to do it.

They finally reached the river and set the boat on the bank. Fenella gave Avelina a big hug, tears in her eyes. "You are sure you will be safe? It will be a long trip back here after you leave him off on one of the islands. You will be tired."

"I will manage."

"'Tis no' the same as when we did this with others as a test of our courage. Or when you go out to fish when the waves are more settled."

"Nay, I'm older now and I've gone out when it's like this." Not usually, but she had to a couple of times when the men were away, and they'd desperately needed more food. Though others had gone out as well, so she hadn't been fishing alone.

"And you will be alone on the return trip, no one to help you paddle, no one to talk to."

"I may return with Wolf. And I can talk to him. *He* doesna ask me all kinds of questions."

"He doesna kiss like a man, either."

Avelina blushed again. She couldn't help it. Not only had Quinn kissed her like a man would a woman he was thoroughly intrigued with, but he was their enemy.

Avelina gave Fenella a hug before she left. Then they set the craft in the water, and Fenella steadied it while Avelina climbed in.

"Godspeed, dear Cousin." Fenella shoved the boat off, tears in her eyes.

"I will be fine. I'll see you before you can even miss me." Avelina waved at her, before paddling hard to reach the place where she would pick up Quinn.

"I already miss you," Fenella called out, then she hurried off.

Avelina knew she'd be worried about her until she returned. And she *would* return.

She continued to paddle hard and couldn't believe it when she hadn't gone but half a mile and saw Wolf running along the bank, wagging his tail at her. Quinn was standing with his bundle at his feet a short distance from him, waiting for her. She swore his bundle looked bigger than before, and she wondered what he'd found to add to it.

Mainly, she prayed they got away without anyone witnessing them now, or her, upon her return.

CHAPTER 7

Quinn had mixed feelings when he saw Avelina and the coracle loaded down with bundles, but he was still worried about her going with him to one of the islands.

"I know what you are thinking, and no, you are no' taking the boat yourself," she said.

He saw that she'd brought his sword and was glad for it.

"Aye, I brought your sword, though I see you have the dead man's sword, but dinna use either on my kin, should they find you on the island. Only on *your* kin, if they should discover you there. I wish you'd had it before, but you are handy with your *sgian dubh*. What did you do with the dead man?"

"Buried him in a bog. I didna have a shovel. Hopefully, he willna surface, ever."

"Or if he does, no one will ever see him. Thank you, for saving me," she said again.

"You have done much more for me at a risk to your own life. You could have drowned when you were trying to help me past the tide waters." He lifted her into his arms, startling her, and set her down in the craft.

"Come, Wolf," she called, and the wolf jumped into the boat.

"He looks like he's taken a ride with you before." Quinn climbed in and took the paddle from Avelina and began paddling them downriver.

"He has. I was going to paddle so you could rest up further."

"You will have to paddle all the way back to your island."

She snorted. "You will have to make yourself a shelter and find food. Though you should have enough to last you a few days." She glanced at the bundle she'd given him that had grown. "What did you add to the bundle I gave you?"

"I saw Judith and repaired some of her byre, enough to keep her sheep from wandering off. In return, she fed me oats and gave me more to take with me, dried fish, and more bread."

"That's why you were so much closer to where I'd be. How did you find your way there?"

"Wolf took me."

"I hope you didna do yourself further injury."

"I will rest up this eve."

She let out her breath and watched the shore. "Neither Fenella nor I learned what your brothers' men said under torture. It isna something we could just come out and ask about unless we wanted to arouse suspicion."

"You willna be missed?"

"I am often off checking on women in the outlying crofts who need some extra help while their men are fighting in clan battles. No one bothers us on the island, normally. We were raided way before I was born, but except for our men being called to fight with our allies against some enemy in Scotland, we are left alone." She shrugged. "We have a simple life. Not much happens here unless we have a violent storm, and rarely, a shipwreck. Your ship must have been getting close to our shores and that was the reason we found so many men, some drowned. We usually don't find any bodies, but sometimes months later, we'll find crates or ship's debris. We assumed the ship had been blown off course, but of course that wasna the case."

"You are sure Wolf willna be missed?"

"He will be missed but he does run off sometimes, so it isna unusual. And with my men finding bodies on the shore, all I have to say is he's out searching for any more."

"They aren't afraid he would eat them?"

"Of course no'. Though if I tell him to attack a man, he will. I didna with the man who promised to kill me because I didna want him cutting Wolf."

"Aye."

"You are no' afraid of Wolf staying with you, are you?"

He fought smiling. "Nay. He will keep me from swimming away."

She gave him a little smile. Wolf was sitting between them, watching the seabirds flying overhead as they paddled out to sea. It was a lot choppier than she'd expected it to be, the coracle bouncing around in the rough water. She sat lower in the craft.

"Go to the island beyond this one. Though most likely no one would see a fire over here, they wouldna see any from the island beyond it. When you build your shelter, make sure it is on the other side, just in case someone comes this way to fish, though I dinna think they do."

"Aye." He knew where to set up the best shelter, but he appreciated that she wanted to make sure he would be safe.

He paddled hard and steady, wanting to get there as soon as possible so she could leave as quickly as she could and arrive home before it was too much later. He was still thinking of how Wolf should go home with her. What if something happened to him, and Wolf couldn't return home? What if something happened to her? If she capsized, could Wolf help her to shore? Or would they both perish?

"Are you certain you can return all right, lass?"

"Aye, keep paddling. I will be sore in the morning, for sure, but 'tis the only way."

"I'm thinking Wolf should return with you." Quinn eyed the birds on the rocks. "Willna he scare off the puffins, gannets, and fulmars? Eat them? Their eggs?"

She smiled at him. "Do you really care about the wildlife on the island? Or are you afraid Wolf will eat all of it, and you will have naught to eat?"

"They are no' used to predators on the island, and aye, I care."

"If I canna return for much longer, and you run out of food, then what will you do?"

"I will be fishing. You found me a fine net. In one of the coves, I can fish." He eyed the shore they were growing closer to. "There are plenty of rocks on this side, and I'm sure on the other, that I could use to build a small shelter. But if Wolf wasna with me, I wouldna have to build it quite so big."

"All right. I will take him back." She watched as gray seals on the beach jumped off the rocks into the sea.

Quinn paddled straight for the beach, and she immediately objected. "You need to set up your shelter on the other side of the island."

"I will, but it will take much longer to paddle around there. You need to return now, so you'll have plenty of daylight."

"Aye. But you are injured."

"Aye, and all this paddling is killing me."

She chuckled. "You will be hurting more if you have to carry all this stuff to the other side."

"I will do it. Dinna come here for several days, so that no one is suspicious of where you're off to. I will manage just fine. I have lived off the land several times and survived. I dinna want you having to travel that far again too soon, nor to risk getting caught."

"Aye, true."

He pulled the boat onto the shore and Wolf jumped out. "Stay here," he commanded the wolf, and Wolf sat. He had forgotten he wasn't supposed to be giving the wolf commands and that Wolf would obey them.

Avelina folded her arms, looking cross. "So he isna your guard after all. Just like when you commanded him to stay and not attack that man to protect Wolf, though I thought he was obeying my order, not yours."

"Aye, he guards. He growls if I dinna feed him enough of my food."

"Och, that food is meant for you! He feeds himself. That decides it. He returns with me or he'll eat all your food and whatever birds he can catch on the island."

"Good. I wouldna want you to miss him, or him to miss you. I couldna sleep nights if he were to howl for you."

Her jaw dropped. "I hadna thought of that." She helped Quinn to unpack the boat.

"Get in the coracle," Quinn said to Wolf. The wolf hesitated, probably not liking the idea that he couldn't have some time to run around the island and chase the birds and seals.

"In," Avelina said, pointing to the boat.

Wolf jumped in, and before she climbed in, Quinn pulled her against his chest for a tender hug. "Be safe. Dinna take any more risks for me."

"I will return."

"No' for several days."

"Aye." Then she wrapped her arms around his neck and kissed him. "You are my prisoner."

"Aye, I will do anything you command of me."

"Rest and heal and stay alive."

"I will." He kissed her back, more passionately than he had the first time, afraid to scare her off when she was his savior. But she fed into the kiss, and he didn't want to let her go. He felt her reluctance to leave also. "You must go, Avelina. Godspeed, lass."

"Take care."

He lifted her into the boat, kissed her as she leaned toward him, and then pulled away. He shoved the boat into the water and watched as she paddled back to her island. She was a strong paddler, but he suspected some of that was for show, that she would weary long before she reached the halfway point. He knew he should move his bundles to the other side of the island, but instead, he watched her go until she was but a speck on the water, and then disappeared altogether.

He'd never felt the loss he felt now, missing her frowns and elusive smiles, even her reserved laughter. But especially the way she kissed him. She was no wanton woman, he could tell from the way she'd so tentatively kissed him and pressed herself against him. All he knew was his body craved having her. He missed the wolf too, wishing he could have stayed with him for companionship. But Quinn wanted her to have him for protection, and to lessen any suspicions she might have aroused by her being gone for so long.

Now he had the arduous task of moving the bundles to the other side of the island, every muscle in his body aching something fierce. He gathered all the bundles, but didn't think he could manage that way. He rummaged through the items and found rope, and taking driftwood and one of the plaids, he created a travois. Using that, he packed the bundles on top and proceeded to climb the hill, hoping there was fresh water on the island.

***

Avelina didn't think she'd make it back to Lendon's

croft. She was dog tired, and she was so sore, she didn't think she could use her arms for anything. But she still needed to carry the boat to his croft and secure it. She considered getting Fenella to help her, but she was afraid once she returned to the keep, she wouldn't be able to go back to get his coracle, and someone would surely notice it out here.

Wolf was running all over, happy to be on solid ground again. She still wished he'd stayed with Quinn, but not if the man was going to feed Wolf half his food! She couldn't believe Quinn had been pretending the wolf was truly guarding him, when he'd easily befriended him!

She didn't know anyone who could so easily win her wolf over. Wolf loved women and children, but he was wary of most men. Mainly because they said such disparaging things about him. She kept telling them Wolf understood what they were saying, and if they were kinder to him, he would be their friend too. But they didn't trust the wolf.

She was trying hard to carry the coracle over her head like the men did, but her arms were aching, and she kept stumbling. She couldn't drag it like she wanted to, because the skin covering the hull would be scraped and possibly torn, and she'd be the one responsible. Not to mention, she couldn't use it to return to Quinn if she tore a hole in it. She prayed he would be all right, and as much as it killed her, knowing he was right, and though she wanted to do just as he'd said—to wait several days—she already wanted to return to him, to make sure he was going to be okay.

She had to leave straight away in the morning to replenish Judith's food supplies also. She finally managed to leave the coracle in Lendon's byre, and then ran as fast as she could toward the keep, Wolf racing ahead of her.

She slowed her run when she saw men carrying bodies out through the gates. The mercenaries. All three. Dead.

Hamish was helping to carry one of the men and glanced in her direction. She had to know what the men had told her people. Had they implicated Quinn? Did Hamish know she'd been helping the man in charge of the mercenaries? Her heart was racing with concern, and she fought wringing her hands like Fenella did when she was worried.

Avelina waited respectfully for the men to pass, and then when they had moved away, she hurried to the gates. One of the guards shook his head at her. "You will have to return sooner than later from your trip to the outlying crofts. If your da or your uncle were here, they wouldna allow you to be wandering around on the island all day, right up until the sun sets, with the possibility that any other shipwreck survivors might be wandering around."

"The men died," she said, hoping Dar would tell her what they had said. But since he wasn't accusing her of aiding Quinn, maybe he didn't know about him. Maybe the mercenaries only mentioned Cormac, but she doubted they would have kept from naming Quinn as a co-conspirator, especially if they believed he might have survived.

"Aye, that's what happens when you try to steal the chief's daughter."

Which meant the same fate awaited Quinn, should they discover him nearby. "Did they tell you that Cormac was behind it?"

"Aye, and his brother, Quinn. There was another man too, but the two of them must have perished in the sea and will feed the fishes because we've found no sign of them. You best be off to supper then, lass."

"Aye, of course." Avelina hurried to the keep and saw Fenella rushing out to greet her, Wolf at her side, and she wondered if Wolf had alerted her cousin she had returned.

When they were beyond anyone's earshot, Fenella said conspiratorially, "I worried when Wolf found me, and you were no' with him. Then I saw you speaking with Dar and waited until you were free."

"And you were no' wringing your hands?"

"Some. I am trying to break myself of the habit as I know it gets me into trouble with my da. What news have you?"

"He is safely there. I hope that he is able to make a shelter for himself and can find enough food when he runs out of what he has."

They walked into the great hall together.

"I thought you were going to leave Wolf with…um, there." Fenella amended when a woman walked past them.

"He was giving half his food to Wolf!"

Fenella glanced at Avelina and whispered, "Bribing him, so he could control Wolf?"

Avelina snorted. "I believe he'd already won him over." She frowned. "Mayhap because he *had* bribed him!"

"They have called off the searches because they have no' found any other men and need to keep after their own chores, but you know they will continue to search for anyone else while they are doing them."

"Aye. If they dinna hunt for him elsewhere, and he can survive on his own, everything will be well."

"For now, aye, but how long can he live on the island by himself?"

Avelina had thought about it a lot, and she wasn't sure what to do about him. Fenella was right. He couldn't live there like that forever. "I dinna know. Mayhap we could find him later and name him by another name. Say he is from a different clan. A fisherman who fell off his vessel during another storm?"

"We would have to wait for another storm, and what if it was long in coming?"

They took their seats.

"And let's say our people took him in, then what? He isna a fisherman," Fenella said.

"For now, he is."

"What if they make him a fisherman here? When he truly is a warrior and a brother to a chief?"

"He would be at just as much risk returning home, if his brother only wants to kill him." Avelina could imagine somehow getting him to the mainland, and then he would die at the hands of his brother.

"You could...wed him," Fenella said, then took a bite of her bread.

Avelina choked on a mouthful of honeyed mead. "Cousin," she said, hoarsely, between spasms of coughs.

"Sorry." Fenella patted her back. "He is braw, and he kissed you. You are blushing again!"

"I am...coughing."

"Dinna tell me you have no' thought of it." Then

Fenella's eyes widened. "You dinna plan to run away with him. He is a Highlander and you are—"

"Gaelic, some Scandinavian, and some Welsh. You know our forefathers made alliances with numerous other kingdoms through marriages, so they could fight against their enemies."

"Even the Anglo-Normans."

"Aye."

"So, see, you have considered it."

Avelina looked heavenward. "Now how could we do that? Swim to the mainland of Scotland?"

"Take Lendon's fishing boat."

"And perish."

One of the women must have overheard some of their conversation, though they'd been speaking low, but most likely it was when Avelina had a coughing fit when her mead went down wrong.

"Who were you interested in marrying?" Gwyneth asked.

"No one," Avelina said. The woman was attracted to her da, and she was always trying to find some way to get his attention. He always laughed at her jests and smiled at her, but Avelina had never seen him truly act drawn to the woman. Mayhap she thought if Avelina wanted to marry some man, her da would take more of an interest in having female companionship—a wife perchance.

"You can tell me. It would be just between the three of us. Unless you've told others," Gwyneth said, tucking a loose black curl behind her ear.

"There is no one."

"It's hard to believe there is anyone since you've shown no interest in anyone that I've seen."

Gwyneth had been spying on her. That made Avelina uneasy. She had always been careful around the men, Hamish, in particular, because he watched both Fenella and her when their das were not here.

Then Gwyneth frowned. "He isna a farmer, is he? That's no' why you keep leaving to see the women who have no men to help them on their farms? Is it?" The woman's brown eyes sparkled with intrigue. "Your da wouldna approve. You are the chief's niece. Both of you will make alliances with some other clan."

Then why ask if Avelina was interested in some man? But she didn't like the disparaging way Gwyneth talked about the farmers. Her mother had been one, and her mother's parents had been. Mayhap that was why Gwyneth didn't seem to like them.

"Your da asked me to look out for you." Gwyneth glanced at Fenella. "And your da as well."

Avelina didn't think her da had asked Gwyneth to watch out for her. He had never done so before. That was Hamish's duty. "Has my da told you whom I'm to wed?" If Gwyneth knew that, then maybe she did have her da's ear.

"Nay. Though dinna be surprised if your das come home from this latest conflict with contracts in hand for both of you. You dinna think they left with such a large force just to fight, do you? They wanted to show prospective allies what they had to offer to back up an alliance."

Avelina and Fenella cast each either looks. Neither had

heard any news of this. She was disheartened to think her da wouldn't have spoken to her about this before he left. Not that she had any choice in the matter, but her mother had assured her that her da had promised he would talk to her first about a prospective contract. Her mother and da had been happy together and when she had died of a fever, he'd been heartbroken. Avelina wished she'd have the chance to marry a man that she loved like that. Her mother had been only a farmer's daughter and had hopes of marrying a farmer's son, until Avelina's da had seen her working in the fields one day, and carried her off on his horse to the keep, declaring she would be his bride. Her mother had always spoken of how gallant he was, and how much she loved him.

Her da had not married to make an alliance with anyone. Why should she? Because half of the men that worked and trained here, were under her da's allegiance, and he was under his brother's, the chief. That meant he could command his men to fight in someone's battle, if the chief consented.

Gwyneth began to speak to the woman sitting on the other side of her, but Avelina and Fenella sat in silence, having a hard time finishing their meals. When the meal ended, they hurried off to speak to one another in Fenella's chamber in private.

Fenella paced across her small chamber while Avelina collapsed on her bed. "I knew this would come to pass sooner or later. I hoped later, no' that I wouldna love to have a man kiss me," she said, glancing at Avelina. "Did you know anything about this?

"Nay. I would have told you had I known. I never suspected..." Avelina clapped her hand to her forehead.

Fenella hurried to sit on the bed. "What? Tell me."

Avelina touched the shell necklace at her throat. "'Twas my mother's. Da finally gave it to me before he left. I thought it was because he was going into battle, and he wanted me to have it, to remind me of him and of my mother. He had given it to her when they wed, and he was going off to battle for the first time after they married. I...I had no idea it could mean more."

"To say it was time for you to wed." Fenella collapsed on her back on the bed. "If I were you, I would return to Quinn and steal away with him."

"And do what? Even if we could make it to the mainland, his brother wants to kill him, and my da would too. Probably yours also."

"Ah-ha! You do care for him."

"He saved my life when I was trying to save his in high tide."

Fenella rolled onto her stomach. "You dinna tell me that. Oh, oh, you kissed him back to thank him! How was it? The kiss? Tell me." She rolled onto her back and put her hands on her heart. "I may never know such a sweet thing. No' from one I love."

"Pleasurable and tender."

"And?" Fenella turned to study her. "You wouldna be blushing so if it wasna more than that. Give."

"And passionate. He made my world spin."

"He was holding you close?"

"His ribs were bruised."

Fenella slapped the bed with her hand. "I knew it! What was it like?"

"Painful for him, because he groaned."

"Mayhap he was groaning because he knew he had to let you go."

"He was groaning because he'd been injured."

"And he was pressing you close to him." Fenella sighed. "You have to keep him. I know you want to. I would want to, if I knew my da wouldna kill us both. Besides, you were the one who rescued him and went out of your way to make sure he would be safe. You canna tell me you did so just because you were being nice. I suspect you wouldna have done the same for the other men."

"Nay. The one tried to kill me, and Quinn saved me."

Fenella gaped at Avelina. "When did this happen?"

"When I returned for Quinn, and told him I'd said too much to Hamish. The brigand was one of the mercenaries, and he was planning to cut me. Quinn killed him."

Fenella's eyes widened. "How? He wasna armed."

"I had given Quinn his *sgian dubh*."

"But he was injured."

"Aye. He threw his *sgian dubh,* and his aim was true. The man released me and fell."

"Oh, Avelina." Fenella gave her a hug. "Where is the dead man?"

"Quinn had to bury him in the bog. I canna imagine how difficult that had to be for him because of all his injuries. The other man had fared much better from the shipwreck."

"Until Quinn took care of him. See? He would be a

good husband. A good protector."

"I canna believe our das are planning to marry us off, yet, I can. We knew this would have to happen before long." Avelina laid back on the bed.

"When are you returning to see Quinn?"

"A few days from now. I will have to be careful Gwyneth doesna begin to suspect something."

"She never leaves the keep. Unless she pays someone to follow you. Are you going to tell Quinn about your da finding a husband for you?"

"Nay. Why would I?"

"So he can steal you away."

CHAPTER 8

Quinn kept busy, building a small stone shelter out of a cropping of rocks on a hill so it wasn't higher than the land, hoping no one would notice it. He'd fished and supplemented his stock of food that Avelina and Judith had given him. And he marked the days he'd been here, trying to avoid looking toward the other island that blocked his view of the one where Avelina lived. He craved seeing her worried frown, feeling her touch, smelling her sweet scent, yet he knew she needed to protect herself from her kin learning that she had helped him. And from them discovering he was here.

He worried too, if she'd made it home safely. And about the risk she'd take crossing the water to see him again. For now, he needed to occupy his time with staying alive and healing. And coming up with a plan to make his way back to the mainland. As much as he didn't want to get Avelina into trouble, should they discover what she was doing, he was thinking that once he was healed enough, he would take her back to her island, and then paddle the borrowed coracle to the mainland. He may, or may not make it, but he felt he had no other choice. If her kin ever discovered him, they would kill him. He was certain his brother's men were already dead. Better that than if they were tortured mercilessly though.

He couldn't remain on this island forever.

He'd given many of the gray seals names—Whiskey, because of the tan on his face, Swimmer, since he seemed to be in the water more than out of it, Sleepy, because he basked on the rocks most of the time whether the sun shone or not. Growly always talked to him in a disgruntled way. Flipper always waved a flipper at him.

And he'd given names to some of the puffins too. As much as he loved Wolf's company, especially warming him at night, he was glad he wasn't here chasing the wildlife.

The wind was whipping up, and it appeared he was in for a storm. Besides thinking of Avelina most of the day and when he was awake at night, worrying about whether she and Wolf had made it safely to their island, worrying that no one learned the truth about what she'd been doing, and that no one had found the man he'd killed, he thought about his brother. Would he send another ship with men to attempt to steal Fenella away, or had he sent Quinn and the other men here, hoping to get rid of them? Always brawling with their kin, starting fights that were uncalled for, the mercenaries had stoked Cormac's ire on several different occasions.

But Quinn wanted to be there to protect Fenella and

Avelina, should his brother attempt to send more men. He knew Avelina would try to defend her cousin and could be killed in the confrontation or taken too. Then he pondered the reason his brother sent him when he did. He must have known most of her kin were away. Then he had hoped to really fetch the lass?

Quinn stored all his spare food and clothes inside the shelter before the rains began, the dark gray clouds blending with the dark gray sea, the white caps the only distinction between the sea and sky. With the storm pounding overhead and all around him, lightning illuminating the sky for brief seconds, thunder following seconds later, he was reminded of the storm that had broken the ship in two and had cast him into the salty sea.

He had felt barely any pain as he'd made his way to shore that fateful day, but once there—and thanking the heavens above for delivering him safely—he hadn't remembered getting there. Not until he'd awakened and worried that this was the island they were supposed to land on and steal Fenella away from. Except he had no way to do so, and moving around the rocks to hide himself had been his only thought, until he could think of something else. That was when Avelina and her cousin had found him, and he was certain he'd be doomed to die. That the women would run back to the keep and tell the men what they had found, and they would have taken it from there.

He was grateful to both women for not telling anyone the truth. To Judith also, that she'd kept his secret. He wondered how she was doing and if anyone had finished building her byre for her sheep. He wished he could have finished it for her.

Most of all, he wondered if he'd ever see Avelina or his homeland again.

***

A knock at Fenella's door sounded and both she and Avelina looked at it, neither making a move or saying anything. Normally, no one bothered them at his hour unless there was trouble.

One of the maids said from beyond the closed door, "Is Avelina in there? I've checked her chamber, but she isna there, and Hamish wishes to speak with her in the great hall."

Her eyes wide, Fenella grabbed Avelina's arm. "You are in trouble now. We both are."

"It will be all right," Avelina whispered to her, though she didn't feel as though it would be. "I'm here and I'm coming," she called out to the maid. To Fenella, she said, "I'll return to see you as soon as I learn what this is all about."

"I pray that 'tis naught."

"As do I." Avelina gave her a hug and then hurried to the door. She opened it, but the maid had already left. She tried to quash the anxiety coursing through her blood, her heart racing as she walked down the stairs. She was attempting not to rush and break her neck, trying not to move too slow, making it appear she was afraid or reluctant to see Hamish. She truly liked him and was always eager to see him, so she knew if she acted otherwise, he'd be suspicious and assume something was amiss.

When she saw him speaking to three other men, all

frowning, all her uncle's friends, her step faltered. She scolded herself for her action because all the men turned to observe her and were eyeing her with wariness. Hamish didn't have to speak with her in front of the other men, surely. She hoped he was going to dismiss them before she reached him. But he didn't, and she feared they were all going to question her about rescuing Quinn on the beach.

"Avelina," Hamish said in greeting, no smile, which didn't bode well. "When the ship wrecked off our coast, you and Fenella had gone to the shore. Am I right?"

She frowned and folded her arms, not meaning to sound defensive, but maybe he would realize she wasn't going to cower. "What is this all about?"

"A dead man has been found in a bog."

Her heart beating even faster, she barely breathed, her lips parting in surprise.

Hamish cleared his throat. "A couple of the guards said they saw you return to the keep soaking wet. Everyone was curious, naturally, but they neglected to ask why. Then some of our men discovered the injured men from the shipwreck and brought them here."

"I had never seen them before. No' until I returned and saw them in the outer bailey tied up."

"I dinna doubt that. But you saw the other man, aye? And he threatened you and you killed him. Afraid we'd be angry that we hadna the chance to question him, you managed to weight him down with rocks and left him in the bog. But he floated to the surface and one of our men came across him."

She wiped away tears trailing down her cheeks, so

scared they would have known Quinn had done the killing. She couldn't believe they thought she had ended the man's miserable life. In a way, she was relieved.

"Lass, 'tis all right." Hamish looked at his other men, appearing uncomfortable that she appeared so distressed about killing the man. He let out his breath. "We have half a mind to send Quinn's remains back to his brother, but his body has deteriorated too much. We buried him with the rest of his men."

She couldn't believe they thought the man was Quinn. She didn't know whether to be more upset about it or relieved. She didn't want anyone believing she'd had to kill Quinn because he was a wicked man, but if they thought he was dead, they wouldn't look for him.

"We just wanted you to know we understand, and you have naught to worry about. Your da will be proud of you for being able to defend yourself so well. That is all, unless you'd like to add something."

Unable to speak, she shook her head. She hadn't exactly lied because Hamish had made up the tale to fit the story, and she hadn't agreed, nor had she denied it. She so wanted to tell him the dead man was one of the mercenaries who had tried to kill Quinn. But then they'd wonder how she knew that and if Quinn had survived, where was he now?

After Hamish dismissed her, she hurried back to Fenella's chamber.

Fenella pulled her into the chamber and shut the door. "What happened?"

"They believe I killed the man left in the bog, and that

it was Quinn."

***

Several more days had passed, and Quinn was beginning to feel much better. His ribs were not as painful. The wounds on his head and arm were healing well. But he couldn't stay here forever. He'd thought of swimming to the next uninhabited island, and then resting up for a day and night, and the next day, trying to swim to Avelina's island. He would steal a boat and make his way to the mainland.

The day was gray and foggy, yet he kept up his spirits by visiting the gray seals. They were used to him now. He talked away to them as if they were his clansmen, glad his own kin couldn't see him. The seals proved better companionship than some men he knew.

No one had come looking for him, and he hadn't seen any sign of ships returning to Avelina's island. He suspected his brother knew his men and the ship had been lost. Had it been worth the cost to his brother to try and kill him in this manner? And he hadn't even succeeded. Not yet. Though his brother wouldn't have expected the ship to be lost at sea. As much as he wanted to see people again, Quinn would miss this time spent with the birds and seals on the island. He'd even managed to see red deer one morning early at the inland loch.

He'd taken to swimming in the crystal clear, aqua sea every day, then in the loch to wash off the sea salt, getting himself in better shape for swimming to the other island. He had to find a way to let Avelina know what he was going to do. He didn't want her making her way in the coracle to find him gone and worry about what had become of him. But he couldn't just walk up to her keep and tell her either. He'd try to reach Judith, and she could tell Avelina the next time she saw her.

Pulling the chilly water past him as he swam, he had just finished his swim halfway to the other island and was heading back in when a couple of frisky seals joined him. One bumped him, and he smiled. Then a dog woofed some distance off behind him. Fearing it was a fisherman, though unsure why he would take a dog with him, Quinn swung around, his heart racing.

And saw the most beautiful sight. Avelina! And Wolf, standing in the boat, wagging his tail vigorously. He was afraid the wolf would tip the boat if he didn't sit down at once.

"What are you doing!" she shouted crossly at Quinn.

What he was doing was preparing to leave the lass behind. She was forbidden fruit. He had nothing to offer her, and if her kin found him, he'd be killed for certain, but the notion of leaving her behind went against every other feeling he had for the lass.

When Wolf put his paws on the side of the boat, it began to tip. "No! Wolf! Down!" she said.

Quinn automatically shouted, "Down, Wolf!"

As soon as she tried to pull Wolf down, she upset the boat even further. The coracle tipped too far and flipped over. Both she and the wolf fell into the water. Though Wolf looked as though he might have jumped into the water, eager to swim to Quinn. Avelina couldn't right the coracle, and her soaking wet clothes were weighing her down.

His heart in his throat, Quinn swam toward her as if her

life depended on it. Which it might. He didn't know if she could swim all that well, or survive the cold. "Hang on, lass!

At least she was able to cling to the boat for now. Wolf paddled toward Quinn and greeted him with a lick on his cheek. Quinn couldn't let anything ruin his focus as he swam to reach Avelina. If she drowned, he would never forgive himself. She wasn't returning to her island without him. He didn't want her attempting to paddle back to the island again alone.

He prayed she wouldn't grow sick from being exposed to the cold. "Hold on! I'm coming."

"What...were...you...doing?" she asked, her speech slurred.

"Swimming." Which he thought was obvious. He suspected she knew what he had been planning to do, preparing himself for the time when he would do it. "I am almost there." He saved his breath after that. Even though he had swum this distance for several days, trying to swim faster and not conserve his energy like he usually did, he was testing every inch of his body.

He finally reached her and gathered her in his arms.

"You are no' wearing any clothes," she said through chattering teeth, her body shivering in his arms.

"Nay. Then I'd have to wash them and dry them. Easier this way. I'm going to let you go, flip the craft over, and lift you into it. Can you paddle in place for a moment?"

"Aye, hurry."

He released his hold on her, and pushed the coracle until he managed to lift it enough, and flipped it over. Once it was right-side up, he lifted her, sopping wet clothes and all, and pushed her up into the craft.

"Wolf," she said, and collapsed on the bottom of the boat.

Quinn looked back, but the wolf was eager to chase seals and birds, and he wasn't having any trouble swimming toward shore. "He'll make it." Quinn climbed into the coracle and sat down to paddle them to shore. As cold as she was, her cheeks turned a little red, and she struggled to unfasten the brooch attached to her plaid. He joined her and unfastened the brooch. She handed him her cold wet plaid, but she didn't look away from him as he quickly covered himself with the wool cloth, and then he began to paddle again.

"You shouldna have brought Wolf." The wolf could have drowned her.

She snorted. "As if I canna see that for myself." She had her arms wrapped around herself and was shivering badly.

"When we get to shore, you can swim in the loch nearby to remove the sea salt. And I'll start a fire, and then dry your clothes."

"It will take too long."

"You can wear your brother's clothes and your spare plaid when you return, but you may be questioned about it. No matter what you do, I'm returning with you to your island." He glanced at the bundle she'd brought for him. "We canna keep doing this, and you canna risk losing your life while aiding me."

"'Tis my life."

"Nay, 'tis your da's." He noticed then a line of thunderstorms off on the horizon. They had not been there when he'd looked earlier. He swore with every stroke he made with the paddle, the dark clouds inched closer. "We willna make the return trip before the storm overtakes us. We'll have to wait until it passes."

"Och, can the day get any worse?" She didn't say anything further, and he paddled hard to reach the island as fast as he could.

When they landed on the beach, he lifted her up and out of the boat. He meant to carry her to the loch and then return for the boat, but she objected.

"I will walk. It will warm me. And you can carry the boat. We canna leave it here. Hurry, I must return as soon as I can. But I have some news." She was still too cold, but she was moving as fast as she could in the wet garments.

He tied the now-wet bundle she'd secured in the coracle—the only way she'd managed not to lose it when the boat flipped over—around his waist, and carried the boat over his head. "Are your men returning from battle?"

"No' yet. Some of the ones who remained at the keep found the other man's body in the bog." She turned to frown at him, then blushed when she glanced at her plaid wrapped around his naked body. She quickly turned away.

"He should have been weighted down enough."

"I think Wolf pulled him out."

That reminded him of the terror Wolf would be on the wildlife here. "Wolf! Come!" He wasn't certain if the wolf would mind him, especially when he had so many other distractions, and he was a wolf, not a dog. But Wolf came bounding over the hill straight for him.

Avelina's mouth was agape. Then she shook her head.

"Stay with us, Wolf. To the right on the other side of the hill is my home, Avelina. The loch is this way." He guided Avelina to the loch and then set the boat down. "While you wash, I'll fetch your brother's shirt and your spare plaid, and you can wear them until we can dry your clothes."

"They think I killed you," she said at the loch's bank.

"That I was the man in the bog?"

"Aye. That I killed him and that he was you."

"Then they think I am dead." The notion was finally sinking in.

"Aye."

He let out his breath. "That could be good. Do you need help removing your things?"

"Nay!"

"Aye. I'll be right back with clothes and start the fire. Wolf, come!"

Wolf bounded after him as Quinn carried the boat to his shelter. Then he quickly started a fire and grabbed her dry spare plaid and her brother's shirt. At least he'd washed and dried them a couple of days ago, and she'd have something warm to wear. He fastened his plaid with his belt and slipped on his boots. He needed to rinse off also, but for modesty sake, he didn't want to return to the loch naked. And he only had her brother's shirt, so until her léine dried, he could only wear the plaid. He grabbed her wet plaid too, to wash in the loch.

"Wolf, come." He didn't trust him to stay at the shelter, or to leave him alone with the food.

When he reached the loch, Avelina was naked and up to her neck in the cold water, but it was so clear, he could

115

see her beautiful breasts, her rosy nipples peaked.

"Here, lass. Come out and get dry. I'll wash off, and clean your clothes, and then carry your wet things back to the shelter."

"I've washed my chemise, boots, and *léine* already."

"Good then." He stripped off his plaid, belt, and boots and walked into the water with her sopping wet plaid. She'd seen him naked so many times already, he didn't think it would matter to her. He expected her to hurry out of the water, but then he realized she probably didn't want him to see her naked and was waiting for him to turn his back to her, or leave.

"I'll turn my back, so you can leave the water," he said, rinsing out her plaid that he'd borrowed from her in the coracle, then laid it out on a rock to dry with her other garments.

"You have already seen me fair naked," she said, her teeth chattering again, the whole while watching him.

"I have started the fire so that you can warm yourself."

He heard her leaving the water, and she fell on the slippery rocks, giving a little oath. He was behind her in a shot, grabbing her up and carrying her the rest of the way out of the water. He dried her with his own plaid, then pulled her brother's shirt over her head. He wrapped her in her spare plaid. Once he wrapped his damp plaid around himself and belted it, he pulled on his boots. He tied her wet plaid, belt, boots, and *léine* into a bundle, then looped it around his belt. He finally lifted her into his arms.

"You dinna—"

"Aye, I do. I want to. I need to."

"Thank you. My da would kill me if he knew what had happened between us."

"He would kill me if I didna do everything I could to ensure you dinna get sick." He carried her to his shelter. When they reached it, he set her next to the fire.

"What were you doing swimming in the sea?" She looked at his arm where he'd been injured. "You are healing nicely."

"Aye. Thanks to your care."

"Your ribs?"

"Much better. You didna hear me groan once when I carried the boat or you, did you?" If he had to fight, he was sure that would be a different story.

She shook her head. "You were no' thinking you were swimming to my home, were you?"

"Aye. This works better. I'll leave you on shore, and I'll try to make it to the mainland."

"You intend to steal Lendon's boat?"

"Unless I swim to the mainland." Quinn laid her clothes out to dry by the fire.

"You wouldna make it."

"I canna stay here forever. And you canna continue to risk seeing me. One of these days, your kin will return from battle and then what happens?"

She sighed, and he pulled her onto his lap to share his body heat with her. She nestled her head against his chest, her hair damp.

He kissed the top of her head. "I couldna quit thinking of you."

"Nor I of you. I imagined you starving to death out

here, or going mad with no one to talk to."

"I made friends with the seals and the birds living here. If I'd had enough time, I would have made friends with the deer."

She looked up at him and smiled. She had the most beautiful smile, though he didn't mind when she scowled at him either. Any attention she paid him was well worth it. "I canna believe Wolf minds you so well. You would think you raised him from a pup."

"I've always done well with animals. I think 'tis a gift. You have it as well."

"I'm no' sure I could make friends with the seals." She sighed. "All right. I'll give you permission to steal Lendon's coracle. He will be livid when he learns of it, but if it gives you a chance to make it to the mainland, then I'll aid you. What will you do when you get there?"

He shook his head. "I have no idea. As much as I abhor the notion, I may be forced to become a mercenary like the men who came with me. I take it the others are dead."

"Aye." She gave another heavy sigh, relaxing in his arms.

This felt right to him. Like she belonged here, with him, to him, as he belonged to her.

"One of the women who has an interest in my da said he and my uncle, the chief of our clan, will be bringing contracts back to have us married off to make alliances with other clans," she said.

He didn't say anything for a while, just continued to hold her tight to warm her, wishing he had a place to call home that he could take her to. He'd never felt like that about a woman. That he would take her in, call her his own, take care of her, and provide for her. But she'd touched at his heartstrings from the moment she had come upon him when he was injured on the beach, a perfect stranger, someone who could have been a danger to her. "I would take you with me, if I could."

"I would go with you, if I could." She turned her face up to his.

He kissed her, wanting so much more. And she was just as eager to kiss him back. "Ah, lass," he sighed, tightening his hold on her, loving the soft curves of her body and the heat, the way she stirred his body to life. "You are more beautiful than any lass I've ever chanced to meet. If I had a home of my own, I would take you there. Handfast now, even. You would be mine."

She wrapped her arms around him. "I've never felt the way I do for any man like I do for you. I would never have gone against my people's ruling, or risked my life to do what I have done for you. I must be mad."

"Nay, you love me, just a little," he said.

Avelina chuckled. "A lot." If he truly cared for her as much as he said he did, she thought of how far she would go to be with him. Had he said he couldn't take her with him because he really didna want to feel encumbered with a wife? Then again, his brother was trying to kill him, and Quinn didn't have a place to live. She would be leaving her comfortable home for who knew what.

Something like this? Wrapped in Quinn's arms, she didn't think she could want for more. Her da would be furious with her for running off, especially if he had an

TERRY SPEAR

alliance with someone else, based on a marriage contract for her. But how could she wed someone else when Quinn seemed so right for her? She would always remember him. Always want to be with him. To help him. To love him. She couldn't believe he'd been swimming in the sea naked, though it made sense, or that he'd join her naked in the loch. He seemed comfortable in his skin, and it made her feel more comfortable around him.

She didn't think she'd feel the same way about another man, yet she couldn't burden Quinn with a wife when he was having trouble enough of his own. And she didn't think he would seriously consider taking her with him either.

"Do you know for sure that your da is returning with a marriage contract?" Quinn asked.

"Nay, it could be Gwyneth's own idea. But both Fenella and I are of age, so it could very well be."

Quinn just caressed her arm in a relaxed way, not saying anything. Wolf was sitting by the fire, his ears perked as he listened to the sea birds and seals speaking in their own languages. She thought Quinn might be resigned to the notion she could be married soon. But then he said, "You canna marry anyone else when you want to be with me."

"We have no say in it."

For a long time, he didn't say anything further, and she assumed he realized she was right, but then he said, "Sometimes we must make our own destiny."

She looked up at him. He was serious! And it gave her hope. "Where would we go?"

"I have fought alongside Malcolm MacNeill and his brothers. They have all said I could join them, but that was before my brother accused them of no' bringing as many men to battle as Malcolm had promised and as a result, my da died."

She sighed. "My mother always said my da would give me a choice, especially if he believed the man to be right for me."

Quinn chuckled. "I dinna think he will believe that of me."

"I believe it. We will go then, but I must get word to Fenella. I dinna want her to think I have drowned."

"If you try to get word to her, surely you will be caught. What if she doesna want you to leave and raises the alarm herself?"

Avelina snuggled closer to Quinn, loving the way he held her in his arms and warmed her. "She would take you for her own, if I hadna already." She rested her cheek against his chest. "She knows I have claimed you as my own prisoner."

He chuckled. "I am yours to command."

"No' all men would say such a thing to a woman. Or if they did, they wouldna mean it. But with you, I know you do. When do we leave?"

"On the morrow. When the storm passes. We couldna outrun it. We'll return to your island. I'll stay either with Judith, or if it appears to be too much of a risk, I'll stay at the abandoned croft. You return with Wolf to your keep. Tell Fenella what you intend to do, if you think she can keep a secret. Bring whatever you can with you, and we'll leave early the next morn so that we'll have time to make it to the mainland and be on our way."

"With Wolf?"

"Aye. Unless you think Fenella would treasure having him when you are gone."

Avelina pondered that for a moment, then shook her head. "She would, but if her da had drawn up a contract for her, and she is sent away, what would become of Wolf? Many of the men dinna like him. I would worry they'd kill him when we are both gone."

"Then we take Wolf with us. Between the two of us, we can make him mind."

"We are really going to do this?"

"Unless you change your mind. I will wait for you a day. Send me word if you dinna wish to go with me, and I will understand."

"Or if I am delayed, or stopped?"

"Get word to me. Somehow."

"You must leave without me if I dinna reach you the next day." She didn't want him to leave without her. But she knew he'd have to, if she wanted him to have a chance at escaping the island and her kin.

"I dinna want to leave you behind," he said.

"You take Wolf with you. I know you will care for him. If I should have to wed another, I dinna want to worry about what might happen to him."

"I will. We'll take care of each other."

She was glad they'd have each other. She just hoped Cormac didn't finally succeed in killing Quinn the next time, if Quinn had the misfortune to deal with his brother again. But she hoped she could meet up with Quinn as planned and they'd leave together. If she was able to leave with him, she hoped she wouldn't be making the biggest mistake of her life.

CHAPTER 9

Quinn cooked fish he'd caught for them and they had that and bread and cheese, sharing some with Wolf. As soon as Avelina's clothes were dry enough, she dressed, though she said, "I thought you were going to make a smaller shelter because you wouldna have Wolf here to share it with you."

"I dinna like cramped quarters. I was in a cave-in when I was around eight and, if I have a choice, I willna stay in a place that is too confined."

"Oh, no. How long were you trapped?"

"Three days. My da was angry with me for wasting everyone's time spent digging me out when they had other duties to perform. Our mother had died when I was young, and Cormac made it out of the cave to tell the others. He saved my life."

"It took them that long to dig you out?"

"Nay. I didna hear the men digging until the next day. I

could see a trickle of sunlight when the dawn came."

"Did Cormac trigger the cave-in?"

"Nay. He couldn't have. He said he went for help, but no one believed him."

"Do you believe him?"

"I did. But now I'm no' sure that I do." Quinn had thought about that day since the more recent events. He'd never asked anyone if Cormac had told the rest of their clansmen right away, or if he'd waited until the next day. Quinn had just been so relieved to hear the men moving the stones to free him from the darkness.

"Your da shouldna have been angry with you. You were only a child *and* his son. He should have been grateful you hadna died."

"I've wondered of late what my brother had said to him. Had he told them we'd been together in the cave? That he'd managed to escape? Or that he had warned me no' to go near it and see what happened?"

"Your brother is despicable."

"Aye. Come. Let's watch the incoming storm, and mayhap we can see a bit of a sunset." Quinn turned to Wolf. "Stay here, Wolf." Quinn didn't want the wolf to chase all the wildlife off while he was on the island.

Quinn and Avelina made their way to a flat rock where he often watched the sunset. Tonight, they could watch the storm building and moving closer.

"'Tis like the day we were shipwrecked. It looked as though we'd have time to make it to the island that day, but no' as we'd planned," Quinn said, his arm wrapped around Avelina.

"Does it scare you now? When you see another storm?"

"Only if we were in the coracle, trying to reach your island. But here, with the safety of the shelter to use when we need it, the storms are invigorating."

"I worried about you when the last storm passed over the island."

"I worried if you had made it back to your island all right."

The wind whipped about them and the lightning flashed in the dark sky, striking the dark ocean.

"Will they miss you no' returning this eve?"

"Hopefully, they will believe the storm overcame me, and I stayed with a crofter. I have done so a couple of times before. They would have no need to worry about me unless Fenella is alarmed, knowing where I really had gone. If she thinks I'm in trouble, she might tell Haimish where I went. But they couldna do anything for me anyway, so I pray she doesna say anything to anyone."

"I agree. I will make a bed for us when we return to the shelter. We need to share it for warmth."

She smiled at him. "You didna need anyone to warm your bed before."

"Nay. But I'm more worried about you staying warm."

She sighed and snuggled next to him. "My da will kill us."

"If we agree to be married?"

"He may still wish to kill you. Especially if he has a marriage contract for me."

"He canna marry you off to another man, unless you

agree. And if you ask me, I dinna agree."

"I have fought feeling anything for you, Highlander. But...I canna help myself. I canna think of anything but being with you when we are apart. 'Tis a sickness, I think."

"Nay, it only means you love me." He smiled down at her and kissed her mouth.

"What of how you feel about me?"

"Every moment that I lay awake in the abandoned croft, or the shelter I built here, I think of you. Of being with you. Of seeing your elusive smiles and your scowls, or hearing your soft laughter or scoldings. I couldna want anyone more than I want you. I love you, Avelina. I didna think I'd ever feel that way about a woman so deeply that I canna get her out of my mind. I imagined being in battle and the only thing I could see was your beautiful blue eyes willing me to return to you."

"Then 'tis decided. I agree to be your wife, though remember, it still might be the death of you."

"I am hard to kill." He rose to his feet and was about to take her up in his arms, but she tugged at him to come with her back to the shelter. He suspected she was afraid she'd wear him out overly much if he carried her. When it came to taking care of her, he had the strength of ten men.

Right before they reached the shelter, he pulled his hand away from hers and lifted her into his arms and carried her inside. Then he set her down next to the bedding. He needed to expand it for the two of them.

"I think you planned all of this."

He chuckled. "If it had been in my power, aye."

She helped him prepare the bedding, but then he was

hurrying to remove his belt and once he'd set it aside, she began to remove his plaid. When she'd dropped it near their bedding, he took her face in his hands and kissed her mouth long and deep. He didn't want to rush this, their first time, not when they had all night, and not when he wanted to show her how much he truly loved her.

She melted in his hands and clung to his waist, kissing him back, as tentatively as before, then growing more adventurous, their tongues colliding and hers seeking entrance into his mouth. She tasted of sweet honeyed mead, and he wanted to devour her, his body burning with need. He only had to think of her, and he was aroused. But kissing her, touching her, feeling her warm body pressed against his, he was past needing to have her.

He pulled slightly away from her to help remove her plaid and her brother's shirt. The air was growing chillier, the wind whipping about outside and the lightning grew closer, the thunder following much sooner. Wolf was sitting at the entrance of the shelter, observing the storm, appearing fascinated.

"He loves storms, crazy wolf," she said.

"Good." Quinn could imagine a cowering wolf trying to get under the covers with them for his protection.

Then Quinn dropped her plaid next to his, and they sat to remove their boots. He wanted to get her under the covers as quickly as possible, so she wouldn't get chilled. The fire had already gone out.

Once they'd removed their boots, he touched her full breast, admiring her beauty, the red gold curls at the apex of her thighs, and looked up to see that she was looking him over too, though as much as she'd seen him naked, she didn't seem concerned, except that this time he was fully aroused. She looked more intrigued than anything.

"Do you know what happens next, lass?" he asked, gently moving her onto her back and settling in beside her, then pulling the covers over them. They would get warm while they made love, but he didn't want her chilled before then, and he didn't want to just finish this without thoroughly pleasuring her.

"I've seen the hunting dogs do it," she said, quite honestly.

He wanted to laugh, but instead, he kissed her lips again, his body half covering hers to keep her warm, his leg in between hers, while keeping his weight off her and resting instead on his hip.

"Are you hurting?" she asked, and he thought she was confused about him not just plunging in like a rutting beast.

"Nay." He kissed her again, and ran his hand over her breast, while her hands explored his back and then lower. Her touch made him all the more desperate to have her, and he slid his hand down her waist, her skin velvety soft against his fingertips. Until he reached her short curly hairs and he paused. "You are sure about us, about me, about us marrying?"

"Aye. We have agreed. Dinna make me so hot and achy for you and then stop again."

He smiled at her. He knew he had made the right choice for a wife, sweet and fiery.

Then he stroked her between the legs, hoping she understood something about foreplay and that he was trying to prepare her for when he entered her. She made little sounds of desperation, and he smiled.

"We are out here in the middle of the water and with a storm overhead, no one will hear you. Enjoy this and share your joy with nature."

"If I scream out, Wolf may think you are killing me."

Hell.

Quinn glanced at Wolf and wanted to tell him to go chase seals or something. But Avelina pulled at Quinn's arm to get his attention, and he continued to stroke her, hoping that she kept her pleasurable moans low so as not to alarm Wolf. Avelina was panting and grabbing at his waist, her face tight, her eyes closed, and then she cried out.

Quinn missed kissing her mouth before she worried Wolf, but he only glanced back at them, then continued to watch the storm. Breathing a sigh of relief, Quinn inserted a finger into Avelina's feminine folds and said, "You are wet for me, but you will feel a pinch, and you may believe I am stretching you too far when I enter you the first time."

"Fenella told me."

He raised a brow, thinking her cousin was a virgin.

"A maid told her. I am ready."

"You may be sore for a while." He had to warn her. He didn't want her to feel that it would always be like this, but he did want her to know how she might feel the first time. He would stop now too, if she changed her mind, but he was hoping she wouldn't because he knew this was right between them, no matter the consequences to him.

"Do it, unless you are afraid my da will kill you."

"The only reason I wouldna make love to you, is if you

choose for me no' to."

"Then do it."

"Aye." He spread her legs farther apart. And then, praying she wouldn't hurt too much and the soreness would go away sooner than later, he drove into her. She cried out and he felt his own pain—his ribs and arm killing him.

Wolf came over to check on Avelina and they both said, "Go, lie down!" He returned to his spot by the entrance to watch the storm.

"I love you," Quinn whispered against her face, tears filling her eyes.

But she was smiling. And he loved her for it. He began to thrust, kissing her breasts, licking and sucking on her nipples, bringing her to the crest again, and he felt her tremble beneath him right before she climaxed.

He hurried to finish now, not wanting to make her any sorer than he was sure she was now. She continued to cling to him, kissing him back as he kissed her mouth, not seeming to need him to hurry and finish. Maybe because she wanted him to find his own pleasure in her. He found it, with bringing her to climax.

And then he came. He groaned with release. He stayed there for a moment, then slid out of her, and pulled her against his chest where his ribs didn't hurt quite as much, though to hold her and keep her warm, he would suffer any consequence.

"How do you feel, lass?"

"Glorious. Sore, but it canna be anything like how you are still sore from your injuries. And dinna deny it. You may be a hardened warrior, but I am your wife and you can be honest with me, as I plan to be with you."

"I dinna want you to fear that it will always hurt like this."

She looked up at him. "How many lasses did you have that you know so much about it?"

He smiled down at her and ran his hand through her silky hair. "I have heard men telling such tales."

She chuckled. "Why is it men can do wild and foolish things, and they are cheered on, but women..."

He kissed her mouth. "I will only be here," he said, and ran his hand down her breast, to her mound.

"Good."

"You dinna regret that you didna receive your da's blessing first?"

"Nay." She sighed. "I couldna imagine being with another man other than you."

"I couldna have been any luckier that you and your cousin found me. I wanted to tell you why I was there, thinking she wanted to be rescued from her kin, but then I worried she might no' have told you and you would tell the rest of your people. I never imagined the woman who saved me would end up being my wife. Though I was smitten with you from the first time I saw you."

"Even when I was half drowned?"

"You were beautiful."

She frowned at him, as if she didn't believe him.

He ran his hand over her bare back and buttocks. "The wind was blowing your clothes against your beautiful body, making me hunger for you."

She laughed. "Even when you were in so much pain?"

"Aye. I couldn't help it. And when you were soaking wet, holding me close, you canna know how much I longed for this."

"Hmm." She kissed his naked chest. "My mother told me any man who held a woman close, *any woman*, would react in the same manner."

"To an extent. But not when a man is cold and in pain. You stirred me in a way that no other woman could."

She sighed. "I hope this friend of yours takes us in."

"We were on good terms at one time. He wasna with my brother. If he doesna hold my brother's actions against me, I'm sure he could use another swordsman at his beck and call."

"I wish I could tell my da about us, but I dinna trust that he wouldna want to kill you."

"Aye. So we return to the island, you get word to your cousin, and then we leave."

"Aye, and pray that everything goes as planned without anything going awry." Then she frowned at him again. "You knew my cousin was there when we found you injured?"

He sighed and told her everything, hoping she wouldn't be angry with him for keeping the secret all this time.

***

Avelina never thought she could sleep in a shelter like this with the wind howling and the rain pouring down. Wolf was guarding the entrance, while she was wrapped up in her Highlander's arms, snuggled under their plaids. She loved how much he had worked to give her pleasure last night, and not just taken his pleasure in her, like she'd heard other women say about their men. After they'd done the deed, the women had wondered what all the excitement had been about.

They must have married men who didn't know how to pleasure a woman, and she was glad that her Highlander did. She kissed his shoulder and listened, realizing the wind had died down, and the rain had stopped. Wolf was gone, and she hoped he wasn't scaring off Quinn's newfound friends—the birds and the seals. She couldn't believe Quinn had picked out names for them, but thought he was for sweet for it.

He finally stirred, and she was glad he'd seemed to sleep well.

His hand stroked her hair, then he kissed her forehead. "Ready to go?"

"Aye. I dinna want to stay away too long or they will worry about me, and Fenella will be anxious to learn I'm all right."

"I'll be right back and"—Quinn glanced around at the shelter—"where's Wolf?"

"I'm afraid he's off disturbing the wildlife. I'm sorry, but I didna want to wake you."

"'Tis okay. They'll get out of his reach. Let's break our fast and be on our way. I'll be right back." Quinn left, and when he returned, he made them oats while she went to relieve herself and find Wolf.

Wolf came racing toward her, wagging his tail, his tongue hanging out. "How many seals did you chase off the island?" she asked in a scolding way. When she returned to the shelter, Wolf stayed with her, and she had breakfast with Quinn.

He fed Wolf some of his fish, and then they packed up the bundles. She and Wolf climbed into the boat, and Quinn pushed it into the water a bit, then climbed aboard and paddled to the next island. They made it around that island and were halfway to hers when she motioned to the sea. "Och, it canna be."

He studied the horizon. "Your ships are returning? It will take them as long to reach the island as it will us. But they will be celebrating their return home upon their arrival."

"Aye, and no one will miss me for a while."

"No' even your da?"

"No' unless he has a marriage contract for me and wishes to see me right away. I suspect he will just be glad to be home and willna miss me for a while."

"Do you always greet him upon his return?"

"Aye, but he is so busy with all the well-wishers, that he doesna pay me any mind. But what if he does have a marriage contract in hand?"

"What if you decide someone else would be better for you. Mayhap it will be for someone who will elevate your position? Someone you already know and care about? That would improve your children's positions?"

"I care about you."

"Aye, lass. But with me, you dinna know where we'll end up, if we can even pull this off."

"With you, I'll have some idea about you and what I'm up against. No' to mention I can still be with Wolf. But if they discover us together... I wish I could make up a tale that you were shipwrecked some other time and that you didna come from your brother's clan." She let out her breath in exasperation. "No matter what, Highlander, I willna give you up. You are my husband now. I wouldna lie to say I am no' married to you. Though I dinna wish to tell anyone right away."

"According to your people, you already killed me."

"I fear if they catch us, or you alone, you will still be a dead man."

"Then we canna let that happen."

Avelina loved Quinn, but she was still torn about what to do. She was afraid telling her da that she had married Quinn would throw her da into a tirade. But she didn't regret agreeing to marry Quinn. She didn't want to hide that she was married to him either. She wanted others to celebrate that she'd married him, and she wanted to be with him, like she should be.

"What are you going to do? Tell your da?"

"I'm afraid of how he will react. What do you think I should do?"

"If it were me, I'd tell him, but I dinna know your da, or how he'll respond."

"He will want to kill you."

"What about you?"

"He needs only to kill you, and then he can marry me off to someone of his choosing."

***

They finally reached her island, and they hurried to take out the bundles. Avelina commanded Wolf to stay with them. He looked eager to race off to the keep. Or maybe he heard something else that made him want to run off, his tail stiff, his ears perked.

Quinn lifted the boat over his head, and Avelina carried the bundles, while Wolf ran here and there, smelling scents. Quinn had to return the boat and the fishing net to the fisherman's byre before Lendon discovered it was missing as Avelina led the way, since he had no idea where she'd borrowed it from.

As soon as they neared the croft, Wolf ran forward, barking, and Quinn feared the worst. They were already too late.

***

Avelina's heart nearly stopped when she heard Lendon whistling a tune, headed for his croft, and Wolf racing to intercept him. She dropped the bundles, all but the fishing net, wrapped it around Quinn's arm, and whispered to him, "Return the boat to the byre. I'll try to stop Lendon from reaching it to give you time to drop both the coracle and fishing net off and then get safely away."

"Aye." He waited for her to race off to intercept the fisherman.

"Lendon! You have returned! I borrowed your coracle and fishing net, but I didna have any luck catching anything. What news have you from the battlefield? Oh, Lendon, let me see to your wounds." The poor man was bleeding, a rag wrapped around his arm and his leg, his step slow.

"You may have to fish for me for a while," he said, his voice gruff, but tired. "But you would have to have better luck. What about that wolf of yours?"

"He catches fish, aye, but I haven't taught him to

release them to me." She prayed Quinn had time to leave off Lendon's things and get out of sight. "Tell me, how is my da?"

"In bad spirits, I'm afraid, lass. We lost a lot of men. He suffered a sword cut to one of his legs. You best be off to tend to him or he'll be in a worse mood."

"Nay. I'll see to yours first and then run along. We will still be celebrating your return home, will we no'? What about my uncle? Is he well?"

"He is dead."

Avelina stopped in her tracks. "Nay."

Lendon stopped and looked as bad as she felt about losing their chief. "Aye, lass. We were victorious, but at a great loss."

Fenella would be devastated. Her eyes filling with tears, Avelina had to return to the keep as soon as she took care of Lendon's wounds and comfort her cousin.

"We heard about you killing Quinn, brother to Cormac. You were a brave lass to do so."

She wanted to ask if he knew if her da had returned with contracts to have her cousin and her married off, but he might no' know about it. Still, she couldn't wait to learn the truth in case he knew of it. "I'll hurry to your croft and start a fire for you." He was moving so slow, she hoped he had not been wounded so badly that he would die on her.

She ran to the croft and saw that Quinn was nowhere near the byre. Then she started a fire at the hearth. She rushed out to where she'd dropped the bundles, fetched bread and cheese, then returned to the croft. At least Lendon could eat a little and rest until everyone was ready to "celebrate" their hard-won victory and their return home. But she knew they would be busy taking care of their wounded first.

Then she wondered who would become chief. Her da, maybe, if he hadn't been wounded too badly. Hamish, maybe, if her da couldn't lead. She'd never given it any thought because her da and her uncle had always returned home from battle with only minor injuries. Fighting the tears welling up in her eyes again, she quickly wiped them away as they spilled down her cheeks. She'd miss her uncle. He'd been a good and fair chief. She managed to stop the tears, her eyes blurry, but she thought Lendon should be here by now.

She hurried out of the croft to see what was taking him so long. He was sitting on a stone some distance off, his body stooped, his hand on his injured thigh. "Lendon!" She ran to meet him. "You are no' going to die on me!" She couldn't stop the tears this time.

"Dinna fret, lass. I willna die. I just needed a rest." Lendon never needed a rest.

"Who shall lead the clan?" she asked, helping Lendon to his feet, and wrapping her arm around him. He leaned on her strength, and she hoped they didn't both fall. But she kept her pace slow and steady. Even so, she was afraid he'd collapse at any moment. Then she saw Quinn behind Lendon, motioning to her that he could carry him if she needed his help. She shook her head. Quinn had to be crazy if he thought her people wouldn't end his life, just because he aided one of their men.

But when Lendon stumbled, she couldn't stop their

downward fall. Lendon cried out and grew silent, lying on the ground. "Nay, Lendon!" She tried to wake him, but Quinn was at her side in an instant. He lifted Lendon off the ground and carried him to his croft. "Is he...is he—"

"He passed out. His heart is beating strong, lass. Dinna worry."

Grateful for Quinn being there after all, she finally reached the croft, and Quinn laid Lendon on his pallet.

"I'll fetch some water. I have bread and cheese for him. When I return to the keep, I'll send someone to bring him there, if he is well enough to go to the celebration." She reconsidered the notion. "Mayhap I can have Judith look in on him."

"He needs rest and food," Quinn said.

"I agree." Then Avelina grabbed a bucket to fetch water from the river and headed out.

Quinn took the bucket from her. "You canna leave now."

"If my da has a contract for my marriage to someone, then aye, I will be leaving," she said, her voice just as hushed as his, in case Lendon came to and wondered whom she could be speaking with. "Dinna think you can help my people, and they will spare your life. I will tell my da later that I've married you and live with you wherever we end up."

"You needed my help."

"Aye, and they will want your head."

Quinn let out his breath. "I'm sorry to hear about your uncle, and your da. Lendon didna say who would lead."

"My da would have been the natural choice. But if he's

too injured…"

"Others will vie to take over."

"Hamish, mayhap."

"Will you want to stay here for your cousin?" Quinn sounded genuinely concerned that she might leave him to stay with Fenella.

"We will be separated before long, no matter what."

"Now that her da is dead, will any marriage contract stand?"

"If my da is in charge, then yes, because she'll be his ward. But if someone else is in charge, mayhap no." She frowned at Quinn. "Dinna think that means any marriage contract for me will be negated if my da should lose his position. Though if my da should lose the backing of his men, whoever would wish to marry me, may no longer want to, and mayhap my da willna be as angry that I married you." She sighed.

"While you're taking care of Lendon, I could see if Judith could come to stay with him for a while."

"Aye, that would be good. No one should be at her croft but her. You could stay there or at the abandoned croft until we can make new plans. If I learn that one of our fishermen has died in battle, we can use his boat. Someone will be coming for it, but mayhap not right away."

"Aye." Quinn set the bucket of water down outside Lendon's croft, then took Avelina in his arms and kissed her mouth. "I have never met a woman so lovely, both inside and out."

Tears filling her eyes again, she hugged him warmly, wishing life's choices were easier ones than these.

He smiled down at her and held her for a moment more before they heard Lendon shout. "Avelina!"

"Coming!" Avelina called out to him, her heart racing.

"I will be at Judith's or the abandoned croft. Dinna worry about me, and see to Fenella and your da. I will wait to hear word from you before I do anything else," Quinn whispered to her.

"Aye," she said, everything so up in the air, she wanted to rush back to ensure Quinn didn't leave before she could tell him the news. She just worried about his safety. Then she kissed him again, feeling as though her heart would break in two if he left without her. "We are married now," she told him, "you dinna leave without me."

"Aye, lass. I willna leave without you." He released her and took off for Judith's croft.

Avelina said to Wolf, "Go, follow him." Then she headed inside with the bucket of water and saw Lendon resettling on his pallet. She frowned at him. "You should've been lying down." She prayed Lendon hadn't seen her kissing Quinn, or overheard any of their conversation.

Lendon snorted and reclined on the pallet. She poured the water into a pot and began heating it over the fire. "Who is taking over the clan?" she asked again.

"That remains to be seen. Several are vying for the position."

She began to remove Lendon's trewes, and when she'd pulled them off, she saw that the leg wound would need stitching. "Do you have a needle and thread, so that I can sew up your wounds?"

"Aye, in the box over there."

She washed the wound, and then grabbed his flask and handed it to him. "Drink." She retrieved the needle and thread and sat down next to him to begin stitching it. "My da's men are still following him, are they no'?"

"Aye."

"Gwyneth told Fenella and me that our das were making marriage contracts, so our clans would have more alliances. Do you know anything about that?" She finished stitching Lendon up.

"She is right, lass. One is Ewen, who would wed you, and the other, Cormac... and he has pledged his support with a marriage to Fenella."

"Cormac? Nay! He tried to have Fenella stolen away."

"His brother, Quinn, did, we were told."

"Nay! His brother tried to have him murdered on several different occasions. Cormac isna to be trusted. Fenella canna marry the swine. Cormac told Quinn that Fenella wanted to leave to join him. He lied to him. Fenella didna even know the brigand."

Lendon frowned at her. "How do you know so much about this Quinn? Has he told you these things?" Then his eyes widened. "You are protecting him. He isna the one you killed. As to Fenella, things will change now that her da is dead."

Avelina thought her cousin would be glad that she wasn't marrying the man, but then she worried that Fenella would be upset that she might never find a suitable husband. Fenella had always lived at the keep. Avelina had always been sure to embrace her other roots—where her mother had come from, farmers, like both their parents before them. That's why she always helped them out as much as she could.

"I thought you might be more concerned about the man *you* are to marry. You havena met him before," Lendon said.

She helped Lendon on with his trewes, and then proceeded to remove his shirt. His arm had a bad laceration also, and she would need to sew it up. Then she had to leave for the keep. She cleaned the wound, then began to sew it. All she could think of was going away with Quinn.

"You wouldna be thinking of marrying some other man, would you?" Lendon was studying her like a man who had seen more than he ought to.

Her gaze shot to his face. Had he seen Quinn?

"You have always been a willful lass."

"Who would I be thinking of marrying, pray tell?"

"You tell me. He looked like he could be a warrior, handy with a sword, and he was armed with one. He was wearing a *sgian dubh* in his boot. Hamish told us the story about how you killed the man who had accosted you. But I'm wondering if this man was the one who did the killing. I know you're capable. But when I saw the one you were kissing, of your own free will, I doubted you had killed the other man. And I suspect he is Cormac's brother, Quinn, since you are defending him."

She finished sewing Lendon up. "They will kill him if they discover him on the island." Not to mention Lendon was sure to tell on her because he'd want to protect her and be loyal to her da. He'd pledged his allegiance to him.

"We have lost twenty men. If he is handy with a sword,

your da may make allowances. Especially if your da learns he saved your life."

"But I would still have to wed Ewen." Not that she would, or could, but her da would not see the situation as she did.

"Aye. To gain an alliance, it would be necessary. I know your mother said you could decide this for yourself, like she did. But she didna have a position in the clan like you hold. Your da will listen to you—to an extent—but in the end, his own position could hang in the balance. Our people count on the alliances we make."

She didna want to hear it, though she knew how important it could be to her people. The more men they had fighting on their own side, the better. Though even with marriages and alliances, allegiances were known to shift. And she was already handfasted to Quinn, though she worried someone might try to kill him, so she would be free to marry Ewen.

CHAPTER 10

Quinn had made his way in the world for so long, despite his brother's repeated attempts on his life, because he was always one step ahead of the game. He knew he should steal a boat and make his way to the mainland. Attempting to stay here would surely get him killed.

As much as he knew all these things, he stayed. He was a fool to remain there. But he wasn't about to give Avelina up. No matter how much he told himself her da may never accept his marrying her, and that taking her on the run with him, until they could reach Malcolm's castle, was dangerous for her and for him, he couldn't give up the notion of wanting her.

He found Judith corralling her sheep when he arrived at her croft, and she hurried over to give him a hug and a smile. That cheered him. "You are like the son I lost a few moons ago, Quinn. Thank you for the kindness you have done for me."

He gave her a hug back, afraid if he said she was like his great aunt, she might be offended. "I would finish repairing your byre if I could, but I've come with news. Lendon has been wounded and is at his croft. Avelina asked me to fetch you to see if you could care for him for a few days."

"Aye, of course. No' that he will want my assistance. He will bristle all the while, mark my words. Is he all right?"

"I had to carry him into the croft. He'd passed out from the pain, so I'm no' sure how bad off he is."

"Oh, oh, all right." Judith grabbed a satchel and filled it with herbs and a few other things, then hurried out of her croft. But then she paused. "Where are you going to be? If the men have returned from battle, will it be safe for you here?"

"For now, I await word from Avelina. Rather than get you into trouble, I'll stay at the abandoned croft."

"The one that is haunted? Och, no one goes there." Judith hurried off to see to Lendon.

Quinn gathered the bundles Avelina had left behind and headed for the abandoned croft. Wolf circled around him. "Stay with me, Wolf." And then they walked toward the croft. He'd been in so much pain when he'd gone to that croft in the beginning, he would be so much better off this time. He didn't think the ghosts would keep others away for long though, if the word got out that he was very much alive and living there.

***

Avelina helped Lendon on with his shirt, and plaid, then heard someone coming. Her heart started racing.

"'Tis me, Judith. I received word Lendon might need

my help for a time."

"No' me, woman. I'll be fine on my own," Lendon grouched.

Judith entered the croft and frowned at him. "See to your da, Avelina. I'll take care of this crusty, old fool."

Avelina nodded and said to Lendon, "I beg of you, dinna say anything about him to anyone."

Lendon snorted. "About who?"

Avelina breathed a sigh of relief and told Judith, "Thank you."

"May no' be my pleasure, but sometimes we've got to do what we have to do in this life." Judith smiled at her.

Avelina nodded, and then hurried out of the croft. Though she meant to go straight away to the keep, she detoured out of her way to go to Judith's croft. She had to warn Quinn that Lendon knew she'd been kissing him, and that he knew he was Quinn and a warrior also. When she reached Judith's place, she saw no sign of Quinn. Maybe he had decided it would be safer to stay at the abandoned croft instead.

Too far to backtrack to the abandoned croft, Avelina finally made her way to the gates of the keep and saw men coming and going, several wearing bandages, some greeting her, others lost in their own thoughts. She hurried to the keep to see to her da and saw Fenella taking care of some of the wounded in the outer bailey. Avelina detoured to give her a hug.

"Oh, Avelina, I canna believe he is dead." Tears streaked Fenella's face, and she brushed away the new ones falling down her cheeks.

"I was taking care of Lendon's wounds. He told me what had happened. I'm so sorry. I adored my uncle, and we will all feel his loss." Avelina hugged her tight.

"What of Quinn?" Fenella whispered.

"He is at the abandoned croft. Lendon saw him. Quinn carried him to his pallet when he passed out."

"Och, will he tell?"

"I dinna think so. Lendon said you were to wed Cormac, the beast."

"Aye, but the contract willna go through any longer, your da said. But your da is angry with you."

Avelina frowned at her cousin.

"You are now to wed Cormac and your da believes you have killed his brother."

"I've made a contract with Quinn to marry him. 'Tis done."

Fenella's mouth hung agape. "You and he...on the island...were...were...together as man and wife?"

"Aye. We consummated the marriage, though we need no' have to make it binding."

"Och, Avelina, your da will be more than furious."

"Most likely." If he thought to have an alliance with another clan. "What about the contract with Ewen?"

"Apparently, he isna as powerful as Cormac, and if your da leads, you will be married to the most powerful man."

"Unless da doesna lead the clan."

"Aye, and if he doesna, and his loyal men continue to be loyal to him, you will wed Cormac, unless whoever takes over the clan has a daughter eligible to wed him. Except I guess you willna be able to with this business of handfasting with his brother."

"Avelina!" Hamish called out to her from the entryway to the keep.

Avelina gave Fenella another heartfelt hug. "I will see you as soon as I can. I'm so sorry about your da."

"Aye." Fenella sniffled. "I know you loved him as much as I did. I'll pray for you, Cousin."

"I fear I may very well need your prayers." Then Avelina hurried off to the keep and joined Hamish. "How is my da?"

"Furious with you, I'm afraid, lass. We thought it was a good thing that you killed Quinn when he attacked you. But now that you are supposed to wed his brother, we may never speak of how Quinn died. He drowned at sea. That will be the end of the matter."

As much as she respected and liked Hamish, she bit her tongue, so wanting to tell Hamish that she wouldn't and couldn't wed Cormac, and that he'd tried to murder his brother Quinn. The man had no morals. But she had to tell her da first.

"How is my da? Besides being angry with me." Though she supposed he would be glad she hadn't killed Quinn, he wouldn't be happy to learn she'd fallen in love with him. Or agreed to marry him.

"He was injured. But according to him, not badly. See to him and we'll speak later."

"Aye." Now she was truly worried about her da. Had he been injured worse than he'd let on, concerned that the council would want to replace him? That his own men would find someone else to lead them?

She hurried up the stone stairs to her da's chamber, expecting a servant to be tending to him, and was surprised to see Gwyneth was in his chamber, nursing her da like she should have been doing.

"Gwyneth," Avelina said in greeting to her, a chill in her voice. If Gwyneth wanted to comfort Avelina's da, she was fine with that, glad even that he was not alone. Gwyneth might even be good for him. But Avelina didn't want her here, listening in on what she had to say to her da. "Da, I'm so sorry about Uncle."

"He died a warrior, which is all we can hope for—fighting our enemy until we draw our last breath."

She reached over and took his hand and squeezed, glad when he squeezed back, his grip strong, not weak, like she worried it might be. "I was taking care of Lendon's wounds, when he told me you had been wounded."

Gwyneth was tenderly wiping her da's brow, and Avelina wanted to dismiss her, but it was her da's place to do so, and he didn't seem to want to, or he would have already.

"How badly injured are you?" Avelina frowned at her da, telling him she wanted to know the truth and not some made-up tale he might have given to Hamish and the other men.

"Not as badly as some, who would like to replace me, would hope."

She took a relieved breath. But she knew that even a wound that seemed inconsequential could become infected and the death of the warrior could soon follow.

"It would seem I have a daughter and a niece to marry

off now."

"Lendon told me about Cormac and Ewen." She waited for her da to tell her what he had planned, just in case it was different from what Lendon had told her. She cast Gwyneth an irritated look, wishing the woman would get the notion she wanted to be alone with her da.

"If I lead the clan, you will wed Cormac. If I continue to lead my men, you will wed Ewen."

"I willna wed Cormac." Avelina hadn't meant to say it quite in that manner. Certainly not in front of Gwyneth, who was smiling a little at Avelina's impudence.

Her da raised both his brows, surprised, Avelina was certain, to hear her defiance. She normally did everything she was told to do, because she knew it was right. And, yes, if her marrying someone else made for an alliance with a powerful clan that could help them fight in battles and win, that was the right thing to do. Except, not when the man was so dishonorable in attempting to kill his brother, the man whom she'd fallen in love with.

Which gave Avelina an idea. "If you want to make an alliance with another clan, *you* are the perfect one to do so. Any woman would be happy to wed you and if you make the right choice, she could help you to make an alliance with another clan." Even if he wasn't chief, he still had his own men to command.

Gwyneth's surprised expression soured, and she looked sharply at Baudwin to see his take on it.

"Aye, I have plans to make this happen. Gwyneth, if you will give us a moment, I wish to speak to my daughter in private."

Gwyneth smiled sweetly at him, though her smile looked strained, and she inclined her head, then left the chamber, closing the door after her.

Immediately, Avelina gave her da a warm hug, tears filling her eyes. "I'm so sorry, Da. Are you truly all right?" She'd never known him to take to his pallet when he'd been wounded in previous battles. He had to show his men he was ready to fight the next one, and many more after that.

"Aye, lass, and we'll go down to the celebration as soon as everyone is able. Tell me what disturbs you so about marrying Cormac. You made no objection about Ewen, and you dinna know him either. 'Tis because you killed Cormac's brother in self-defense? He tried to steal Fenella for his own when he learned Cormac was arranging this treaty between our people and theirs."

"Nay, he lies."

"What would you know of it?" Her da was looking at her sternly now. He knew her well enough to realize she had some real knowledge of the situation, rather than that this was just her imaginings.

She explained about Fenella overhearing that the mercenaries they had tied up in the outer bailey intended to kill Quinn. That Quinn hadn't known that Fenella hadn't agreed to marrying Cormac, and that Cormac was the one who had sent his brother with the men to face their fate. Quinn hadn't known that his brother was arranging to wed her cousin while making an alliance.

"Aye, and then you killed Quinn," her da said, but the way he spoke the words meant he believed otherwise. "How would you know what Quinn knew or didna know?"

She could never easily lie to her da or to others whom she was close to.

"You were no' helping the women who were without their menfolk while they were fighting the clans," he accused, when she didn't answer him.

"Aye, of course I was. You can ask any number of them. I always reach out to them and aid them with their chores, even fish for them when their men or sons are away. You know I would."

"Aye, and I'm proud of you. Your mother would be proud of you. But if you dinna kill Quinn—"

"He killed one of Cormac's mercenaries who was about to slice me in two, Da. I didna kill Quinn. He saved my life. And I saved his. He was badly injured, and the tide would have drowned him. But when I tried to move him to the hill, I was caught in the undertow, and he saved me. He repaired part of Judith's byre, and when Lendon collapsed in a faint from the pain from his wounds, Quinn carried him into the croft to lay him on his pallet. He has done everything that could be called honorable. I canna marry Cormac. He is the most despicable of men."

"You have feelings for this Quinn?"

"Aye. You have always been a fair and just leader of your men. Quinn is a good man. How would you feel if you had a brother who sent you to battle for him, but he was always trying to sabotage you so that he would be assured you would die?"

"My brother and I had a special bond. I held him in my arms as he took his last breath, his dying wish was for me to take care of Fenella like I would my own daughter. Which he knew I would, just like I knew he would have for me."

"He was loved by us all."

Her da's expression darkened. "Why would Quinn's brother wish to murder him?"

"Quinn doesna know the reason. Cormac saved his brother when they were young, but Cormac has been trying to kill him for the last couple of months. Some think Quinn is invincible."

"I have an agreement with one or the other of the clans, depending on where I stand with the council and our men. You marrying Quinn isn't one of the options."

Then her da could make an alliance through his own marriage, but she'd decided what she would do.

"Where is he?" her da asked.

"Who?" she asked. Playing innocent wouldn't work for her.

"If you didna kill him, and he just helped Lendon to his pallet, Quinn is on the island. Where is he?"

Avelina folded her arms and narrowed her eyes. "You will have him killed."

"Nay, he deserves to participate in the feast. He saved my daughter. If he had not survived, and you hadna saved him, you wouldna be here today."

"A feast. And after that? You will kill him."

"He is Cormac's brother. Even if Cormac wishes to kill his own brother, we willna do it for him. No' when you could be marrying Cormac. Instead, Quinn can work for me. If he is so indestructible, a good fighter, and loyal, I could use another man. I've lost too many men as it is. *If* he can be trusted, where you are concerned."

Now she had a choice. Pretend she hadn't married Quinn and they would feign that there was nothing going on between them until they could plan to leave the island? Or tell her da the truth and still risk that he would have Quinn killed?

"Let me speak with him and see what he wants to do. Our people killed the mercenaries, and he has no reason to believe you willna have him put to death too."

"You have my word. But you willna be going alone to meet with him. Hamish and two other men will go with you."

"For heaven's sake. I am safe with him. Your men may scare him off."

"Take it or leave it, Avelina. You willna be seeing him alone again, and if we find him, and we *will* find him, who knows how he will react. If he fights our men, he could very well be killed. If you go to him now, accompanied, he may listen to reason."

She chewed on her bottom lip. "All right. But no one is to hurt him."

"Aye, as long as he doesna fight back."

"Aye."

"Send Hamish to me, and then you and he and two others will go in search of this Highlander."

"Thank you, Da."

"Be sure to return in time for the celebratory feast."

"Are you sure you should attend?"

"I must. If I stay in my chamber, who knows who might be in charge by morn."

She had to speak with Quinn alone and see what he

thought they should do. They were in this together.

She hugged her da, and then hurried out of his chamber. She practically ran into Fenella coming up the stairs, just as she rounded the curved wall.

"Fenella!" Avelina said, throwing her hand to her breast.

"What news?"

"I'm to send Hamish to see my da. We have to go fetch Quinn, and he'll be welcomed to the clan."

Fenella's eyes widened. "Your da doesna mean it."

"He said they wouldna kill him."

"You trust your da? The other men?"

"Aye. They want Cormac's clan to ally with ours, so they willna want to kill Quinn. Though all bets are off if anyone knew he'd been kissing me, and well, mayhap the rest."

Fenella's cheeks reddened, then they hurried down the stairs. "Your da willna let you wed him?"

"Work for him, aye. Wed him, nay."

"What are you going to do? You have to tell your da the truth."

"For Quinn's sake, I will have to go along with bringing him to the keep, until we can decide what to do. He would be safer living among our people, than being hunted down. And you know my da would do it to keep us from meeting in a clandestine way."

"But you are already married. Will he no' want to claim you for his wife? I doubt Quinn would go along with pretending no' to have claimed you for his own. No' as braw as he looked."

"He willna have a choice. I'm to go with Hamish and two other men. Once we can find a way to speak privately, Quinn and I will talk of our plans. We are in this together. I canna tell my da until Quinn is in agreement. No' when this will affect both of us."

They saw Hamish speaking with a couple of the guardsmen, and when Hamish caught her eye, he seemed to know she needed to have a word with him.

"How are you doing, Fenella?" Avelina asked her cousin, not wanting to be insensitive to Fenella's loss.

"Holding it together. I still canna believe my da is gone, or...or that so many changes will be taking place. I've heard men trying to make alliances, figuring who would be next in charge, and discounting your da as a viable leader. Everything is unsettled. I just...just never expected him no' to return with the others, though 'tis always a concern when the men go off to fight."

"Aye, the same here. I just expected them both to return as they always do, a little battered, but no really serious injuries." Before they reached Hamish, she added for Fenella's hearing only, "Mayhap Quinn can help my da keep his position."

Fenella's expression brightened. "Aye, because he can never die."

Avelina let out her breath. "Anyone can die. He's no' invincible."

Hamish waited for her to reach him, and when she did, she said, "My da wishes to speak with you."

"Aye." Hamish turned to the other men. "I'll be right back." Then he took off for the stairs.

"How is your da?" Dar asked, his black hair tied back, his beard trim. She'd overheard him saying once to some of the men how he wished he'd had a chance to wed her, but he knew he couldn't because of her da's position in the clan.

"He is well. Ready to fight again. You know how he is."

The two men exchanged glances. She knew then that they truly believed he was bedridden for the time-being. She folded her arms and looked crossly at them. "He will be down for the celebration."

They smiled then.

"We didna doubt it," the other man said. Fagin was a redhead, his bushy brows knit together, his beard not nearly as neat as Dar's.

Dar agreed.

Sure, they didn't. But what worried her most was what would happen when she took them to see Quinn. She prayed she could call out to him, and he wouldn't come out fighting. They would kill him.

CHAPTER 11

Quinn had repaired the roof on the abandoned croft so that he would stay warmer and drier this eve, and for however long he might stay here. He wished he had time to help Judith out also.

As soon as Avelina had left to return to the keep, he kept expecting a troop of men to arrive, and take him prisoner, then drag him to the keep where he would be whipped and tortured. Then killed.

Not because she would tell on him, but the more people that knew of his being here, the more of a chance the truth would slip out.

After cleaning her brother's plaid and laying it out on the shore, he swam in the loch to wash off some of the dirt and sweat from rebuilding the croft. Wolf had been paddling around in the water nearby, but he suddenly perked up his ears, looking in the direction Avelina had gone. Wolf swam toward shore, and Quinn headed in, worried that someone was coming.

Wolf reached the shore and shook off the water from his fur. Then he raced off. Quinn swam as fast as he could to reach the shore. Once he climbed out, he dried off, and dressed in Avelina's brother's shirt and Quinn's own plaid. He grabbed his sword belt and fastened it, though he wouldna fight Avelina's kin if they showed up. He thought maybe Avelina was coming to see him, the way Wolf ran off like he was greeting someone he liked, not racing off to attack someone, or chasing a deer. But he could be reacting in the same manner if it was any of her people. They would be considered his pack.

"'Tis Avelina, come with some of my da's men," Avelina called out from beyond his sight. "They wish to welcome you to our clan, Quinn."

She didn't sound like she was speaking under coercion. He was certain she would have shouted for him to run away, if she knew the men were planning to attack him. On the other hand, they may have led her to believe they meant him no harm, when they meant just the opposite.

"My da wishes me to marry a man named Ewen, or your brother, Cormac, depending on the position he ends up with. I will wed neither, if he loses his position. In the meantime, he welcomes you to our clan for saving my life. 'Tis all right. I vouch for these men."

She couldn't really mean to wed either man. Not when they had wed each other. He assumed she hadn't told her da the truth yet.

"I am here," Quinn said, still not trusting the men, but he knew he wouldn't be able to outrun them. He didn't know the island like they did. And if her da was being honest about allowing him safe passage, Quinn would be willing to attempt an alliance with the man. Maybe her da decided not to kill Quinn because they thought his brother would be angry with them for ending his life. Little did they know...

When the three men and Avelina came into view, Wolf dashed off to greet Quinn as if he hadn't seen him in eons. Avelina didn't look happy. No doubt she had some concerns as to how safe Quinn was as much as he did. If he were to stay with her kin, he knew he and she would never be allowed to be alone together again until they told her da they were married, or they slipped away to the mainland. He suspected her da would not be happy to see him either, knowing fair well that Quinn and his daughter had been together without anyone chaperoning them.

Quinn eyed the men—all looking ready to draw swords and end his life, their expressions dark and foreboding.

"This is Hamish, Dar, and Fagin. The feast will begin shortly. Come with us," Avelina entreated, unsmiling, trying to look at ease, but her shoulders were stiff. "You will be safe."

"Baudwin has said you will be allowed to keep your weapons, as long as there is no trouble," Hamish said, frowning at him. He had to be the leader of this group.

The other men continued to look just as hard-faced.

Quinn knew they were angry because she had taken care of a wounded stranger in secret.

"I will be honored. And if I can be of assistance to you and your people, I will be happy to oblige," Quinn said.

"You planned to steal Fenella away," Hamish accused him, growling the words.

Before Avelina could object, her mouth opened to speak on Quinn's behalf, he said, "Cormac, my brother, said she wished to marry him. I would have learned the truth from her and let her be. I am no' in the habit of stealing women away from their kin."

The men looked at Avelina, and her cheeks turned red.

Well, yes, he had planned to steal Avelina away from her people, so that much was true, but he had no intention of speaking of it, as long as she didn't. He trusted the men would beat or torture him, just to learn the truth about what had gone on between Avelina and him. Still, they'd allowed him to keep his weapons, and that helped to lessen his concern a little.

Avelina and Wolf led them back toward the keep, the three men walking beside him, guarding him in case he bolted, he imagined.

He hated to admit he felt somewhat anxious about making a good impression on Avelina's da, in particular, and her people, in general—if he had any hope of gaining their approval for him marrying Avelina.

When the castle came into view, he considered the fortifications, the stone wall surrounding the keep, two towers, the keep in the center. The portcullis and gate were open, and he moved with the others into the outer bailey. Another wall stood between them and the keep and the inner bailey.

Men and women stopped doing their chores to stare at him, most likely believing him to be just like the mercenaries his brother had employed. They were probably also wondering why Avelina was helping to escort him through the bailey with a guard force. Maybe wondering why he was still armed too.

He couldn't help but glance around at the fortifications—the fifteen-foot thick stone walls, the guards posted on top, watching him, not the surrounding area, the guard towers—and the wounded being taken care of on pallets next to the stables. Bread was baking in the bakery, filling the air with the aroma.

"Keep moving," Hamish said brusquely, though Quinn hadn't slowed his pace while observing the place. He didn't like that Quinn was tactically checking out the fortifications.

Avelina was ahead of them, but she looked over her shoulder at Quinn as if wondering what he was up to. He gave her a wee smile, trying to reassure her that everything would be all right, though he wasn't sure at all.

She didn't smile in return, but the men were all watching her behavior, so he understood.

They entered the inner bailey where more people stopped to watch the procession. He kept his bearing straight at all times, despite that his ribs and his arm were hurting again. He'd done too much work on the abandoned croft, and now he figured it was all for nothing unless someone was brave enough to use it for their home.

They passed the well where a woman was gathering water and then they climbed up the steps to the keep where tapestries hung on a couple of the walls and trestle tables were set up for the festivities in the great hall.

A redheaded man was seated in the middle of the head

table, his back to the wall. His beard was long and curly, his blue eyes settling on Quinn in a judgmental way. Avelina had her da's coloration, blue eyes and red-gold hair. Everyone else began filling the great hall as if his arrival let them know it was time to feast.

Everyone who'd been conversing grew deathly silent, all waiting to see what Baudwin would do.

He shifted his attention to Avelina, and she looked at Quinn and took a deep breath. She inclined her head to him, as if she wished she could say something to him, but instead, she moved around the head table to take her seat.

"You are Quinn of the Clan MacDuff," her da said.

"Aye, brother to Cormac, their chief."

"Your chief."

"No longer. I would have died in battle for my brother, but I willna fight for him any longer. No' when he has tried to have me murdered on several separate occasions."

"Why is that, do you think?"

"I dinna know. I've questioned several of our kinsmen, trying to learn the truth. If any know, they wouldna say."

"And yet you didna leave when it would behoove you."

"Aye. I was still loyal to him, and to the clan."

"You saved my daughter's life."

"Aye."

"Twice," Avelina said, and her da looked sharply at her as if rebuking her for speaking at all. But she only looked piercingly back at him, her chin lifted, defiant, unyielding, and Quinn contained the smile that was fighting to be set free.

He didn't want her to get into any trouble if her da

should see that Quinn approved of her action regarding him. "Aye, if I may be so bold to say so. Twice. The lass is right."

Her da's attention swung back to Quinn. "If I am to be chief, she will wed your brother. Will you have a problem with this? If so, speak your mind now. I will allow no one to interfere in my rule."

Quinn suspected he spoke to the gathered clan with respect to his untenable position right now, as much as he was speaking to Quinn about this matter. Quinn glanced at Avelina. She was barely breathing, her eyes wide. He could state what her da wanted him to say, or he could be honest. He was not a political man, and, though honesty had gotten him into trouble more than once, he would not lie about this. Avelina was too important to him.

"Aye, I will have a problem with this, but I hope to change your mind about me and wedding your daughter, rather than marrying her off to either Cormac or Ewen."

Her da narrowed his eyes. "You wish to marry my daughter?" Baudwin practically bellowed, yet there was a twinkle in his eye, and Quinn suspected he had surprised her da to such a degree, he approved. Else, he would have just had Quinn killed now. "What have you to offer, that I canna get from powerful clans?"

"My undying loyalty to you, to your people, and to Avelina."

Several men grumbled, three shouted their disapproval. One said, "She has to make an alliance. What good is a single man to help aid us in battle?"

"He is hard to kill," Baudwin said, smirking. "So I've

been told."

Her da had a bit of a sense of humor. That was good.

"We can see about that," Odran said, standing.

God's knees, Quinn was afraid someone might challenge him to a fight, just to see how invincible he was.

"After the celebration. Eat, drink. We fought long and hard. Some of us didna make it, but they were good men who fought fiercely, and died hard. We will celebrate in their memory." He motioned for Hamish to take Quinn to one of the lower tables where the other men joined them.

Quinn suspected they were his guards for now.

Hamish shook his head at Quinn as they took their seats and conversation filled the air. "You may no' live through the eve here, Highlander. You could've said you were agreeable to Avelina marrying one of the men who will provide us support in upcoming battles. Even if neither of you wish it. If Baudwin did agree to allow you to wed his daughter, he would be removed from his position at once. Our clan would see that as a weakness on his part. Clan alliances can mean the difference between losing your life and everything you hold dear, and beating the odds. You canna have her."

"Odran will kill him to make a point," Dar said. "Quinn is foolhardy to believe this would go his way."

There was only one way Quinn could think to make it work then. He would have to accuse his brother of trying to murder him. But he would need eyewitnesses who would corroborate his claim. Many of his clan approved of Quinn. They knew of his leadership and fighting skills. They would follow him, if Cormac was no longer in power. Except he had to do this right. And Cormac still had a core of men he counted on to watch his back. If Quinn could fight Cormac one on one, without his men interfering, he stood a good chance to win. Though he'd never beaten his brother ever in practice combat. The likelihood that his brother would risk having a fair fight between them was slim, Quinn thought. Otherwise, Cormac would have fought him long ago and would have tried to finish him off on his own. Instead, he had to try and get rid of him in some sneaky, despicable way.

"My brother canna have her," Quinn said with resolve. "Neither can Ewen."

Hamish chuckled then, as if pleased to hear Quinn was determined to pursue this. "She is well worth it. Though I doubt you will live long enough to enjoy the fruits of your labor." Then he narrowed his eyes at Quinn. "Unless you have already done so."

Quinn didn't respond, drinking his mead, then eating some of his stew.

"No' for lack of wanting, aye?" Hamish asked.

Quinn continued to eat, not responding to Hamish before he got himself into more trouble than he was in already. The man who challenged him would fight him, and Quinn suspected he'd kill him if he could. But Quinn knew he couldna kill the man. Only fight him the best he could and knock him out if he was able.

"Odran is vying to be the chief, aye?" Quinn finally asked.

"Aye, and he has a strong following. He's a strong leader. You would have done well no' to have created an issue between the two of you."

"He can fight me to the death?"

"Aye, naturally. He is eager to prove to the others that you are mortal."

"What if I have to kill him to prevent him from killing me?" Quinn knew the answer before Hamish offered it, but he had to ask.

"You may have to fight several others at the same time."

"I will try my best no' to kill him then."

The other two men were watching Quinn and grinning. "If you think you can best Odran, think again," Dar said. "Only Baudwin and his brother have ever beaten him."

Which didn't bode well, not that he expected anything less. They didn't know about his own fighting skills, so no one who wasn't well-trained would challenge him, he suspected. Not until they saw how he fought.

"Which is why Odran is vying to be chief," Hamish said. "And if anyone beats him, others will follow to try and take you down. They'll wear you down until there is no chance that you can win. Not as an outsider. And not as one who means to ruin our chance at an alliance with another clan."

"You mean that if I win against them all, I still willna be offered the position of chief?" Quinn was jesting, of course, and the three men laughed. At least they enjoyed his company before their clansmen tried to kill him.

He glanced over at the head table to look at Avelina. She was watching him, quiet, anxious, saddened. He didn't want to see her like that. He wanted her to be happy, to be with him. He hoped he didn't accidentally kill her clansmen.

He hoped he could best one or two of them, and the rest would worry that he might be truly invincible and leave him be.

Her da caught Quinn's eye, then glanced over at Avelina. He spoke to her, and she shook her head.

Quinn considered telling her da what he planned to do concerning his brother, but he would have to wait and see. First, Quinn had to prove himself to her kin. They had no idea the kind of fighter he was, so why should they even want him to be part of their clan? Though he didn't know their strengths or weaknesses either.

Hamish watched Odran for a moment. "I see you are no' drinking the whiskey." He pointed his bread toward Odran. "Only the honeyed mead. He can drink barrels of the harder stuff and still be steady on his feet. Any mon worth his salt could."

Not true. It could numb the pain the fighter was feeling in battle, but it could make him slower on his feet, and that's what Quinn was hoping for. He had to use every trick to his advantage, if he was to succeed.

"He has a mighty swing," Hamish said. "If you can stay beyond one of his killing blows, you might stand a chance, for a little longer."

"He favors his left shoulder," Dar said, "because of an old injury he suffered." Then he frowned at Quinn. "You had suffered injuries from the shipwreck, hadna you? The wound on your head looks fresh."

"Aye."

Hamish and the other men shook their heads.

Dar said, "You will never last. Even on his worst days,

Odran is a real killer."

It was true that if Odran hit Quinn in the ribs, he'd probably howl in pain, incapacitating him, and the man would have a good chance at beating him. Even his arm was aching from all the work and paddling, and swimming he'd done. He knew it would take more than a few days to completely heal. Though he wasn't one to rest when there was work or training to be done.

"My daughter says you are still recovering from injuries you received when you were shipwrecked. Can you fight?" her da suddenly asked Quinn, speaking over the loud conversation in the great hall.

Everyone grew quiet.

"Aye." Any man born and bred to fight had to be able to do so even when injured. Quinn couldn't back down from the challenge.

Most of the men nodded in approval.

Avelina was scowling at Quinn, but she had to know he had to fight. Then he smiled at her. Had she mentioned this just so that if he were to lose, her da could stop the fight before the man killed him, and he'd still save face? To say if he had been at full fighting strength, the man may never have beaten him? To remind everyone he was like so many of her people, recovering from injuries?

He adored her.

She looked away from him, appearing distraught. He wished he could hold her close, kiss her, and chase away her fears. The only way he'd be able to was to prove his worth to her da and her clan was to fight whoever challenged him though.

"You can fight in any manner that gets the job done," Fagin said to Quinn.

Quinn wondered if he was only giving him a tip now because Avelina had said how he was still recovering from his own injuries. But fighting men couldn't afford to be sentimental in this business.

He nodded his thanks to Fagin. Odran was still pouring the whiskey down his gullet. Quinn could do many things well, but drink like that. When Quinn had too much to drink, he'd been on his arse, babbling some nonsense, and thinking his words were as clever as could be. Which, to others in the same inebriated condition, probably were. But to any sober man, not.

When the meal was done, they headed out of the keep to the outer bailey, but Hamish allowed Avelina to speak with Quinn for a moment before the fight began, everyone looking on, and eager to see a new man fight their own.

"If you manage to take him down—" she said.

"When."

"*If*...he will have three of his friends—the ones seated at the table with him—try next. But my da willna allow them to attack all at once. It willna matter. You willna be able to take Odran down. My da says he is limping on his left side, but he feigns naught is wrong. Mayhap you can use that to your advantage."

Quinn glanced at her da. He was looking as stern as before, but Quinn appreciated that he would attempt to aid him in the fight. Maybe because he knew his daughter cared for Quinn. Maybe because Baudwin knew, if Quinn could make short work of Odran, her da would stand a better chance of claiming the position of chief. "Hamish and the other two men gave me a couple of tips also."

Avelina's eyes rounded, then she glanced at them and thanked them with an incline of her head.

"We stand by your da, lass," Hamish said, "And if Quinn can knock Odran down a peg or two, it canna hurt."

"If he doesna kill Quinn," she said, reminding them this was not a game.

Quinn knew it wasn't. He would have to make the best of it. Then he cupped Avelina's face and kissed her, wanting everyone to know he loved her with all his heart. That she wasn't chattel to offer for an alliance. "I will confront my brother, we will fight, and should I win, I will take over the clan. And then I will be your da's ally."

Tears filled her eyes, and she wrapped her arms around his neck and kissed him back.

Then he released her and kissed her forehead. "We will do this."

"If you get yourself killed, I will never forgive you."

"Neither will I." Then he turned to hear what her da had to say.

Looking stony-faced, her da ordered, "Last man standing is the winner. Begin."

CHAPTER 12

Fenella took Avelina up to the ramparts, so she could watch from the wall-walk. They could be trampled down below, as wild as all the men were. She would think they'd had enough fighting to last their lifetimes. Not men. They were always eager to fight, even after suffering their own recent injuries in battle.

"You were brilliant to mention Quinn is still healing from his injuries. Odran will think him weak and leave himself open to attack."

"Aye," Avelina said, but she had no stomach for this. Quinn was her husband. Could he truly win her da over if Quinn was able to fight his brother and take over his clan? She worried that his own injuries could sabotage his fighting abilities here.

Out of the corner of her eye, she saw her da joining them. He stood next to them and leaned over the wall to watch.

"Thank you, Da, for trying to aid him."

Her da snorted. "If he bests Odran, that will aid me." Then he looked down at her. "You love him, dinna you?"

"Aye. Da, he said he'd fight his brother and rule his clan. Then you would have an alliance with him, no' Cormac. Quinn would be true to his word."

Her da shook his head. "That is a lot to expect. I wouldna get my hopes up." He frowned as they watched Quinn dodge Odran's killer blows. "He is quick as a bunny."

But Quinn would have to strike decisive blows to take Odran down. Dodging him wouldn't be enough.

"Quinn doesna want to lose faith with you, or me, or our people, should he kill Odran," she said.

Her da chuckled. "He will never best Odran." But then he was frowning again.

Avelina was frowning just as much as she saw Quinn leap at Odran, striking his padded vest at the shoulder. Odran actually stumbled back and fell on his arse.

Everyone was quiet, then low conversation filled the outer bailey, several nodding their heads at Quinn's decisive blow.

Odran sat on his arse and didn't get up right away, breathing heavily.

"Quinn dances like a deer," her da said.

Then Odran was on his feet, staggered, and lunged forward, trying to kill Quinn with one pivotal blow. But Quinn was too quick. He feinted like he was falling back, but dodged to the right of the warrior instead, and kicked out with his booted foot, striking Odran in the leg.

Odran howled in pain and fell back on his arse,

dropping his sword, and holding his leg.

"Odran had suffered an injury to his leg during battle, but no one saw to it?" Avelina guessed.

"He said he had no injuries, though some of us saw him attempting to hide a limp," Fenella said.

"Serves him right," her da said, smirking. "Here he planned to prove he should be in charge because I had been wounded."

"He has won. Odran isna getting up. Tell our people Quinn is the winner," Avelina commanded her da, not that her da would do what she ordered. But she didn't want anyone else to step in to fight Quinn.

"Quinn hasna proven himself yet."

She scowled at her da. "What? He has to die before he has proven he is a remarkable swordsman? He is injured, for heaven's sake, Da. And he bested the man, when no one thought he could!"

"He has to fight whoever is willing to take him to task. 'Tis our way, lass." Her da motioned in the direction of another man who was heading toward Quinn, his sword in hand. "Padruig is up next."

"This is barbaric."

"'Tis the only way to prove who is the strongest and can lead the clan."

"So if he wins, he can lead the clan!" Avelina said, not believing it for a moment. Her da had to be speaking in generalities.

Her da gave her a small smile.

"Truly?" She didn't believe it! This was her da's plan? She didn't think the council would agree to a stranger taking over their clan though. "Are you jesting?"

"Nay. If he is as invincible as you say he is, then he could lead us to victory."

"Och, that is ludicrous." She still believed her da was jesting. If she hadn't saved Quinn from the sea, he would have died. He was not invincible.

"Aye, but you only have to make others believe it and it will influence the way people view him."

His comment made her wonder if her da really did believe the council would consider Quinn for the position. She wasn't sure the other men would support him though.

Quinn was preparing himself for the next man's assault, as a couple of other men moved Odran out of the way. The injured clansman was howling the whole time.

"We didna give him any tips on how to fight Padruig," Avelina said, angry with herself for not having given Quinn more information about the other men who might fight him.

"We didna need to. Quinn appears to be a skilled tactician. Consider the way he observes Padruig's movements. He's studying him, watching to see if he favors any old wounds or new injuries. Or if he will give away his tactics before he fights. Odran is so big and his blows so dangerous, he uses his brute force to attack and intimidate his opponent. Quinn could see that and used it to his advantage. He is like your wolf. Observant and careful. Other men might see Quinn as too cautious, but he has to use whatever techniques he can to survive. He is at a strong disadvantage, everyone wanting to see the stranger fail, and so he might have to fight numerous opponents, when he is suffering from his own injuries as well. Padruig willna be the last to challenge him. Of that I am certain." Her da pointed out another man. "Braddach might appear relaxed, but he's just itching to get into the battle."

"Then you will allow it until all have fought him and Quinn is dead!"

"Silence, Daughter! He wouldna be the one for you if he canna fight well."

She was about to tell her da that she was married to Quinn, but if her da thought her husband couldn't fight well, then he would be glad to see him die, eager to have her married off to someone who was more powerful than him in men and supplies.

Swords began to clash and clang, each man holding his own. Padruig fought more like Quinn, their strikes not wild, but measured, each of them determining the other's strengths. *And weaknesses.* She was certain Quinn's ribs weren't fully healed. His head wound was healing nicely, but he still had a cut across it, and his arm had to be on the mend. Even so, he fought well, thrusting, slashing, advancing. Now he was more like Odran, pounding on Padruig until he knocked his sword from his grasp. Both men heaving to catch their breaths, Quinn quickly had his sword at Padruig's throat. Padruig's hands were outstretched in defeat.

"Do you yield?" Quinn asked Padruig, loudly for all to hear.

"Aye," the man said, sounding angry that he couldn't have bested the stranger.

"Good fight, mon." Quinn lowered his sword.

Padruig went to retrieve his sword, though Hamish picked it up for him and said something to him. Padruig nodded, glanced back at Quinn, then took his sword and sheathed it. Avelina wondered if Hamish had told him to go in peace, and not fight Quinn further or he'd fight him. She hoped so.

No one advanced on Quinn, and she prayed that was the end of the fighting. Though she was eyeing Braddach because her da said he would fight Quinn next and being a battle-hardened warrior, she was certain her da knew best. Then she saw Braddach unsheathe his sword, proving her da was right. Braddach's stance low, he advanced on Quinn. She wanted to kill the man herself for fighting Quinn next. Couldn't they see that he'd already fought two men successfully, even though he was himself injured and had to be worn out? Not only wasn't it fair, but wouldn't it make Braddach appear callous? That he couldn't fight a man who was as fresh as him?

"The more men Quinn can fight, the better," her da said.

"Until the last one cuts him down!" She couldn't believe how men could go to war and come home ready to fight all over again.

"Quinn proves how hardy he is with each man he brings down. If he only bested one man, it wouldna be enough. He needs to take down—"

"A whole army!"

"Any who wish to challenge him," her da said.

"That could mean the whole lot of them."

"Aye." Her da looked over at her. "Remember, if he

wishes to fight his brother and take over the rule of his clan, he will have to be prepared to fight any number of men. No' just his brother, but those who would want to succeed his brother, any one of them wanting to take Cormac's place, or who are loyal to him and try to protect him."

She let out her breath in utter exasperation, but she knew, as much as she hated to admit it, her da was right.

"The same thing if he takes over our clan, lass."

She glanced at her da, but he was watching the fight. Her da was serious!

***

Quinn was glad he'd managed to defeat two of the men without causing serious injury to either of them. At least, in Odran's case, he hoped he had not. But when fighting Odran, he'd had to take drastic measures. The next man wasn't as wary as Padruig, and he must have thought Quinn wouldn't have enough stamina to fight a third man who charged in, slashing away at him. The truth was, it was easier for him to fight such a man. With Padruig, Quinn felt he'd been playing a deadly game of chess, winner take all, including the loser's life.

The man was quick and determined, and like Padruig, he'd had time to study Quinn's perceived weaknesses. What he didn't know was Quinn had been feigning that his left arm had been injured and the man kept trying to strike it. Quinn's ribs were killing him, and his injured arm was too. With every clash of swords against swords, he felt the pain shoot acutely up his right arm and through his ribs. His head was pounding too.

But the swimming he'd been doing for all the time he'd

been on the island had strengthened his arms and legs, and he felt nimble and quick. More so when he'd fought Odran, he had to admit. The blood coursing through his body was filled with purpose—fight to win, or lose and possibly die. Worse, he would lose Avelina, and that's who he was truly fighting for. The right to have her. With every fiber of his being, he fought to win, and he would continue to fight if it meant dealing with every one of her clansmen.

Quinn was careful to not overexert himself, as much as he wanted to end this quickly. Ending the fight too quickly would mean another man would entertain the notion of battling him next. If he drew it out a bit, he had more time to rest. Not much, but some. The other man seemed not to be injured, and he appeared tireless.

He proved to be an able adversary. If Quinn had to deal with only him, he would have easily taken him down. But the man was cagey, and he kept drawing Quinn forward, striking, and retreating.

Quinn waited this time, breathing heavily, trying to pace himself, attempting to draw on his inner strength like he always did during a long battle where he didn't have time to rest before he was fighting another of the enemy. Though in those cases, the men had been fighting, just like him. They were on more equal terms. This man was well-rested, taking his time to try and wear Quinn down. Maybe he hoped to draw Quinn into a confrontation, to make an ill-thought-out move, but Quinn had fought in too many battles, even when his brother sent the enemy to take him down. He wouldn't let this man best him.

Quinn set the tip of his sword on the ground as if he

needed to rest or he'd fall. Taking the bait, Braddach raced forth to strike him down. Quinn raised his sword so fast, he sliced Braddach's cheek, the man crying out, and slinging an oath of curses at him before he charged forth, and they clashed. They struck swords and broke away. Before Quinn could prepare for Braddach's next assault, he slammed his body into Quinn's.

Pain shrieked through Quinn's whole body, and he groaned. Stars sprinkled in front of his eyes before he could clear his head and react. He quickly kicked out his leg and swept it behind Braddach's legs. He shoved him back at the same time and the man's legs were swept out from under him. He landed hard on the ground on his back with an oof and an oath.

Before Braddach could get to his feet, Quinn slammed his boot down on the man's chest and pointed his sword at his throat. He wasn't asking this time. He demanded. "Yield!"

Everyone waited for Braddach to say he would yield, his breathing labored, and he finally gave Quinn a smirk and raised his hand to him. Quinn had to acknowledge that the man was offering his hand in friendship, but he also knew he could be feigning friendship and continue the fight.

When Quinn offered his hand to him, the man clasped it with a solid grip.

As much as it hurt, and trying not to groan again, Quinn pulled him to his feet. He felt like he was dying, and it would take him time to heal again. He couldn't fight his brother until he was in better shape.

Instead of stepping off to the side, or fighting him

further, Braddach stood next to him, his sword in hand, his arms outstretched, and said, "Anyone else?"

Quinn couldn't believe it. The man, who was vying to take over the leadership of the clan, was now offering to fight on his behalf?

Padruig joined them and offered his support as well. Odran couldn't if he'd wanted to. Not that Quinn thought he would want to after he'd injured him.

His hand on his sword, Hamish came over to stand with them, observing the rest of the clan. "If no one else wishes to fight, I'd say it was time to celebrate further!"

"Aye," a chorus of men and women said, and then everyone hurried back to the keep.

Padruig slapped Quinn on the shoulder. "Good fight. Honorable. At least when you fought me and Braddach."

A couple of men were carrying Odran into the keep. He was swearing at them to take care, that he wasn't a sack of potatoes, and more.

"No one could fight fair when it comes to Odran," Braddach said, assuring Quinn that he had done right by them. "Good fight!" Then he grinned at Quinn. "Ribs a little sore?"

"God's wounds," Quinn said. "How did you know?"

"Your left hand covered your ribs a couple of times when you were fighting Padruig and your face expressed your pain." Then Braddach frowned. "I thought your left arm was injured, but every time anyone struck at it, you didna look as though you were feeling any pain. No' from that. Your ribs, aye. Mayhap your head."

"That's because I wasna injured there." Quinn pulled

up his right sleeve and showed the gash that was healing.

Smiling, Padruig and Braddach both shook their heads at him. "You are a good fighter," Padruig said. "I dinna think you could take Odran down and then best the two of us also. You earned a lot of men's respect today. But I suspect your success has all to do with winning Avelina's da over."

"Aye," was all Quinn would say.

Before they could walk to the keep, he was looking for Avelina and saw her come out of one of the towers leading to the wall walk. She ran straight for him and the other men waited with him.

"You still canna have her," Hamish said. "No' unless you are a chief of a clan or have an army of men to lead."

"I would fight in support of Quinn," Padruig said.

"As would I," Braddach said. "And I believe, once Odran has healed, he will feel the same way. He highly respects those who can best him. No' too many can."

Quinn was glad to hear it, though all that he cared about for now was feeling Avelina in his arms, and hoping he didn't wince or groan when she pressed against his ribs. He didn't have to worry about it. Once she was in his arms and kissing him, he thought of nothing else.

Her da was coming and Fenella was at his side. He was looking stern; Fenella was smiling.

"You are truly undefeatable," Avelina said against Quinn's mouth.

"Only when I think of naught but holding you tight. Will your da agree to our marriage?"

"We have to see what the elders decide on. Who will lead whom."

"And if I can oust my brother and take over my clan from him."

"We will go with you and aid you," Padruig said.

"Aye," Braddach said. "Odran also, once he's able."

Her da reached them and he said, "Well done, Quinn. You will sit at the head table with me and my daughter and my niece from now on. You have earned some allies this day."

"I have agreed to marry your daughter."

"You will have to do more than that to marry her," her da said.

"I will do whatever it takes." Quinn had never thought he'd feel that way about a woman, but he had never known a woman like Avelina before either. He knew he shouldn't be kissing Avelina in front of her kin or her da before they knew they were married, but he wanted everyone to know she was his, and he would fight every last man for the right to have her for his wife. Thankfully, her da seemed to approve.

But then her da must have assumed he should set some rules where his daughter was concerned. "You willna be seeing my daughter unless 'tis in the company of others. Do you understand?"

"Aye." Quinn understood, and he would feel the same way if Avelina were his daughter. He would be just as protective of her when it came to a stranger who wished to take her to wife, but had no properties or an army to call his own. Especially when Baudwin had other plans for her, if Quinn couldn't succeed at removing his brother from power. He was glad some of Baudwin's men had pledged to aid him. He hadn't thought that would come about. He thought some might admire him for his fighting ability, as many did. But the men he fought? He'd believed they might resent him for bettering them, especially when he had to fight three of them, when they each had only to fight him.

He had his arm wrapped around Avelina as they headed into the keep, and she asked him, "How badly are you injured after fighting with the men?"

Avelina had to know he wouldn't admit to how much he hurt, not in front of her da or the men he'd fought.

"I'm fine."

She looked up at him with such an incredulous expression, he assumed she knew he was hurting. She shook her head and tsked. "I told my da how honest you were."

"Give the mon a break," her da said, as if Quinn was one of them now. "He canna admit to you or the others here that he is in pain. How would that appear to the rest of us?"

"Aye, then he can finish rebuilding Judith's byre and patching up her roof to her croft," Avelina said, sounding disgruntled.

The men all looked at Quinn.

"You survived the shipwreck, knew our kin had killed the other men who had come with you, and that the same fate would await you if you were caught, were suffering from injuries, and yet you were repairing Judith's byre?" Padruig asked, sounding astonished.

"She needed the help," Quinn said, not about to mention he would have done anything for her for offering to harbor him and look after his injuries. Just as he would do anything for Avelina and Fenella.

"I will assist you," Braddach said.

"As will I," Padruig said. "With three of us working on it, we'll have it done in no time."

"I was going to recommend Quinn rest after all of you ganged up on him, but now I willna. No' when he is perfectly fine. Dinna let him shirk his responsibility either," Avelina said, sounding annoyed.

The men all laughed. Quinn smiled down at his bonny wife. He loved her.

CHAPTER 13

When they entered the great hall, whiskey was freely flowing. Music was playing, and several men and women were dancing.

Since her da had declared Avelina would not see Quinn alone, she was making the most of being with him here and now.

"When do we tell your da we are married?" Quinn asked.

"After 'tis decided who will be chief." Yet she didn't want to wait to see Quinn alone. She hugged him lightly. "How are your injuries?"

"They are sore, lass."

She smiled up at him and kissed his mouth tenderly. "I knew so. I was so proud of you. Angry with my da for allowing the fight with so many men. Angry with the men for battling with you. Especially Braddach and Padruig for fighting you after you had to deal with Odran. And knowing you were still suffering from your own injuries. Though I understand why my da didna stop it, and why the men did what they did. They were making you one of them."

"Aye. 'Tis a great thing to be welcomed, instead of hunted. I didna think the men who fought me would be willing to protect me. Odran may still be another story. We just need to tell your da about us."

"As soon as the council decides on who will lead."

"Aye, but it may kill me no' to be able to be with you this eve."

She chuckled, and he kissed her again. "I love you," she said. "They should decide the leadership soon."

***

Quinn danced with Avelina, intending to stay with her until her da forced them apart. He still limited himself on his drinking. He didn't want Avelina to think poorly of him should he step on her feet, or say things he didn't mean under the influence of the whiskey. But everyone kept offering him another tankard in friendship and respect. So he drank as little as possible, sharing in the celebration.

In the middle of all the revelry when he and Avelina were seated at the high table taking a respite, he hadn't expected Avelina to whisper to him, "Join me in my chamber, fourth chamber up the stairs on the south tower, my husband."

"What of your da, lass?" Quinn could see all the good cheer he had managed to create, turning to animosity in a heartbeat.

"We are married. I leave it up to you whether you wish to join me or no'." She kissed him in a way that said she wanted him, now, her tongue caressing his, her hand sweeping over his plaid, and she smiled when she felt him half aroused.

"Dinna wait too long, or I'm bound to be asleep." She kissed his mouth, then left the table and found Fenella dancing, took her hand and pulled her toward the stairs to their chambers. Fenella looked back at Quinn, smiled, and the two of the women slipped out of the noisy hall.

Quinn watched the women go, and Hamish leaned over to him and said, "You may never have another opportunity, and if she's willing..." He shrugged. "If it were me, I wouldna be sitting here. You've declared you want her for your wife. She's declared she wants you for her husband. Her da took her mother from a farm and married her. No one would fight you for the right to have her. Not after the way you fought today."

Still, Quinn wanted her da's permission, even if it was after the fact. Baudwin glanced at Quinn, and he raised his tankard to him.

Quinn raised his in a salute, drank deeply, wiped his mouth, and said to Hamish, "If this gets me killed...I will come back and haunt you. But know this, we are already married." If Quinn drank anything more, he would forget he had a wife.

Hamish threw his head back and laughed. Quinn didn't wait another moment and left the table to find Avelina's chamber. He thought someone might try to change his mind, but everyone was so busy celebrating, no one bothered. He also hoped that if anyone did try to follow, Hamish would stop him.

At the bottom of the stairs, Quinn met Fenella, and he was glad he was going to make love to his lovely wife, despite that he still hadn't gotten approval from Avelina's da.

"She is waiting for you in her chamber. Just in case anyone looks for her, and for you, I'll stand guard and warn you. Be quick. I want to retire to bed after seeing you fight. It wore me out."

"Thank you, Fenella."

"Thank you for saving my cousin. And she told me you were already married, which is the only reason I agree to being a co-conspirator."

He smiled and headed up the stairs. Startling him, Avelina was just around the curve of the wall, looking anxious, but she quickly smiled. Then she led him into a chamber. "Is Fenella downstairs guarding?" she asked, her voice hushed as she closed the door. "Just in case anyone tries to check on me at my chamber?"

"Aye. You know you dinna have your da's permission for this." Quinn took her face in his hands and kissed her.

"You have to know how to understand him. He said you might even take over our clan. Either way, if you take over your own, or ours, I am yours."

He kissed her soundly. "I havena done either."

"This is just in preparation and to give you even more of an incentive to fight well. You are mine, Highlander. We have pledged our love and our marriage to one another. It is done. Naught that my da can say will undo it."

Quinn smiled down at her. "Do you still think of me as your prisoner?"

She wrapped her arms snuggly around him. "Aye, you are."

"Then I am all yours to do with what you will."

"You willna hurt too much if we make love?"

He chuckled and swept her up in his arms and carried her to the bed. "Naught would keep me from making love to my beautiful wife."

She was glad he was brave enough to join her.

"You said we would tell your da we were wed as soon as the leadership was decided."

"I did, but I couldna wait. When no one else was too close to us, I told my da we were wed. He said, 'That's nice, lass.' My da was in his cups. I doubt anything I said to him this eve, he would remember on the morrow."

"Hamish encouraged me to see you. I told him we were wed, just in case he wished to defend me, should any of your clansmen attempt to stop me from being with you."

She tugged at Quinn's belt. "Mayhap Hamish also overheard me telling my da we were married. He is good at overhearing things." She finished removing Quinn's belt. "I love you, Quinn, and naught was keeping me from being with you tonight."

"I wasna planning on letting you be alone." Quinn's voice was already rough with urgency, and he was hurrying to pull off his plaid and shirt.

She treasured how eager he was to make love to her and ran her hand over his glorious, naked muscles, his arms, his back, his arse. He was already hard with need, and she prized that he was always ready and eager for her. He began pulling off her plaid, and she kissed his shoulder, nuzzling her face against his chest, heard his heart thrumming with desire, just like hers was.

Their mouths connected. He ran his hands over her breasts, and she moaned against his mouth. He pulled her *léine* off. Then he slipped her chemise over her head and dropped it to the floor. With a fire blazing in the hearth, the light on their faces and hair, the warmth heating their already hot bodies, he lifted her off her feet. She wrapped her legs around his hips. And then she was hugging his body, his staff pressed against her mound, making her feel deliciously wanton.

They were still kissing when he carried her to the bed, laid her down, and he moved on top of her. She ran her hands through his hair, and he leaned down and pressed his mouth against her lips. He slid his hand down her belly and started to stroke between her legs. She felt hot and wet and achy.

She arched against his questing fingers, wanting him to finish her off like he'd done before in the shelter by the ocean with the storm pounding all around them. Then she felt lifted up, loving the way he excited every part of her with his touch.

He kept stroking her, kissing her. His eyes were smoky with desire.

"Beautiful," he whispered against her cheek, and then he inserted a finger between her legs and stroked.

Not expecting that, she went over the top and cried out with pleasure. Wolf came out from underneath the bed to check on them, and they both told him, "Go lie down."

Wolf returned to his spot underneath the bed, and

they hoped he would get used to them making love soon.

Avelina ran her hands over Quinn's arse, and he groaned before he pressed his staff between her legs and pushed.

"Ohmigod, you are incredible," she said, and he continued to thrust.

"As you are." Quinn loved his wife. She intoxicated him, made his head spin, just from her touch, the whisper of her breath on his cheek, the way her heart pounded, and she wrapped her legs around his.

Deeper he thrust, hoping no one would hear Avelina, and worry that she was in trouble, but he was glad she found pleasure in his making love to her. He kissed her mouth, and she parted her lips to take him in. He tasted the mead on her tongue, and her blue eyes fluttered open. She smiled a little, and stroked his tongue with hers. And then he moved his mouth over her nipple, and sucked and she arched against him.

"Ahh," she groaned, her inner muscles contracting around his rigid staff. "You are amazing."

He groaned with exquisite release and continued to thrust until he was spent. "Lass, *you* are amazing."

***

Before dawn, someone was banging on Avelina's barred door.

"I will see to it," Avelina said, as if she intended to defend Quinn from anyone who would attempt to fight him for being in her chamber through the night.

"Nay, lass, I will." Quinn threw on his shirt and headed for the door. He would straighten out whoever it was.

When he opened it, he found her da standing there, frowning at him. "You were to sleep in the barracks with my men," Baudwin said, but he wasn't armed, and Quinn suspected her da already knew the truth.

Quinn motioned to the cloaked bed. "My wife had other plans for me."

Baudwin smiled. "I'm finally free of my duties to the lass then."

"I heard that, Da," Avelina said from the cloaked bed.

"You could have told me. I shouldna have had to learn it from Hamish."

Avelina came out of the bed wearing her chemise and *léine*. "I told you last night, Da. See? You dinna even remember." She began wrapping her plaid around her.

Baudwin rubbed his bearded chin. "Mayhap." He frowned at Quinn. "We need to know how you plan to oust your brother from power, so we can prepare."

"You will back me in this?" Quinn said, surprised that Baudwin would want to aid him after Quinn took Avelina for his wife without her da's permission and when her da had a contracted marriage for her already.

"Aye, if you are true to your word that you intend to have an alliance with us once you remove your brother from power. You have put me in a bind with your brother's clan. It's only right that you straighten this matter out. Now that you are my son by marriage, you have my support. And Hamish agrees. We'll wait until more of our people have healed so that we're at full fighting strength. We'll send word that I've taken over and that we'll be bringing Avelina to wed Cormac."

"I would give anything to be the messenger," Quinn said.

Baudwin gave him a dark smile. "As would I, but it would be too dangerous. He'd kill you, and I'd have to give my daughter up to the bastard, if we were to be allied. I'll send someone else. But later. I want to be ready to leave once my messenger gives Cormac the news. I'm sure Cormac will understand after all the fighting that we've had, we need time to recover."

"Aye. Mayhap he will send one of his men to see what has happened here though. He might have learned Fenella's da died in battle and may want to learn what is happening about the contract."

Baudwin rubbed his chin again. "God's wounds, we would have to kill the messenger. He would be sure to learn that you still live." He slapped Quinn on the back. "Come, we have a wedding to attend."

"Da?" Avelina said, frowning.

"I know this is already official, but I want my only daughter wed in the chapel."

"Aye, Da."

"Come," Baudwin said to Quinn. "We must talk. Your wife needs to finish dressing." Then he frowned at Quinn. "As do you. Meet me in my solar."

Then he left, and Quinn shut the door.

Avelina threw her arms around Quinn. "I told you my da wouldna remember what I spoke to him about last night."

"Good thing I told Hamish. I canna believe your da would back me in this."

"He would do anything for an alliance when he felt his ally wouldna turn on him, especially after he saw you fight yesterday."

Someone knocked on the door, and Quinn released Avelina to answer it, surprised to see Fenella there. She glanced at his state of undress, her cheeks blushing, and she stammered, "I...I came to help Avelina change for the ceremony."

"Of course." He smiled and hurried to finish dressing. He gave Avelina a hug and a kiss before he left, and Fenella sighed.

As soon as he began to shut the door on his departure, she said, "I hope Ewen is half as braw as your Highlander."

"I do as well," Avelina said, and Quinn finished shutting the door and headed to Baudwin's solar.

They had a lot of plans to make if they were to ensure they were successful. Quinn wasn't expecting to see Hamish in Baudwin's solar too. Both cheered him for having married the lass.

"She is a handful, as no doubt you already know," Baudwin said, offering Quinn a tankard of ale.

"Aye, she is a fighter too, and yet she aids everyone she can who canna do for themselves. She will be sorely missed here," Hamish said.

"'Tis no' enough that I love her, but that my people will love her also. I have no' doubt they will adore her. What about Ewen? What kind of a mon is he?" Quinn asked, hoping that Avelina's cousin would be happy as well.

Baudwin and Hamish smiled at each other.

"See? What did I tell you, Baudwin? Quinn would be

just as concerned about your niece as he is about your daughter."

"Aye. When we escort Fenella to see Ewen, you can judge him then," Baudwin said. "But we must get this other business done first."

Quinn was surprised Baudwin would be willing to take him with him to see to Fenella's welfare. But he knew Avelina would also want to go, and he would take her with some of his men. If he didna like the man? He wasn't sure what he'd do then.

Odran came to Baudwin's chamber, still limping badly, but he wouldna let it keep him down. "Your daughter is ready to be married." He sliced Quinn a glower. "Some say I would fight on your behalf, Highlander. They misspoke."

"Aye, but I will watch yours."

Odran growled and limped out of the room as fast as he could.

"They didna misspeak," Hamish said. "Believe me, if anyone made a move to cut you down, he would be at their throat."

"Aye," Baudwin said. "What are we waiting for? I need to marry my daughter off."

***

Avelina didn't know why she was so nervous about marrying Quinn in the chapel, when they were already wed. But she'd been coming here as a bairn and with everyone's eyes on her, she felt self-conscious. Some of the women had made a flower garland for her hair, and Gwyneth had surprised her by giving her a blue gown that many of the women had worked on so she would be ready for her wedding day. Fenella had also worked on it and had selected the color, knowing it was Avelina's favorite. She should have known the women would have done so because she'd been working with others to create Fenella's gown. Also blue, but darker.

When she saw her beautiful husband standing beside Hamish, and to her surprise, Odran, she smiled. Quinn smiled back at her, looking as though he wanted to sweep her off her feet and carry her to the altar.

"He looks eager," her da told her as he escorted her to him.

"As eager as you were to wed my mother?" she asked.

"Aye, lass. Though I dinna think I stood as straight and tall and still as Quinn is doing. I was rather anxious to have it over and done with. And just so you'll know, we handfasted on the way from her farm to the chapel."

She smiled at her da. She loved him.

Before she knew it, she was looking up into the eyes of her adoring husband, and she knew he was the only one for her—as long as he didn't get himself killed when he tried to take over from his brother.

***

After three days of feasting and a week later, Avelina was taking supplies to Judith while Quinn had been teaching the men his sword-fighting skills. She would miss helping her people, and she knew they'd miss her.

When she returned to the outer bailey, everyone had dispersed to do their chores, some of which meant to help rebuild crofts and byres. The wall surrounding the castle had already been finished. Avelina couldn't find Quinn, but she suspected he was helping others somewhere else on the island. He'd become a valued member of the clan and many would miss him also.

"Have you seen Quinn?" she asked Hamish as he was giving some of his men orders on what they needed to do next.

"He went to see Lendon, to help him fish after he did some sword practice with the men. You should have seen Odran trying to fight Quinn with a bum leg."

"Do you think Odran's leg is broken?"

"Nay. But he is still limping, so Quinn must have done some more damage after Odran injured it in battle."

"Is Odran angry with Quinn?" Avelina couldn't believe he'd hold a grudge against Quinn for fighting him the best he could. *He'd* been injured too.

"Nay, he respects Quinn now. It had to be done."

"What has the council decided?"

"They were no' happy you took things into your own hands and married the Highlander. But they agreed that Quinn will be valuable to our clan, in any event. I canna say what the council has decided, only that they are fighting amongst themselves as to who should lead the clan."

"Did I hurt my da's chances of being chief?" She'd worried about that. Perhaps she and Quinn should have waited a little longer to declare their intent, but she hadn't wanted this to be decided for her.

"Aye. If you had said you would willingly wed Cormac to gain the alliance, one of the men on the council would have voted for your da. As it stands, he willna. Though, everyone appears to like the Highlander. Except his brother, it seems. Quinn is a strong fighter and a good and fair leader of men. Even while he was teaching the men some of his fighting techniques, and I was attempting to lead, he had it well in hand. I'll warn you though, the council and everyone else in the clan are watching everything he does, lass."

"Thank you, Hamish. I thought you might be our new chief."

"Or mayhap your da will, and I will lead his men."

She smiled. "I would vote for that."

"But then your Highlander would have to fight his brother, take over the clan, and ally with us."

Could Quinn even fight his brother? Or would it feel wrong? Could he fight his clansmen, if more of them should back their chief? Would his council even support Quinn's bid for power? She supposed he could fight his brother, if he attempted to kill Quinn. And Cormac would, she was certain, when Quinn went there with the intention of taking over the clan.

More than that, she didn't want to risk losing Quinn in a fight, yet she knew it was always a possibility when he went into battle. "I'll return. I'm off to see how my fisherman husband is doing."

Hamish snorted. "From what Lendon has told me, Quinn should stick to fighting rather than fishing."

She smiled. She knew Lendon would teach him the tricks of the trade, sooner or later. She left the keep and headed for the beach. When she came up over the sand dune, she saw Quinn looking out to sea, no sign of Lendon and his boat. She assumed they'd quit for the day, and Quinn had carried Lendon's boat back to his byre for him.

Wolf ran to catch up to her.

"Where have you been for most of the day?" she asked Wolf.

He wagged his tail at her. He'd accompanied her to most of her visits to the farms, but he smelled of the sea, and she thought he must have been looking for Quinn when she returned to the keep. He preferred when Quinn and she were together, so he didn't have to protect only one or the other.

Quinn was standing still, looking out to sea, braw as ever. At hearing her approach, he turned to see her, inclined his head, and then looked back out to sea.

He seemed in a contemplative mood. She joined him, placing her hand on his arm and pressing her head against his back and shoulder as the sun was beginning to set, coloring the sky in a wash of pinks, yellows, and oranges, the dark blue water turning golden. She didn't say anything, wondering if he was thinking of returning home and what would happen then. She wanted to ask him about his brother and what he would do, but she was afraid to.

Instead she asked, "Did you catch a lot of fish?"

"If I had to prove my worth to your clan by fishing for my lot in life, I would fail." He continued looking out to sea, and she felt his tension, as if he was eager to leave, ready to do something, anything, other than stay here.

"You dinna need to prove anything to my kin, or to me either."

He pulled her arms around his waist and continued to look out to sea.

"I mean what I say." She knew in the way he didn't

speak, he didn't feel as she did. "Quinn—"

"I must earn my respect like any other man in your clan. 'Tis the only way. I have promised I will take over my clan and become an ally to your people."

"But…can you fight your brother and no' feel badly about it?"

"Nay. But it must be done." He turned around then, and drew her into his arms, and she nestled her body against him.

"You dinna have to go. Fight for our chief, whomever they choose to lead our men. Fight for my clan. Be one of us. Da is making an alliance through a marriage for himself, and with Fenella marrying Ewen, that is two more alliances than we had before."

"Your da promised your people an alliance with your marriage to my brother. He will get one, only with me instead."

If Quinn didn't die.

"You will stay here for the time being," she said. The longer he remained with her people, the more they would see he could be a help to them and maybe they would convince him to stay, to be one of them, that they could live without another alliance. But she knew the men were only preparing for another battle, healing their wounds, ready to fight Quinn's cause this time.

He leaned down and kissed her head. "Will you and Wolf make me stay?"

She smiled through her tears. "Aye. For the time being. Come, 'tis time for the meal. You are teaching the men many good fighting skills."

"They are teaching me as well." He wrapped his arm around her and he, she, and Wolf headed to the keep. When they reached the keep, Hamish greeted them. "The council has decided who will lead us. They will tell us at the meal."

***

At the feast, one of the council members stood and said, "We have unanimously decided Baudwin will lead us. Hamish will lead his men. Fenella has agreed to wed Ewen." He looked at Avelina. "And we have Baudwin's agreement he will be making another alliance through his own contracted marriage."

Quinn squeezed Avelina's hand, then stood to make his declaration to the council. "I will provide an alliance."

She was both proud of him and worried for him at the same time.

Everyone grew quiet.

"My clan will ally with yours."

Everyone cheered him, though Avelina still felt he would get himself killed.

CHAPTER 14

Quinn had kept busy helping others of Avelina's clan, just like he would when he was back home. He fought when he had to fight, but he was good at doing many things. The longer he stayed, the more men offered to go with him to take down his brother. His beautiful wife had been right, as much as he had wanted to return home and settle this between him and his brother as soon as possible.

The longer he waited, the more everyone healed, and were more eager to fight again. But as he was returning from fishing with Lendon, he saw a square sail fluttering in the wind—a ship headed for the island. Wolf joined him, and they watched the ship for a long time, until it was close enough he could make out the markings. It was one of his brother's ships.

Maybe Cormac had tired of waiting to hear from Baudwin about their agreement to wed Fenella to him.

"I'll carry the coracle to the byre. You warn the chief of

the trouble that could be on the horizon," Lendon said.

"Aye." Quinn slapped him on the back. "Come, Wolf." Quinn raced to the keep while Wolf ran at his side. The wolf could run much faster than him, and often did, but this time he stuck close to Quinn. He swore the beast knew he had to warn their people of the incoming ship.

He observed several people working in the outer bailey when he ran through the gate. He saw Fagin, who had replaced Hamish as the man in charge of the guards, and headed for him.

"Trouble?" Fagin asked, frowning. He'd been one of the men to bring Quinn in when they'd learned Avelina had been caring for him and hadn't killed him.

"Aye, could be. One of my brother's ships is on its way here. Just one, so it doesn't appear he's intent on waging war."

"Just in claiming your wife, I suspect," Fagin said, smiling.

Quinn snorted. Then he frowned as he and Fagin headed into the inner bailey. "Where is my wife?"

"Helping the midwife with birthing a bairn out at one of the crofts. I'll tell Hamish the news if you can warn Baudwin."

"Aye." Quinn and Fagin split forces and when Quinn reached Baudwin's solar, he knocked on the open door.

"Aye, come in, Quinn. What is the news?" Baudwin was on his feet and coming toward Quinn, buckling on his sword.

"My brother has sent one of his ships."

"Just one?"

"Aye, a messenger, mayhap. He may have sent an 'escort' to take his bride-to-be home."

"I want you to stay out of sight until they leave. No one needs to know you are still alive, and I'll tell my people to watch their tongues."

Quinn didn't like the idea of hiding from his kin, but he knew Baudwin was right. If anyone from his home learned he was alive, they'd send word back to his brother. It was better to keep that a secret, until he was ready to travel with Baudwin's men to take over the clan. "I must see my wife. She's helping Elizabeth to assist Mai in the birth of her bairn."

"They willna want you at the croft. I'll send Gwyneth. You stay here. Out of sight. I know it goes against all your training, but for your safety, and ours, it needs to be done this way."

"Aye."

"Trust me."

"I do."

"Good. Stay above stairs and we'll send food up to you. I'm sure your wife will want to see you."

"It will be a couple of hours before they land on your shores."

"Then do whatever you feel you must, but retire as soon as we have word they are here."

"Aye. But I will see to my wife." Quinn left the solar and soon headed out of the keep. He had to speak with Avelina, even if her da felt the women would send him away while Mai was giving birth.

He wished he had his own horse here, but no one who

had a horse offered for him to use theirs and it took him a good half hour before he reached the croft, Wolf running ahead of him. He didn't want to alarm Avelina, but they needed to discuss what they should do. Would her da pretend she was marrying Cormac? Did his clansmen intend to take her back with them, if Baudwin was too preoccupied to send her along? He suspected that would be the case.

"Wolf, out!" he heard Avelina command him.

Quinn smiled, glad he wasn't the only one who would be unwelcome. When he was near enough to the croft, he called out to Avelina, "I need to see you, Avelina. Though no' right this instant."

"No wonder Wolf is here. I am busy, Husband."

"Aye." He hesitated, then figured he could talk, and she could still do whatever needed to be done inside the croft. "I just came to tell you my brother has sent a ship."

Avelina poked her head through the open doorway. "Cormac?"

"Aye. He might no' be with them. I wouldna put it past him to—"

"Avelina," Elizabeth hollered at her.

"Just a minute, Quinn." Avelina returned to her duty and a woman cried out.

He wanted to rush in and help, but he knew they wouldn't need his aid, and he would be in the way. A baby cried out, and then he heard Avelina say, "She is a beautiful bairn."

Wolf sat by the croft door as if protecting the baby and mother. Quinn suspected the wolf believed this to be his pack, and he was protecting the newest member.

Quinn glanced back in the direction of the castle. He couldn't see it from here because of the distance they were from it. He'd already waited another half hour or so and was anxious to get back to the keep with Avelina, but she was busy inside, helping the new mother and the baby to bond. Which made him think of a time when she would be carrying their own bairn.

He walked around the croft, looking for anything he could do. He fetched water and set it next to the croft, took the sheep out to pasture, returned them to their corral, milked the cow, leaned against the byre, his arms folded as he waited some more.

"Your Highlander is anxious to be with you," Elizabeth said. "Send Maria to help out here, and we'll be fine."

"Are you sure?"

"Aye. Quinn has banged around long enough out there, and done all the chores that needed to be done. See what the matter is."

He smiled.

"Aye." Avelina came out of the croft, her hair in disarray, and he quickly moved away from the byre and joined her, brushing her hair out of her face. She threw her arms around him and hugged him tight.

He just held her there like that for a long moment.

"Send Maria!" Elizabeth reminded them.

"Aye." Avelina took hold of Quinn's hand and headed off to another croft in the distance, even farther away from the keep than this one. "You said Cormac has sent a ship?"

"Aye. Your da wants me to hide away." Quinn couldn't help how disgruntled he sounded.

She glanced up at him. "You will do as my da says."

Wolf raced past them as if he knew where they were headed.

"You canna be seen or heard. Or we could be forced to kill Cormac's men. And how would that set with the men you hope to lead?" she asked.

"Aye, lass, I know. I just wish I could speak with them and solicit their help in this. But one, or all of them, could return and warn Cormac that I'm coming with a force to take him over. So I will hide." His words sounded just as disagreeable this time.

"Good. I would hide with you, but I will be your eyes and ears and report back to you about all I witness."

"I was hoping we could be locked away in your chamber instead." He smiled down at her then.

She chuckled. "And keep me in bed with you for as long as they stay?" She shook her head. "You can observe some of what goes on through a hidden passage and secret holes for observing what's happening in the great hall. Only my da and my uncle, my brother, when he lived, my cousin, Hamish, and I know the locations. We, at times, were employed to watch there, to see if we had any traitors among us. But mostly to watch strangers when they visited."

"Can you hear any conversation?"

"Some. Not all. It grows too noisy. But I will show you the way so that you may see who came on the ship. But I warn you, dinna attempt to speak with any of them. Even if you think them to be a friend. A friend could tip the wrong person, not meaning to, and then you wouldna have the advantage upon your return home."

"Aye." As much as he hated to admit she was right, he would go along with the plan.

They finally reached Maria's family's croft. She was five and ten years of age, but she was eager to help with the new bairn.

After leaving her off at Mai's croft, Quinn, Avelina, and Wolf headed for the keep. "I will take you through the postern gate, but we might still be seen. I'll need to go first, and talk to one of the guards to ensure none of the men from your brother's ship are about, then sneak you into the keep."

He hated the idea that he had to sneak in. He hadn't thought he'd have to worry about such a thing once he and Avelina had married, though he had considered his brother might send a messenger.

"Stay here. No one from the ship will be back here." Then she made her way along the wall walk until she reached one of the guards. "Dar, we need your help. Quinn came to fetch me while I was helping Mai give birth. Now we need to get him to my chamber without him being seen." She prayed this would work. His future success at ousting his brother could be directly affected otherwise. She did think that he could just live with them, though, and never return, if someone did see him and reported that he was still alive.

Dar leaned over the wall walk and shouted down to the courtyard, "Tell Fagin he is needed on the wall walk at once!"

A lad nodded and ran off to fetch him.

"Since Fagin's in charge of the guards now, he can decide how to handle this."

"Thanks, Dar," Avelina said.

"You are welcome. Quinn is one of us now, and we protect our own."

She smiled at him. "Thank you." She wasn't sure Odran felt that way about Quinn yet, but she was glad many of the others did.

She hurried to join Quinn and told him what they would do. They waited until Fagin ran up the stairs and saw them standing there.

"You are no' in your chamber," Fagin said, frowning at Quinn.

"No statement could be truer."

"But we have to get him there now. Where are the men from the ship?" Avelina asked.

"In the outer bailey still. My men are disarming them. I'll hold them there until you can reach your chamber."

"Is my brother with them?" Quinn asked.

"Nay. The man in charge was called Liam."

"Liam," Quinn said.

Avelina didn't know if that was good or bad news, but they had to leave now. "Thank you, Fagin." Avelina took Quinn's hand, and he quickly thanked Fagin before she rushed Quinn down the wall walk stairs to the inner bailey. "Who is Liam?"

"A loyal and good friend to me."

"You canna speak with him, or let him see you, Quinn. You know that. Even if he's a good and loyal friend. Why would Cormac put him in charge to come here, if Liam is so loyal to you?" Avelina said.

Fagin followed behind them, and then separated from them to return to the outer bailey to supervise their guests.

"Mayhap he hoped that Liam, as the messenger, wouldna live to tell the tale. I wouldna put it past my brother to send him into danger now that I'm gone. Liam and Lorne wanted to kill the mercenaries Cormac sent with me, if they returned and I didna, sure they would attempt to murder me. They wanted to come with me and help protect me against them. They are both good friends. I suspect Lorne would have come if my brother had sanctioned it."

"You canna see any of them," Avelina warned Quinn. She knew from his intense posture and determination that he wanted to see his friends. "Quinn."

They entered the keep and when they reached the stairs to her chamber, he lifted her into his arms and carried her up the stairs. "You can take my mind off it."

"I need to join them in the great hall to hear what's being said." Not that she wanted to be away from her husband right now. "Thank you for coming for me, even if you were supposed to be protecting yourself from your clansmen."

"You come first. And this canna wait." He carried her into the chamber, and then set her next to the bed.

She rushed to pull off her clothes while he removed his. She wanted to hurry so she wouldn't miss anything that was being said during the meal. But she wanted this too.

Once they were naked, he cupped her face and kissed her mouth. She tunneled her fingers through his hair, pressing her body against his. She savored the time with him, these intimate moments, his tenderness. His thick muscles pressed against her softness. She reached between them to touch his manhood and loved when his rigid staff jumped against her fingers. She grasped him in her hand and stroked. He groaned. She loved being in control.

He was everything that was masculine and desirable, his body, his scent, his touch. Even now, his hand, kneading her breast, made her hot with need, the place between her thighs aching and wet. He kissed her throat, and then lifted her onto his staff. She gasped and took him. She was as ready for him as he was for her.

He kissed her neck as she clung to him, feeling the heat building, the pinnacle coming as he moved inside her, slow and steady, then fast and deep. She fought for release, her heart—and his—wildly beating. The pleasure splintered into a million pieces, and she treasured the way he made her feel.

Except now she was so boneless, she didn't want to leave him alone and go to the great hall. That's what Quinn did to her. Made her melt into the bed, satiated, and with thoughts only of him and his enveloping her with his body for the rest of the night.

"We must go," he said, snuggling with her against the bed.

"Aye." But she wasn't moving a muscle.

He smiled. "We both must listen to the conversation."

She sighed. "Aye." She rubbed his arm. "All right. Let's get dressed."

***

Once they were dressed, Avelina led him to the secret tunnel that hid him from those in the great hall. The walls were so thick, Quinn wasn't surprised that someone had hollowed out some of it to make use of it for an escape route if the chief and his family needed to escape. He still couldn't get his mind centered on what needed to be done next. All he could think about was the way Avelina had taken his staff in her hand and began stroking him to completion.

She peeked through a hole, then motioned to several others. "They canna see you," she whispered. "They're coming in now. I must go. Stay here or return to our chamber. I'll meet up with you later. I'll tell one of the servants to take your meal up to the chamber and leave it, so we dinna have to worry about leaving it there at some particular time."

"Be careful," he whispered back to her. "I'm sure they'll be on their best behavior. But...just be careful."

She knew it was killing him that he couldn't be there to protect her. "Which one is Liam?"

"Seated beside your da. I dinna see Lorne."

"All right." She gave him a hug and kiss. "It might be late by the time I retire. I may learn more once they are in their cups."

"Aye. I will be waiting for you."

"I suspect you will still be here," she said, kissing him again, and then she left him alone in the secret passageway, wishing they could go down to the meal together. She didn't worry that anyone might try to harm her. All the men would be watching the women, as protective as the men were. And her da and others would know Quinn couldn't be seen and wouldn't be there to protect her, so they would watch out for her.

CHAPTER 15

When Avelina took a seat at the table beside her da, he leaned over and said, "This is Liam. He is representing Cormac."

Liam inclined his head slightly to her, but he wasn't smiling.

She thought it was odd that he wasn't at least trying to appear pleasant about escorting Cormac's intended to her new home. But then she remembered what Quinn had told her. Liam was his good friend. Was he upset that Quinn wasn't alive then? What had her da discussed with him already? She was glad she had spent the time with Quinn, but she wished she could have been listening to what had been said already.

"Quinn was your good friend, aye?" she asked, knowing she shouldn't, but she wanted to say something, if Liam was truly loyal to Quinn still. He'd need allies among his people.

Liam's eyes widened. Her da's narrowed when he looked at her.

"Aye, and you are?" Liam asked.

"The chief's daughter." She looked away from Liam's intense stare. She knew he wanted to know more, why she knew Quinn was his good friend and what had happened to him.

Her da quickly spoke. "Avelina, Liam comes here asking about fulfilling the contract between Fenella and Cormac. But I've told him that her da died in battle, and she is my ward now."

Liam was studying Avelina, watching to see if she'd give anything away.

"Have you heard the rumor that Quinn intended to steal Fenella away from her da? Because she loved Cormac and wished to leave here?" Avelina asked.

"Cormac sent Quinn with five mercenaries to bring Fenella home to marry Cormac. Quinn didna intend to steal the lass for himself. He thought the lass wished to wed Cormac."

"She didna," Avelina said, her chin raised.

"So I have learned." Liam tilted his head to the side. "Did you perchance meet Quinn? Everyone has said the men must have all drowned at sea. No one said they had seen him."

"He canna be killed, so I've been told." Avelina smiled.

Liam's mouth curved up, his dark brown eyes smiling. "You *have* seen him. Do you know where he is?" He glanced around the great hall as if expecting to see his friend.

"He was returning home. Has he no' already arrived?"

She arched a brow in query.

"Nay. If I had learned of it, I wouldna be asking about his fate." Liam frowned again. "Why would everyone else say he must have died?"

She shook her head. "Mayhap they worried you would fault us for no saving more of the men."

Liam eyed her warily. "You met him? Spoke with him then?"

"He was well, the last I saw of him. A braw warrior. He walked out of the sea like a god."

Her da choked on his ale.

Liam smiled and leaned back with obvious relief.

"Some of our men helped him to reach the mainland. We had no idea Cormac had made a contract with Fenella's da to wed her. Quinn showed no interest in taking Fenella to be his wife. We had a lot of damage to our crofts due to the storm, most of our men were away at battle, and Quinn volunteered to help us rebuild. That was why our people helped him. He is a good man. I hope he finds his way back home soon. Though he did say the mercenaries his brother sent tried to murder him. Thankfully, they didna survive."

"Good. I told Quinn I would kill them if they returned without him. I didna trust them in the least."

"You were right no' to trust them."

"Your da said you would marry our chief, instead of Fenella doing so."

"Aye." She had already married him. Their chief would be Quinn.

"We hoped to take you back with us if your da is too busy to attend to it at this time," Liam said, his focus switching to her da.

Baudwin slammed his tankard on the table. "Nay. Our men are recovering from their injuries. We will be there to celebrate the wedding in a couple of weeks' time," her da said, giving Liam a growly look.

She had wanted Liam to know Quinn was alive, if he was as good a friend as Quinn said he was. And she knew Cormac would be on the lookout then for Quinn's return, once he received word he'd survived, but he'd never suspect Quinn would come with her da and their clansmen when they arrived to see Cormac. She had also wanted Cormac to know he couldn't kill Quinn. Maybe that would put the fear into him, and he'd give the clan up to Quinn without a fight.

Liam was smiling and shaking his head. "I canna believe he is alive. His brother will be livid."

"Because he can never kill him?" she asked.

Liam looked a little taken aback that she would know that. "How much did he tell you?"

"My daughter is a good listener. Men and women tell her things all the time. She was never alone with him though," her da quickly said.

"He told me everything," Avelina said. "Cormac tried to kill him numerous times."

"Aye and that his da died on the battlefield in an earlier conflict?" Liam asked her.

"Aye. It was obvious he cared about his da." Even though Quinn hadn't spoken a lot about him, he never said anything disparaging about him.

"Quinn and his brother were fighting their enemy.

Their da too. Quinn was nowhere close to his da to see him fall in battle, but Cormac said a man has come forth as a witness who saw Quinn kill their da."

"He lies! The man lies! What about Cormac? Where was he when their da was struck down?" Avelina asked, furious that Cormac had contrived the accusation, or that someone else might have.

"From all witness accounts, their da was knocked off his horse and had to fight the enemy on foot. Cormac indicated he was going to his da's aid."

"Then he had the opportunity!"

"He says Quinn killed their da."

Avelina frowned at Liam. "Nay. He is lying. Quinn wasn't anywhere near his da when he died. You already said so yourself."

"Aye. He was near me. He saved my life. If he hadna been there to stop the man from swinging his sword at me again, I would have been cut down. But Cormac has found witnesses to say that Quinn killed their da, that Quinn feigned going to their da's aid, and then struck him down."

"Cormac had the motivation. And if others saw Cormac riding toward their da, I canna believe how twisted this could be and that anyone would believe it. Cormac became chief, no' Quinn. Why would Quinn kill his own da, if he gained naught from it?" Avelina was furious with Cormac. She couldn't even pretend to want to marry the man.

"I agree. And since Cormac was fighting nearer his da, if Quinn had killed him, Cormac *would* have ended Quinn's life. Ever since the battle where their da lost his life, Cormac has been trying to have his brother eliminated." Liam drank some of his ale.

"Why send word of this to us now?"

"Because Cormac hasna heard anything from your chief or your clan, and he's been dying to learn if Quinn survived or no'. Mayhap he hoped the news that Quinn murdered his da would persuade your chief to hand him over to us for Cormac's disposition, if he was staying with you here. It makes me wonder if he suspects Quinn knew what Cormac had done to their da and wants to eliminate Quinn before he tells the council the truth. Or mayhap he is worried that someone else had witnessed what had happened and is too scared to say anything. But if Quinn learns of it, he would take his brother to task."

"If Quinn had known, he would have said something when it happened. He might have even challenged his brother then." Avelina was sure of it.

"I believe someone had to have seen what happened on the battlefield."

"That's why you suspect Cormac murdered their da."

"Rumors have been floating around ever since many of us believed Cormac sent Quinn to his death this last time. Their da favored his first born: Cormac. Quinn had always tried to prove himself to his da and the clan as a fearless and fearsome warrior. He was well-liked by everyone. His da thought Quinn couldna lead men because he wasna as ruthless as his brother." Liam shook his head. "Thank you for telling me the truth about Quinn. You canna know how relieved I am to learn he still lives. I just hope he willna return home and give his brother another chance to kill him."

"But you are a witness to prove Quinn didna have anything to do with his da's death."

"Aye, but I have to find others who will say he wasna anywhere near his da when he died. More importantly, I need to discover someone who witnessed that the enemy actually killed their da, or if someone of our clan did."

"You said that some say Cormac went to rescue his da when he was unseated from his horse."

"Aye, but you have to remember that in a battle, we're always fighting someone. Some saw him ride toward the chief, but after that, they were involved in a fight. The fact remains that Cormac was nearer to his da, on his way to join him, and then his da died."

"As long as you dinna believe Quinn had anything to do with his da's death."

"I know he didna."

She sighed with relief. "I'm certain when Quinn can, he'll try to reach you." Avelina hoped when Quinn met up with Liam again, he would be on his side in overthrowing Cormac.

***

The hidden passageway was cramped, but Quinn was going to make the most of learning what he could from the men who had accompanied his friend Liam. He wasn't going to try to listen in on Liam and Baudwin's conversation because Avelina would tell Quinn what he needed to know after the meal. For now, Quinn was trying to hear what he could from others, though the great hall was noisy with conversation. Six men really stood out to him. They were the ones he was sure would back Cormac when Quinn came to oust him as chief. Did they believe, if Quinn were still alive and living among Avelina's clan, they could kill him? He wouldn't be surprised if they had that in mind. He was certain when the mercenaries hadn't returned, and neither had he, that his brother was dying to know the truth, and that's why he had sent them. Maybe to learn who was in power after the battle too so he'd know if his alliance still stood.

"Everyone I've spoken to says Quinn's body was never found," one of the men said.

That meant his brother would still worry whether Quinn had survived or not. He guessed that it was better they said that than confirming he had died. They might have wanted to dig up the body and return it to his brother. At least that's what they would tell Baudwin. They'd truly only want to confirm he was dead and then toss his body into the ocean.

"He canna have survived if no one else did. They were probably lost too far from the island. As bad as the storm was, I doubt anyone could have managed to survive."

"How many times have we said that?"

"Too many to count. He canna have survived, but I'm no' placing any bets that he's no longer among the living either."

"Cormac willna be happy to learn we dinna have positive proof."

"He should have killed him himself when he learned the news. No one would have faulted him."

Learned *what* news?

"Their da was a good chief. I canna think of anything

more despicable than dying at the hand of your own son."

God's knees! Their da had died in battle. Had Cormac made up charges against Quinn, blaming *him* for their da's death? Surely someone must have seen what had occurred and knew their enemy had struck down their da.

Everyone loved his da as their chief. If Quinn couldn't prove he had nothing to do with his da's death, he wouldn't have any backing from his clan. Quinn glanced at Liam and Avelina's expressions. Was he telling Baudwin and Avelina what Cormac had said about him? Would they believe Cormac's lies?

Even if they didn't, and Quinn couldn't prove his innocence, would Baudwin's clan believe him to be a hindrance in having another ally, rather than being the one who would secure it?

He couldn't believe his brother would stoop so low. Yet he shouldn't have been surprised. Just in case Quinn had survived, Cormac had to ensure he couldn't return and accuse him of paying the mercenaries to kill him aboard the ship.

Surely someone had been near where Quinn had been fighting on the battlefield that fateful day, other than Liam, and knew he hadn't been anywhere near his da. Unless Cormac threatened anyone who could vouch for Quinn. Maybe no one would, if they thought he wasn't coming back. No sense in telling the truth, if Quinn was already dead and anyone who spoke up for Quinn risked being accused of standing behind Quinn and helping to conceal the murder from the rest of the clan.

Quinn watched Liam, hoping his friend wouldn't risk his

life to protect Quinn's reputation. Quinn and Liam had been like brothers. More so than Quinn's own. But that had been mostly since they'd both lost their da in battle. Though he could understand why Quinn would feel animosity toward him, if he'd been told Quinn had actually killed their da. He wondered then if Cormac hadn't been the one to make up the falsehood, and instead, someone else had for some nefarious reason. He had to set his brother straight. If his brother wasn't behind the deception and he could convince him Quinn wasn't to blame for their da's death, he didn't think he could oust him from the clan, despite his brother's attempts on his life. In all honesty, if Quinn had murdered their da, he would have been tried and put to death.

Which made Quinn wonder why his brother hadn't done that, instead of trying to have him murdered in a sneaky way. That made Quinn suspect his brother had made up the whole tale, just to ensure if Quinn returned, Cormac would have no other choice but to publicly put him to death.

Quinn had wanted to see Liam in the worst way, but even more so now. He had to let him know that he didn't want Liam putting his own neck on the line for him.

At the high table, Avelina was shaking her head.

Quinn wanted to go to her and reassure her, if Liam was telling them what his brother had said.

Below where Quinn was hidden, he overheard some more conversation. "Cormac willna be pleased," Dogmael said, one of Cormac's staunchest supporters.

"Aye. If he wants to go fishing in the ocean for Quinn's body, he's welcome to do so," Accalon said.

The men began to eat and that was the end of any conversation about what Quinn was supposed to have done to his da. The men started to talk instead about which lass they wanted, and Quinn moved around through the hidden wall to listen in on other conversations, but no one talked about anything worth hearing. He wanted to be with Avelina, sharing a meal and conversation, and then taking her to bed. He just hoped she didn't hear the news about what his brother was saying he'd done, but that if she had, she would know his brother lied.

He noticed Baudwin shifting in his seat and that was a signal he was getting ready to end the meal. They usually feasted longer than that. He hoped Baudwin didn't believe Quinn had murdered his da and that he was planning to have Quinn arrested, tortured, and turned over to Liam and the rest of Cormac's men.

Quinn needed to leave the secret passageway, return to Avelina's chamber, and wait there to hear what would be done next.

As soon as he made his way out of the hidden passageway, Wolf greeted him. "You would have given me away, if anyone had wondered what you were doing standing there next to the guest chamber. I should have left you in Avelina's chamber. Why didna you go down to the meal?" Quinn never thought the wolf would be more interested in being with him than with eating. "If you think I'm going to share my food with you..."

Wolf looked up at him, his golden eyes fixed on him, and Quinn swore he smiled.

"You think you know me too well, dinna you?"

CHAPTER 16

After the meal, Fenella and two of his guards kept Cormac's men, including Liam, away from Avelina. Though Liam continued to study her, as if waiting for a time when she wasn't so surrounded by guards.

Not hearing anything further from anyone of any importance, Avelina told Fenella she was retiring to bed.

"I'll go with you," Fenella said. "I'm tired, and I'll help protect you."

Assuming Quinn was still observing his clansmen from the secret passageway, Avelina had to get word to Quinn that she was returning to the chamber. She couldn't tell her guards because they didn't know about the hidden walkways. She told Fenella, "I need to speak with you."

Fenella and Avelina entered Avelina's chamber. "I canna believe you told Liam about Quinn," Fenella said. "Everyone else was saying he must have drowned with the rest of the men aboard the ship."

Wolf crawled out from under the bed and loped to greet them.

"There you are. I missed you at the meal." She rubbed Wolf's head and suspected he'd been looking for Quinn. "Liam had to know. I need you to get word to Quinn that I've returned."

The bed curtain moved aside, and Quinn pulled aside a blanket, but was fully clothed. "Are you coming to bed, Wife?"

"Och, I'm leaving." Fenella's face turned red, and she hurried to leave the chamber.

Avelina smiled at her cousin, and then at Quinn, who looked displeased. She told the guards outside her door, "Quinn is here with me. You need no' stay."

"Your da has ordered us to remain here in case one of Cormac's men come looking for you and try to learn more about Quinn and the other men Cormac had sent," Dar said.

"Or attempt to steal you away," Fagin said. "We dinna trust these men."

"All right. Good night then." She closed the door and barred it, and Quinn was behind her in a heartbeat, wrapping his arms around her.

"I missed you."

"I told Liam you live."

"I heard, lass. What did he say?" Quinn hadn't expected her to tell Liam the truth.

"He was glad to hear it. I told him we helped you to the mainland, and we dinna know what happened to you after that. Although I mentioned you would be seeing him as soon as you could, I was sure."

Quinn couldn't believe she'd come up with the idea. It was a great notion. "You were clever to tell him I had survived and left."

"I admit that I wanted your brother to know you are invincible. Mayhap he will worry you're returning to deal with him. But your brother willna believe you are returning there with my people. My da wasna happy with me for telling Liam you survived the shipwreck, but Liam seemed so disconsolate about what had happened to you that I had to tell him. He seems to be just as loyal as before. I felt as though he'd come here to learn about you, more than he wanted to learn about the status of Cormac's marriage contract and who was now in charge."

"That sounds like Liam."

She knew Quinn wanted to speak with Liam still, but she figured this was the best plan. She took hold of Quinn's belt and began to unfasten it, then removed it. She put it on the bench at the foot of her bed.

Quinn unfastened her brooch and pulled off her plaid, and she began to work on his. She knew he wanted to make love to her, just like she couldn't wait to join him in bed, but she had to tell him all that Liam had said. "We have to talk."

"Aye." Quinn sounded darkly concerned, and she wondered if he'd overheard something his clansmen said while he was listening from the secret passage.

"Liam said that Cormac has accused you of killing your da on the battlefield the last time you fought your enemy."

He continued to help her out of her clothes, and once she was only wearing her chemise, she helped him remove his boots.

"I overheard one of the men say that my brother said that." Quinn looked up and frowned at her. "I didna kill my da."

"Liam knows you didna. But he's worried about you. If you return home, everyone will believe what Cormac says. They'll think he has the right to kill you."

"You dinna believe Cormac, do you?" Quinn pulled off his shirt and then took Avelina in his arms.

"Nay, what do you take me for? Your brother took over when your da died. He had everything to gain. Do you believe he killed your da? And then planned to pin the murder on you?"

"Or someone else told him I had done it. But I was nowhere near my da when it happened."

"That's what Liam said. He is your witness. Like he said though, we need to find anyone who saw what really happened. But for now, I want you."

He kissed her mouth and then pulled away. "As long as—"

"I believe in you." She pressed her mouth against his. "Always."

He slid her hands over her chemise-covered breasts. "I love you."

"Oh, Quinn, I love you." She ran her hands up his bare chest. "You're so braw. And we'll learn the truth. I'm so sorry."

Then she kissed him back, their tongues tangling, her fingers sweeping over his nipples. He pulled her chemise over her head and tossed it on top of the rest of their clothes. He lifted her, wrapping her legs around his hips, and carried her to bed.

They needed to talk, but she needed this more right now. The connection between them, the love...she couldn't believe how rotten his brother could be, and Quinn needed to know that she and the others in her clan believed in him.

He laid her in the bed, then covered her with his body. "I worried that Liam was telling you and your da that I killed my da—"

"None of us believed it, Liam either, because he is your witness. But he had to learn if you were alive first before he did anything."

Quinn frowned at her. "He canna do anything. If he speaks out against my brother, he's as good as dead."

"I have an idea. What if when your brother's ship returns, he stays with us? That way he can be safe and you can see him. He can go with you to back you against your brother. He can say he's waiting for my da to take me to Cormac's keep. We'll have to get my da to agree, but I think it would work, dinna you?"

"Aye. I'd much rather he stays here than get himself killed if he tried to defend me in front of the clan. He isna leaving any time soon, is he?"

"Your brother wanted him to return with his bride as soon as they could set sail again."

"All right."

"Go, tell the guards."

He snorted. "I wouldna leave you for any other reason at a time like this"—he caressed her breast—"unless we were in the middle of a battle." He moved off her and covered her with the blanket, kissed her smiling mouth, and then wrapped his plaid around himself before going to the door.

When he opened it, Dar said, "Aye?"

"Can you send word to ask Baudwin if he'll allow Liam to stay here while the chief 'makes preparations' to escort his daughter to wed Cormac?"

Dar glanced at Fagin. "You'll be all right by yourself, protecting them?"

"Aye."

"I'll be right back then." Dar hurried off.

Quinn thanked him and then shut and bolted the door. He yanked off his plaid and pulled aside the blanket before climbing on top of Avelina again, warming her.

And then there was no more time for anything but kissing and touching. He nuzzled her face with his. She swept her hands down his back, loving the silky feel of his skin, though she also felt old wounds in several places.

He began kissing her mouth, his hand sweeping down between her legs. And then he began stroking her. She loved the way he made her feel hot and needy. She moved against him, wanting him to stroke her faster, harder, and he did, as if he knew from her body language just what she needed.

He began kissing a breast, suckling, making her heart race. Then he inserted two fingers and pushed as deep as he could into her and the climax hit her hard. His mouth covered hers in the next instant, kissing her, tonguing her.

"Aww," she moaned against his mouth, feeling her world coming apart in his hands. He lowered his mouth to her breast and licked her nipple. "Aye, oh, aye." She ran her fingers through his hair and arched against him. She felt like she was flying through the clouds and cried out his name.

He centered on her and thrust home. Quinn loved Avelina, the way she wanted him, just as much as he wanted her. She was so receptive, so willing.

He kissed her mouth, and she opened it to take him in. Their tongues caressed, and he tasted the honeyed mead she'd had with her meal. "Hmm," she murmured against his mouth.

"Aww, lassie." Then he was thrusting harder, faster, deeper. She wrapped her legs around his and he dove even deeper. He couldn't believe her hot moves that sent him right over the edge, luxuriating in the feel of her wrapped around his staff until he came. He finally pulled out and moved off her. "You are a wonder." He pulled her into his arms and kept her against his chest, stroking her long hair.

They heard Wolf chasing something in his dreams underneath their bed, and Quinn was glad the wolf hadn't charged out to protect her this time when Quinn was making love to her.

"I love you, my unbeatable warrior," Avelina said.

Before Quinn could respond, someone banged on the door and Avelina moved off him so he could see who it was. He left the bed and grabbed his plaid, then wrapped it around himself, and stalked to the door.

"Aye?" she called out.

No one answered.

Avelina was out of the bed in a flash and grabbing her chemise. Quinn dressed, belted his sword, then helped her finish dressing.

She whispered, "We'll use the secret passageways. They run throughout the castle."

He grabbed a candle.

Someone banged on the door again, but Avelina belted her own sword, and then led Quinn into the hidden passageway. They didn't speak, and he was glad she knew where she was going as many twists and turns as she made.

"We're going to my da's chamber," she whispered. "He'll have guards posted there too, even though your brother's men will be quartered in the barracks in the outer bailey."

"Are you sure whoever was at the door wasna just your guardsman?" Quinn hadn't called out to ask because it didn't seem right that someone hadn't identified themselves, and he hadn't wanted to let on that he was there, if the wrong person was at the door.

"They would have announced who they were. My maids do. The guards would. Anyone does who bangs on the door. But especially when we had guards posted to protect us."

They reached her da's chamber after what seemed like a long time, and then she gently pushed open the secret door, but Quinn moved around her to protect her. The bed hangings had been pulled aside, but no one was in bed. A fire was crackling at the hearth, but the chamber was quiet otherwise.

"He's no' here," she whispered.

Quinn moved around the chamber, checking it further, just to make sure her da wasn't unconscious in the room, or someone wasn't hiding in there, but it was clear. He shook his head.

She started to walk toward the door, but he quickly bypassed her, then paused at the door and listened.

He drew his sword, and he heard Avelina pull hers from its sheath. Then he slowly opened the door, and saw two of Baudwin's men standing guard, both of whom turned, swords drawn.

"Just us," Avelina said. "Where is the chief?"

"He went to see Liam," Padruig said, furrowing his brow to see them in her da's room. "What are you doing in there?"

She frowned at Padruig. "Why didna you go with him?"

"He ordered us to safeguard his chamber, and he took a half dozen other men with him. He was bringing Liam back to his solar to speak with him. I didna think you were in his chamber," Padruig said.

"Someone was pounding on my chamber door, but didna identify himself," Avelina said. "Dar gave my da the message about Liam. Fagin was still guarding my door."

"We would check it out, but we canna leave your da's chamber unguarded."

"No worries. As long as Da is safe, we'll just wait for him in his chamber."

"Aye."

She shut the door and she sheathed her sword and took the candle. "Come on. I'll see if I can learn who all is there."

"Nay. I dinna want you coming to harm."

"You will protect me. Your sword is bigger than mine. Both of them are."

He smiled at her. She never ceased to amaze him.

He was glad she knew the way because, as much as he tried to remember the different paths she took, they were all...different. "You must have spent a lot of time playing in the secret passageways," he whispered to her.

"Aye. Da and my uncle encouraged it, though the two of them had to come searching for us a few times when we got hopelessly lost. We were brave. We didna ever cry, knowing we'd give away the secret of the hidden passageways. Hamish is the only other person who knew about them. We'll be coming out in a chamber that is set aside for guests. Your men will all be in the barracks, including Liam. We'll have to go up the stairs to reach my chamber."

"I'll go first." He opened the hidden passageway door and moved through the empty chamber. Then he listened at the door that opened to the hall.

He heard a man say, "I willna ask you again to tell Avelina she needs to speak to her da."

"You canna force me to get her to open the door. Why do you think I'm here guarding her chamber?" Fagin asked.

Quinn looked back to see Avelina shutting the door to the hidden passageway. "Trouble. One of my brother's men is threatening Fagin to open the door."

"How many are there?" she whispered.

"Just kill him and be done with it," another man said.

"Two." At least. Quinn carefully opened the door, then rushed out of the chamber and up the stairs, hoping Avelina would stay in the guest chamber for her protection, but she was right behind him. If the men rushed down to meet him, they'd have the advantage because he wouldn't be able to swing his sword at his opponent.

"Can you use my sword?" Avelina whispered.

He shook his head, not even wanting her to follow him up the stairs, but he would be above her, protecting her. He made the landing and saw Accalon, his sword at Fagin's throat. In that instant, Fagin saw Quinn rushing to fight Accalon. Quinn's brother's man, Banquo, turned to see who was coming and gasped.

"I told you he was here," Accalon said, his voice angry, but worried at the same time. "I knew he hadna died, and that the woman hadna lied."

The man knew not to take Quinn on in a swordfight, but for this, Quinn needed his dagger. He threw it with deadly aim, and struck Accalon down, just as he had the mercenary earlier. Black-hearted Banquo was behind him. Before he could attack Fagin, the guard grabbed Accalon's sword and slashed at Banquo. Fagin was so furious the men had gotten the best of him and threatened to kill him, he drove the man back. Banquo lost the battle with the enraged guard who struck him in the chest with a fatal blow.

"Were there just the two of them?" Quinn asked.

"Aye." But Fagin was staring at the man Quinn had killed. "Just like the mon we found in the bog."

"Aye."

"You must teach me how to do that."

"I will. What in God's wounds did they intend to do?" Quinn asked.

"Take Avelina with them. When Baudwin said he would

bring her, they knew Cormac would be angry with them for returning home without her. They wanted me to get her to open the door. But then they would have seen you."

"Which they did anyway. Thank you for protecting Avelina."

"Are more of them roaming about the castle? I thought they would have been moved to the barracks," Avelina said.

"They were supposed to have been, but that's why your da had guards posted here, at your chambers, at his, and at your cousin's. Just in case of trouble."

"Is Fenella all right? What if they've taken her?"

"They were no' supposed to take her, but—" Fagin said.

Someone was coming up the stairs, and Quinn pulled Avelina behind him. The door to Avelina's chamber was still barred from the inside. They couldn't get in that way or he would have pushed her inside and had her bolt the door.

The two men acted as a barrier, but it was just Dar. He looked down at the dead men, and then at Quinn and Fagin. "You were no' supposed to kill anyone before I returned. Where did *they* come from?" As if he'd truly wanted them to wait for him to kill the men.

"They must have slipped off from the rest of their group when the other men were escorted to the barracks," Fagin said. "Do you know them? More mercenaries? None of your kin, I hope," he said to Quinn.

"Some of the men who pledged loyalty to my brother. None that are directly related to me or my brother. That will mean two less to have to deal with later. But someone will have to ensure that all the rest of his men are quartered in the barracks. These two were armed also. They were supposed to be disarmed, I thought," Quinn said.

"They had been. But these two somehow slipped by our men," Fagin said.

"I told Baudwin what you asked me to say. He said he'd speak with Liam. But this could change everything," Dar said.

"We're going to Fenella's chamber. I want to make sure she's all right." Avelina waited for the men to agree.

"We'll accompany you and inspect your chamber upon your return," Dar said, then they headed for the stairs and down to Fenella's chamber. "We'll take care of the other men too."

They heard several people rushing around down below and a woman cried out.

"Avelina, I want you to return to the guest chamber and bolt the door," Quinn said.

A lad rushed up the stairs, clutching a wooden sword in his hand, his face red with exertion.

"They stabbed Gwyneth. Can Avelina save her?" the lad asked.

"If there is fighting going on—" Quinn said, holding his wife back so she wouldn't rush down the stairs to help the woman.

"Nay, the guards are there. But the two men..." The lad eyed Avelina. "They were going to your chamber."

"They are dead," Quinn said.

Dar hurried down the stairs to check out the situation, two more guards running to meet up with them.

"Tell us what you know," Quinn said, heading down the

stairs with the boy, his sword readied.

Avelina followed them down the steps.

They found a maid bleeding from a knife wound, clutching her stomach, groaning as she lay in the rushes on the stone floor.

"Those two men from the ship, they were kissing her and…" The lad's cheeks turned rosy. "I…I watched. But it was a good thing I did 'cuz they gave her coin and then she fetched their swords. I was well-hidden from them, but I wanted to run and get the guards. I stayed put instead. I…" He glanced down at Gwyneth as Avelina tried to stem the bleeding with rags that another couple of women brought her. "The one drew back his sword, and I knew he was going to kill Gwyneth. I clasped my mouth before I let out a cry that would've alerted them that I saw everything. They even took the coin back from her."

"Then you went for the guards," Quinn assumed.

"Aye, but not until I had to deal with more of those men. They asked where I was going so late at night and in such a hurry." The boy held up his wooden sword. "I told them I was a guard-in-training, and I was supposed to be at my post already, but my mother made me do chores. They just laughed."

"You did well," Quinn said. "You will make a fine guard someday." He turned to Avelina. "How is she?"

Avelina shook her head. "She is alive, but barely. Still, we may save her yet."

Baudwin joined them. "And then she'll be banished. We dinna allow traitors in our midst. What about the men who did this?"

"Dead. What about Liam?" Quinn asked, sure that he had nothing to do with the men coming for Avelina.

"I spoke to him about staying with us until I was ready to escort my daughter to see Cormac. Liam would then come with us. I didna mention you were with us in the event he was leaving with Cormac's men."

"What did he say to that?" Quinn asked.

"He would give me his decision on the morrow. Considering all that has happened here tonight, they must return to their ship now. They can sail home at first tide. As far as Liam is concerned, he can remain in the barracks, unarmed and under guard, if he so chooses to stay with us. If he does, then you can let him know you are here."

"Aye."

The healer arrived and would take care of the woman the best she could.

Avelina's da issued orders, rallying several more guards to escort Cormac's men back to their ship. "Take Gwyneth with you," Baudwin said to some of his men.

Several men were carrying the dead men down the stairs, and others were cleaning up the mess.

Fagin explained to Baudwin, and the others who had gathered to help, just what had happened.

"Take the men's bodies to Cormac's men. They can carry them to the ship. That will keep them from causing mischief." Baudwin said to Quinn, "We have this well in hand. Take my daughter back to her chamber and protect her there. " Baudwin hugged Avelina and kissed her forehead. Then he slapped Quinn on the back. "Get some sleep."

"Aye," Quinn said.

Dar escorted Avelina and Quinn to Fenella's chamber and knocked.

Fenella opened the door to him. Looking half asleep, she frowned at Quinn and Avelina. "What's going on?"

"We need to return to my chamber," Avelina said, and they walked into her room. Quinn bolted her door for her.

Fenella arched a brow.

"We'll explain later."

Fenella saw the blood on Avelina's hands and her jaw dropped.

"All right, we'll explain now." Avelina gave her a brief explanation of what had occurred, including why they needed to go through Fenella's chamber to reach her own. She washed up in the basin, dried off, and then they hugged each other. "Stay safe."

"Aye, you too."

Avelina and Quinn slipped into the passageway and found their way to her chamber. Once inside, they stripped off their clothes and climbed into bed.

Avelina was shivering, and Quinn tucked her in his arms. "Are you cold?"

"Aye."

He suspected it had something to do with the attempted kidnapping, the killing of the men, and the wounding of the woman.

Avelina frowned. "If they send Gwyneth with them, she may very well tell them that you're living here and that you're married to me."

"Aye." Quinn climbed out of bed, but Avelina grabbed

his hand and pulled at him to return to bed.

"My da will know that."

"Then he will send her with them only if she is dead," Quinn said.

"Aye," Avelina said softly and snuggled against Quinn. "You dinna betray our kin and get away with it."

"I will be betraying my own."

Avelina didn't say anything for a moment, then scoffed at his words. "Your brother has betrayed you countless times. He deserves to be dealt with."

CHAPTER 17

Early the next morning, Avelina and Quinn hurried to dress for the morning meal. She hoped that Liam had stayed, for Quinn's sake. But when they joined her da at the high table, he shook his head, and they saw Liam wasn't at the table.

"Liam was angry about what had occurred and returned to the ship with Cormac's men. So you may no' have an ally in him when you return, Quinn," Baudwin said.

"I suspect he hopes to learn what really happened to my da, now that he knows I'm alive," Quinn said, and Avelina hoped he didn't get himself killed while trying to learn the truth.

"And Gwyneth?" Avelina asked.

"She died, and she and Cormac's dead men were taken aboard the ship last eve," her da said.

"What if she told them Quinn was alive and living with us? Married to me even, before she agreed to get their weapons for them?" Avelina had barely gotten any sleep last night, worried about what Gwyneth might have said to any of the other men for a bit of coin. "What if they hadn't been going to my chamber to steal me away, but instead hoped to find Quinn there and kill him? That Gwyenth hadna lied. The one brigand had said he knew Quinn was there."

Gwyneth might very well have been angry that Avelina had suggested to her da that he marry someone else to make an alliance with another clan, even though her da had already made the decision to do so. If Gwyneth couldn't have whom she wanted, Avelina couldn't have Quinn.

"Aye," Baudwin said.

"If that happened, then his men will tell Cormac that his brother is here," Avelina said.

"Aye." Her da rubbed his beard. "We'll be prepared for him, if he thinks to come here and wage war with me."

"Us," Quinn said, "But I want to take this home and not bring it to your soil."

Hamish was quietly listening to the conversation and finally spoke up. "I think we should go now. We would arrive right after they put to shore. They wouldna have any time to do anything."

"Are you sure you want to do this?" Quinn sounded surprised anyone would help fight his cause.

Baudwin cleared his throat. "I willna have a treaty with your clan if you're no' in charge."

"That's saying the council approves my taking over, if I'm able to remove my brother from power," Quinn reminded him, "and they dinna believe my brother's lies that I murdered my own da."

"Aye. I'm counting on the council and your people backing you," Baudwin said. "Besides, my daughter wouldna forgive me if I dinna protect your back."

"You canna go, Da," Avelina said, frowning. "You just returned from battle and you're still healing from your injuries."

"So is Quinn. I'm going. If I'm there, and they didna know that Quinn was staying with us, they'll believe I'm coming about negotiations over my daughter's marriage to Cormac. If I'm no' with my men, what will they think?"

She couldn't help being bothered about him going into battle again. He hadn't had enough time to heal. She hoped he wouldn't get into a fight. Then again, she worried about Quinn and the other men too. She was certain some of those who had fought, even if they were still recuperating from injuries, would be going too. If for no other reason than they would want to support their kin and friends.

"I want to go with you," Avelina said.

"Nay. What if my brother is successful in killing me this time? He would take you as his hostage. Mayhap wed you to have an alliance with your people."

"He willna kill you. Even though I will stay, I still want to go with you, to see you vanquish him after all he's done to you, and to celebrate your victory." She worried he'd be injured, and that he'd be distraught over having to kill his brother and mayhap the others he might have to fight. If he didn't get himself killed. She wanted to be there for him.

"Avelina..." Quinn pulled her into his arms. "I know what you are thinking, and if you were there in harm's way,

I'd think of naught but your safety."

"I have said I will stay," she said crossly.

"Aye. I will return for you soon."

"You will keep everyone safe until then, aye?" her da asked her.

"No picking up injured men on the shore," Quinn said, then smiled at her.

"Aye, of course, Da." As if he ever left her in charge of everyone who remained behind. She wrapped her arms around Quinn's neck. "Dinna get yourself killed then."

"I dinna intend to."

"We should be readying to leave then," Hamish said

"Aye." Baudwin rose from his seat and said to their gathered people, "We're taking Quinn to see his brother and set this right between them."

Everyone raised their tankards and cheered.

Avelina shook her head. Men were always so eager to fight. Any excuse.

After they broke their fast, Baudwin, Quinn, and Hamish discussed battle plans.

Avelina and Fenella helped the kitchen staff to pack food for the men. "Do you think they'll be all right?" Fenella asked.

"They're good fighters. They'll make it home just fine." Then Avelina changed the subject, not having thought Fenella's own da would die in the last conflict, so she didn't want to think about Quinn and her own da failing in their quest either. "How do you feel about marrying Ewen?"

Fenella finished wrapping the rest of the food. "Your da says Ewen's a good man, that he's around the same age as

Quinn, and he's eager to have a wife and children." She blushed. Then she glanced at Avelina. "What about Quinn? Is he eager to have a bairn?"

This time Avelina felt her face heat.

"Aye," Cook said, waving at them to take the food to the men. "All men want them, so they can prove they have what it takes to make 'em."

The women working in the kitchen all laughed. "That's the truth," another said.

Quinn joined the ladies and took Avelina into his arms. "I have to go. Their ship is sailing, and we need to leave."

"Aye." She hugged him back and then kissed him.

Quinn didn't want to leave her, but he had to say goodbye. She and Fenella went to the beach to see the men off, including Avelina's da. Quinn never believed it would be that difficult to leave his wife behind.

"We'll be together soon," she said, but she sounded worried.

"I'll make it through this."

"And if you do? When you do," she amended, "what will your people think of you? Of me?"

"We will soon learn the truth." If they wouldn't accept him, then he hoped her da would keep him on, and he'd fight for him or do whatever they needed to take care of things and the clan.

They said their goodbyes one last time, and the men sailed off to the mainland.

Avelina didn't watch to see the ship disappear but rushed back to the keep and returned to her bedchamber, Fenella following her like a little lost lamb. Avelina wasn't about to be left behind. She began packing her clothes.

"What are you doing?" Fenella asked.

"I'm leaving with the last ship to sail. When Quinn wins the battle against his brother, I dinna want to waste any time rejoining him, as his wife should. And he shouldna leave there either. No' when he will have just taken over the clan. What if while he's gone to fetch me, someone else tries to take over?"

"I'm going with you then."

"It might no' be safe for you."

"No' for you either. Besides, 'tis closer to where I'm bound. I'll pack my things. Dinna leave without me."

"I willna, but we must no' miss the last ship."

"Your husband willna be happy you followed him there."

"I will make him happy."

Fenella blushed and headed for the door. "You must tell me more. But after I've packed."

Avelina felt in her bones the need to join Quinn. What if he was badly injured? He'd need her. And her place was with her husband. She knew that if she were nearby, he would win. She was so sure of it, she had to go.

As soon as she had her bags in hand, she hurried out of her chamber, joined Fenella in hers and then they finished packing and found a couple of men to carry their things to the last ship.

Dar just shook his head as he was overseeing the men's work. "Neither your da, nor your husband wanted you to join them."

Wolf was watching the horizon, but turned to see her

arrive and came to greet her, then went back to looking at where Quinn's ship had disappeared to, as if waiting for him to return from a fishing trip soon.

"Aye they will change their minds when they dinna have to sail from one place to the other and back again, just to take me to my new home."

"And Fenella?" Dar eyed her next.

"I will be on the mainland and that much closer to the location where Ewen lives. Besides, I wish to see where Avelina will live."

They were helped onto the ship, Wolf not hesitating to join her, and Dar said, "Let us hope you are no' involved in a battle or your da *and* your husband will have my head."

"Your head will remain on your shoulders," Avelina assured him and then they set sail on the last ship, another having already sailed.

"Do you think Quinn will really win?" Fenella asked Avelina as they found a place to sit out of the way of the men who were busy sailing the ship, Wolf staring off toward the mainland where they were headed.

"Aye. If the council doesna approve him taking over the clan, my da will hire him to work for him." Avelina prayed neither of them would be mortally wounded and that her clansmen wouldn't be embroiled in a fight.

***

Quinn, Baudwin, and Hamish watched Cormac's ship sailing for the mainland off in the distance.

"They'll see us," Hamish said.

"Aye," Quinn said.

Bringing others into the fight wouldn't set well with his

people. But Quinn needed Baudwin and his men to support him in this so that he could confront his brother with the truth without being cut down by him, or anyone else in the clan, first.

It was late when Cormac's men landed on the shore. They didn't return to the keep, but waited on shore to see what Baudwin wanted. Quinn suspected that they believed something was wrong for one of Baudwin's ships to join them after they killed two of Cormac's men for trying to steal Avelina away, if that had been the reason they had tried to access her chamber. Especially since Baudwin hadn't told them they were leaving for there so soon.

Then two additional ships would follow, in the event they needed more manpower.

"You wait aboard ship," Baudwin said to Quinn. "We'll signal when you can come ashore."

Quinn shook his head. "This is on me."

Baudwin smiled a little. "I will enjoy being your ally."

As soon as they reached the shore, several of Cormac's men pulled swords, but Liam held up his hand, signaling everyone to hold.

Then Liam stalked forward, grinning. "He canna kill you, mon. He canna kill you." Then he pulled Quinn into a heartfelt embrace.

"Aye. I told you so." Quinn returned the embrace.

"And the men he sent with you?" Liam asked. "The damned mercenaries?"

"They tried to kill me, but they were no' successful."

Liam quirked a smile. "I can see that."

Cormac's men were all standing around, waiting to see

what needed to be done, most ready to unsheathe their swords if this was going to be a fight, some already holding their swords.

"I take it you didna bring Avelina to marry Cormac," Liam said.

"No."

"You…" Liam glanced around at Cormac's men. He said for Quinn and Baudwin's hearing only, "You married the lass, didna you?"

Quinn didn't need to tell Liam the truth. His friend must have surmised from the smile he shared that he had.

Liam returned the smile, then his expression grew solemn. "God's knees, mon. Cormac will be…" He paused and frowned, glanced at all the men, and said to Quinn in a lowered voice again, "You're going up against him." He slapped Quinn's arm. "You know you're going to have trouble. Cormac's told everyone that you killed your da."

"But you know I didna."

"Aye. I was there. I've been trying to learn who was where on the battlefield when your da died. Most say they were too busy fighting to see what else was going on, just trying to stay alive and take the other men out. I couldna contradict your brother without a witness or two to speak up against the accusation, but so far no one has come forth."

"You're bound to get yourself killed."

"Aye. No one would come forth, probably figuring you'd died and it didn't matter what they said. If they spoke out against your brother, they'd end up like you. If you'd been dead, that is. Now that you're here, we'll find others

253

who can verify the truth. I'm with you on this. But what are you going to do now? Just go up to him and accuse him of lying about it? Of hiring men to kill you?" Liam asked.

"Aye."

"Mayhap no one but me will side with you."

Quinn motioned to the men with him. "They will."

Liam chuckled darkly. "Only you can attempt to steal a woman away from her kin and have her kin backing you in a takeover of your own clan."

"He had to prove himself worthy," Baudwin said.

"Aye," Hamish agreed. "He bested three of our fighters, and all three were vying to take over the clan."

Braddach, Odran, and Padruig stepped forth.

"Hamish means us," Odran said. "And let me tell you, only our former chief and our present chief could ever beat me."

Odran had surprised Quinn when he was the first onboard to go on this mission. He was still limping even.

Quinn turned to his clansmen and spoke aloud. "I've heard the horrible accusations that someone has made about me concerning my da. During the last battle, Liam and I were near each other when we were fighting, and nowhere near my da. I didna even learn about my da's death until after the battle ended. I believed, like everyone else, that he had been killed in battle—by the enemy. If this isna so and one of our men murdered him in cold blood, that man must be put to death. With that said, who told my brother that I had murdered my da? That man lied. To cover his own crime? Who is the accuser?"

His clansmen glanced around at each other. Quinn had

a real sense that his people had some doubts about the truth of the matter. Especially when Liam was vouching for him, and like Quinn, he was a well-respected fighter and liked by many. Though, like Quinn, they'd overstepped their bounds with kissing lasses wanting to be kissed when someone else wanted to marry them. And learned about it soon after. How were they to know that some clandestine meetings were going on between the men and lasses, unless the men declared their intent?

"As you might know"—and Quinn couldn't believe his clansmen would be unaware—"I've been sent into several ambushes for the past two months, since my da died. This time, Cormac lied to me about the lass wanting to wed him, not to mention the mercenaries who accompanied me attempted to murder me on the ship. And later, one who had survived, threatened to murder the woman who'd saved me from drowning, and I had to end his miserable existence. Tell me none of you have knowledge of any of this."

No one said anything, but several averted their eyes, looking at the ground, or at each other.

"What are you going to do about it?" Cael asked. He had been frail when he was a bairn, stout now, muscled, his black eyes narrowed, sharp, his wild black hair and beard making him appear to be more like an uncivilized beast, but his name was a reminder of how he'd been when he'd first floundered at his mother's breast. He'd always been loyal to Cormac, and he was one of the men that Quinn was sure he would have to fight if he had to battle his brother.

"I'll fight whoever accuses me of killing my da. And I'll

fight whoever has tried to have me murdered while I was doing my brother's bidding. I'm loyal to the clan and our chief, and have always been, but—"

"But you bring another force to fight your own kinsmen if you dinna get your way?" Cael asked.

Quinn smiled. "You know as well as I that had I come alone, I would have been killed before I ever reached my brother for an audience. Beyond that, everyone would believe what my brother has said. That I killed my da."

"I dinna," Liam said. "Quinn saved my life on the battlefield. We were watching each other's backs as much as we could. We were dismounted and fighting near each other. He never left my side. He couldna have been in two places at once. Whoever has accused him of killing his da outright lies. And for what reason? Everyone thought their da died in battle. Why falsely accuse Quinn now? Another attempt to get rid of him? Just in case he hadn't died when the ship he was on went down? Who gained the most if their da died?"

Cael laughed. "You have been skirting the issue all along. You believe Cormac wants you dead, Quinn? Then come out and say it."

"He might no' have anything to do with it. But someone else wants me dead, set up the ambushes, hired the mercenaries to kill me aboard the ship, and killed my da so my brother could rule the clan."

"What would the motivation be in that?" Cael asked.

"Someone who would be my brother's righthand man? Someone my da would never have elevated in position? Someone who knew if I ever had the chance to lead our people, he wouldna be my righthand man?" Quinn said.

Cael smiled darkly. "You mean me."

"Or the five others who are so fiercely loyal to my brother," Quinn said.

"You attack us for your own misdeeds? Who's to say you were ambushed at all? That the mercenaries tried to kill you? It's all your word against no one else's. There's no one to back you up." Dogmael was itching to kill Quinn now. He could see it in the way he gripped his drawn sword, his blue eyes dark and narrowed, his dark brown hair whipping across his face in the sea breeze.

"I do have witnesses for the ambushes, and I have witnesses concerning the mercenaries." Not who were now with them, but Fenella had heard the men's threats to kill Quinn if he had survived the shipwreck, and the one man intended to kill Avelina and him, thinking he was unarmed. So she was Quinn's witness to that. Whether his clansmen would believe the words of the two women was another story.

Even so, everyone looked back at Dogmael, waiting to see what he had to say to that. He just grunted.

"What are you going to do about it?" Cael asked again.

"Speak to my brother."

"And these men?" Cael motioned to the men with Quinn.

"We are here to make sure he gets to speak his mind before being cut down," Baudwin said.

"You mean to take over from your brother," Cael said to Quinn.

"If my brother is at the root of attempting to have me

killed and has lied about me killing my da, aye. I have no other choice."

Cael motioned with his sword to climb the hill to the castle. "After you."

All of his clansmen stepped out of Quinn's way to make a path for him and Liam, Baudwin, and the others.

"What have you been doing since I was stuck here, missing out on all your adventures?" Liam asked Quinn as they trudged up the hill.

"Same old thing. Trying to stay alive. It was a good thing you hadna come with me."

"I would have helped you to fight those bastards on the ship."

"Aye, but you dinna swim as well as me."

"True."

"Besides, if you had managed to make it to shore, Avelina couldna have saved us both if you'd been as injured as me."

Liam frowned at Quinn. "You were injured?"

"I've been healing up just fine."

"Och, and you plan to fight your brother when you are still suffering from injuries?"

"I fought them," Quinn said, motioning with his thumb to the three men following Baudwin and Hamish. "And I hadna even had that much time to recover."

"I have told the council already what I believe," Liam said.

Quinn glanced at his friend.

"It was a risk I had to take, hoping you were still alive, and afraid you'd make it back home, only to be thrown in the dungeon."

"And they said?"

"They said they needed proof. More than just my word that you are innocent in the case of your da's death. What will you do if your brother is innocent of trying to have you murdered?"

"Then I'll have to learn who is at the root of it."

"Then Quinn will come to work for me," Baudwin said. "If he's going to die, it'll be in battle against our enemies, not fighting his own clansmen."

Quinn smiled at him. "Thank you."

"You are married to my daughter, and I dinna want you to get yourself killed if you were to return here under your brother's rule. I wouldna want to fear for my daughter's life."

"Liam, when did the clan learn that I was stuck in the cave when we were eight?" Quinn asked Liam.

"You're asking about that now?"

"Do you know?" After Quinn and Avelina had talked about it in the island shelter, he hadn't been able to let go of it. He had to know the truth. "Didna anyone question where I was that night?" Quinn couldn't believe no one would have learned from his brother what had happened.

"Your brother said you wanted to prove your manhood and were staying in a cave for the night. Your da thought it would build character. But by the time we broke our fast the next morn, and you were still no' back, he asked your brother which cave you were staying in."

"He lied. Even back then, my brother lied."

Liam shook his head. "That was the only story we

knew. You were sick from the cold and lack of food and water, and everyone was so grateful to have you returned alive, you never said what had really happened."

"I thought he told Da, but it was too late to dig me out."

"You were stronger for it, despite what your brother did."

"He bolted when he heard the rocks caving in. I couldna make it out in time because I was farther back in the cave."

"Did he cause the cave-in?"

"I dinna think so. We were no' supposed to go there. Mayhap he was afraid he'd get into trouble if he said he'd been there too."

"Worse, that he came home and didna tell your da that you were there, until the next morn. He made it sound like he knew naught of the cave-in."

"Bastard."

"Aye."

They came within sight of the castle and Cael said, "These men need to be disarmed."

"They willna be," Quinn said. He wasn't allowing his brother the opportunity to kill Baudwin and his men, if Cormac decided to give the order.

"They canna," Liam agreed. "They're no' here to start a war. They're here only to see that Quinn has his say."

Dogmael snorted. "This is the only way you can take over the clan."

Quinn shook his head. "When have I ever said I wanted to?"

They approached the gates and the gate guards were frowning.

"They willna be disarmed," Quinn said, Liam echoing his statement.

Archers on the wall walk looked down at them, bows in hand, ready to shoot their target if anyone looked like they were going to attack their clansmen.

"They're no' here to fight anyone," Liam called out to those in the outer bailey and the men on the wall walk. "Only to learn the truth about what Quinn has been charged with."

"You canna all go inside," Cael warned.

"Then tell my brother that he can speak to me out here, before all of you. That way it will be fairer," Quinn said. He was afraid if he went in with just Baudwin and Liam, they'd be slaughtered, if his brother didn't want the truth to come out.

"Aye," an elder on the council said, joining them. Two more followed him, all gray haired, no longer fighting battles unless the battle came to them. "I'd like to know the truth. We all would. Here. Among your people, Quinn."

"If you have been wronged, 'tis your right to have the final say in this," another said. Elphin had always liked Quinn and had expressed some concern before when Quinn returned home, injured, when he'd fought the men who had ambushed him while doing his brother's bidding. "There have been too many attempts on your life to be mere coincidence. If I were you, I'd be thinking everyone was out to murder me. And for what reason? You have always been one of us, loyal to a fault. I dinna blame you for bringing our allies with you to see that you have a chance to speak freely."

"Aye," the first council member said. Enda was always a fair man.

Quinn thought he'd have a chance to sway him in his thinking.

The other four council members reserved judgment, not wanting to reveal how they felt about it one way or another.

"I'll ask Cormac to come and meet you here," Dogmael said. Then he hurried to the keep.

Quinn was surprised Cael hadn't gone to see Cormac first, unless he thought to take Quinn down if he believed he was a traitor to his da like his brother had said.

Cael gave Quinn an evil smirk. "If your brother didna want to kill you before, he sure will now."

CHAPTER 18

Cormac took forever to come out, armed, and shouting orders. "Arrest my brother at once! And any who interfere. If they fight, kill them!"

"That is always your way, Brother. Use someone else to kill me. If Da had been alive—"

"He isna because you murdered him!" Cormac spit out.

"If Da have been alive, he would give a mon a chance to plead his case. No' you, eh, Cormac? You'd have me put to death and silence me once and for all? Did you have Da murdered like you tried with me? Or did you kill him yourself? He was knocked off his horse, calling for your aid, from what others have said. Was he injured when you struck him down? Or was he just so shocked his first-born would do anything so odious as to attempt to kill him that he didna fight back? And why do you accuse me now of murdering him? Why no' after the battle? You thought I would die after you had men try to murder me. But I canna be killed."

"All lies. I knew you would twist the truth and return home to try and murder me!"

"I would have been loyal to you until the end. I still dinna know why you wish me dead. Whatever have I done to you?"

"I think I know the answer to that," Lorne said, entering the outer bailey with a dozen men. Like Liam, Lorne had always had Quinn's back. "While you were away cavorting with island beauties, Quinn, and from what I've learned, married the chief's daughter, I was questioning everyone I could about how your da died."

"We thought he'd died in battle. You know that as well as any man here who fought in that last battle with him. The men who took off with my brother to steal my bride away, had told me before they left how Quinn had killed our da," Cormac growled, pointing his sword at Lorne.

"Your paid mercenaries. Your paid assassins," Quinn said. None of his clansmen had liked the mercenaries, so that made them immediately suspect. Cormac must not have told their people that the mercenaries were the ones who claimed Quinn had murdered their da. Conveniently, they were dead and couldn't speak for themselves.

"Two of our men saw Cormac kill your da," Lorne said.

Cormac's face turned red. "They lie. Or mayhap you lie. Who are these men who never came forth with these accusations?"

"They both witnessed the chief call out to you for help when he was knocked from his horse. You rode to his aid, so the men thought. Instead of lifting your da onto your horse, you struck him a mortal blow with your sword. They were engaged in combat after that and you were busy fighting also. They never said anything because they knew you and your supporters would kill them. They thought the same if they told Quinn the truth, he couldna fight everyone, and that all three of them would die. But word has gotten out that you have tried to have Quinn murdered several times, and they finally told me the truth," Lorne said.

Quinn suspected his own brother had murdered their da, but hearing the truth made it seem unreal. "You killed Da to take over the clan! Why try to kill me then too?" But then Quinn added, "You thought I would try to do to you what you had done to Da!" As if he could be just like his brother!

"Is that no' why you are here now, Brother? With your own armed mercenaries?" Cormac waved his sword at the men with Quinn. "Though I dinna know how you could have encouraged them to come here, unless you planned to raid my treasury to pay them."

"We came with him as friends, no' for money," Baudwin said, "and we are more like kin to him than you deserve to be."

"You think you can take over with a handful of men when I have an army to back me?" Cormac had to know that none of his men, but a handful, were here to take his side.

And there were about sixty of Baudwin's men here, not a handful.

A man ran through the gates and shouted, "More come. Two more ships just reached our shore!"

Everyone looked at Quinn to explain why he was starting a war with them. "I only wanted to say what I came to say. I wasna anywhere near where my da was when he fell in battle. And I have witnesses to prove that. Now it seems there are witnesses who can testify to you having murdered our own da."

Two men finally came forth. Fanch and Griffith.

"We are ashamed we didna go before the council and tell the members what we had seen," Fanch said.

He was a sturdy warrior, but Quinn understood why he and the other clansman, Griffith, would have been reluctant to tell anyone the truth, worrying that no one would believe them and fearing for their lives, as well as for their families'.

"You lie!" Cormac shouted. "What is my brother paying you?"

"He has no money to pay anyone. We have to do what is right," Fanch said.

"You can fight me, and this time try to kill me by your own hand, or you can be judged by our people. Da was well-loved, you, no' so much." Quinn knew his people would despise him now for what he had done.

"You think you can take me? Then come and try," Cormac said.

"It willna be the same as sending your thugs to bushwhack me, or killing Da while he was on foot, and you were riding a horse, swinging your sword at him, when the last person he'd expect to betray him would be one of his sons—his eldest. His favorite."

Cormac had his sword out and Quinn unsheathed his. He hated to fight his own brother. He'd looked up to his brother, four years older than him. Cormac had taught him how to fight, to defend himself, and now Quinn was going to have to use everything he'd learned against his brother.

Cormac was sure-footed, fast, and deadly. He knew he was a dead man for murdering the chief. There was no way out for him. He would take Quinn's life at the same time, if he could, so that he couldn't take over the clan.

Everyone, his clansmen and Baudwin's, moved out of the way to give them room to fight.

Quinn had only faced his brother in practice and friendly competitions. He knew his strengths and weaknesses like Cormac knew his.

"Were you injured badly when the ship sank?" Cormac asked, as if mentioning Quinn's injuries would make him fear his older brother. He was eyeing Quinn, looking for any sign of weakness.

"Aye, I was, Brother. Will you do the civilized thing and give me another chance if I begin to falter?" As if his brother had been honorable in the least and would do anything decent regarding Quinn now.

"You are lying now, just as you lied before. Nay, I will give you no quarter."

A few men talked amongst themselves, but Quinn was concentrating on his brother, who wasn't making a move to take him down, just yet. Quinn suspected it was because Cormac wanted him to make the first move. He would have too. When it came to fighting his brother, Quinn had always been eager to prove to Cormac, and their da, that he could best him and would rush forth to take him on. And Cormac always got the best of him. This time, Quinn couldn't be so hasty. Not when it meant his life was at stake.

"You have never beat me in practice before, Quinn. You willna beat me now."

"He beat me," Odran said, slamming his fist to his chest. "And he'd suffered from injuries before he had to fight me. Only the former chief and our new chief could do so."

Cormac snickered. "You've never fought *me*." He turned his attention to Quinn. "Are you going to stand there all day, Quinn, or are you going to fight me? Afraid you're too injured to fight well? Afraid I'm going to beat you like I always do?"

"Why did you kill our da? Afraid he would choose me over you to succeed? Or just tired of being his second-in-command? You couldna wait to take over instead?"

That comment pushed Cormac into engaging Quinn. As soon as Cormac charged in to swing his sword at Quinn, he moved in and cut Cormac's sword arm. Cormac howled in pain and fell back.

Quinn had learned time and again that rushing to engage the enemy could have dire consequences. For the first time that he was battling his brother, he used more guarded measures. But the wound he'd given his brother didn't slow him down, only enraged him further.

His brother swung his sword at him again, and Quinn slammed his sword against Cormac's, blocking the blow, the two weapons clanging.

Heart racing, Quinn readied for another assault. But he wouldn't make the first strike against his brother in the beginning, hoping the tactic would rattle Cormac. Quinn wouldn't do what he normally did when fighting his brother. Maybe this time, he would be the victor.

His brother slashed at him again, and Quinn stopped him. This time, he struck at his brother, forcing Cormac back. And again, hitting hard, their swords striking, sparking. They parried and thrust, defended and attacked until they were both breathing hard, their hearts beating furiously.

"God's wounds, Brother," Cormac growled, his face red with exertion, sweat pouring off his brow, "when did you learn to fight?"

"From the best. You."

Cormac swung his sword, but Quinn finally found the opening he needed and thrust his sword into Cormac's chest. He'd never wanted it to end like this.

You killed our da was running through his mind like a mantra. *You killed our da for naught more than the lust for power.*

"Awww," Cormac groaned. He faltered, and Quinn pulled out his sword. Blood poured out of the wound, and Cormac clutched his chest. "You...would've...done"—he collapsed to his knees—"the same if..."

"Never." Quinn wasn't a murderer like his brother.

Cormac collapsed on the ground on his back and stared up at Quinn.

"It should never have been like this. Between you and me. Between Da and you," Quinn said.

Cormac snorted. "Now what? You'll... take over... the clan?"

"If the council agrees. Aye. But it never had to be this way."

Panting, Cormac closed his eyes, his hand over his chest, his other loosening on his sword grip. "He was...going"—Cormac coughed up blood—"God's knees"—he coughed again—"tell...council.."—his eyes fluttered open—"you...you were his choice."

In disbelief, Quinn stared at his brother. Now it all made sense. Why his brother felt he had to kill their da. The battle was a convenient way of making it appear that their da had fallen in the heat of combat.

"He favored you. Why would he change his mind?"

"Always...plan...once"—Cormac's chest heaved—"you... could...fight...me...and...win."

God's wounds. Why had his da never told Quinn? "Why blame me for our da's death? Why no' just let everyone believe he'd died in battle?"

"We started talking about what we saw," Fanch said.

"Aye, and your brother blamed you so if you returned, the council and the rest of us would think you were guilty and have you put to death," Griffith said.

Rasping for breath, Cormac closed his eyes.

"It didna have to be this way," Quinn said, angry that he had to kill his own brother.

"Aye, you...know...it...did." And then Cormac took a final ragged breath.

Quinn didn't feel any triumph in killing his brother.

"What do we do about the other men coming up the hill?" someone called out.

One of the council members said to Quinn, "The battle is done. We've already made a decision, based on your da's suggestion. We were only waiting until you could prove

yourself better than your brother in a fight. You'll lead us."
He was one of the men who'd reserved judgment, but he'd
come around quickly enough. Afraid Baudwin's men would
overwhelm the clan in a fight?

One of Baudwin's men approached Quinn. "Your wife
and Fenella came with our ship. They're still waiting aboard
to hear the outcome of what went on here today."

Quinn said to some of his clansmen, "Remove my
brother's body."

He couldn't believe his wife would come. Then again,
he could. "I accept the responsibility of leading the clan. I
will return with my wife, and we will be allied with Baudwin
and his men."

Before Quinn left to join his wife and escort her to the
keep, he turned to Cael and Dogmael. "You'll follow my
leadership?" He didn't need to have trouble with them also,
but if they wanted to fight him, it might as well be now.

Cael shrugged. "We were only waiting for you to make
a stand against your brother."

Dogmael agreed. "When the rumors surfaced that
Cormac was the one who murdered your da, we knew his
time to rule the clan was coming to an end."

Quinn considered the rest of Cormac's loyal men.

"We pledge our loyalty to you, our Chief," one after
another said.

"'Tis only right that we celebrate our new chief and his
bride's arrival. And the alliance with Baudwin and his
clansmen," Enda said. He knew how Quinn had to feel
about celebrating anything right now.

But it was important for Avelina to see his people

rejoice in her arrival and for Baudwin and his men to be treated as respected allies.

"Aye, make it so." Quinn heard his horse whinny at seeing him, and Quinn turned to observe a lad bringing Warrior to him.

"To fetch your bonny bride," the lad said.

"Aye." Quinn took hold of the reins.

Baudwin slapped Quinn on the back. "Go. Bring them here. You will have to counsel your wife to obey you better. I must speak with Fenella."

Another lad hurried to bring Cormac's horse to Quinn. "'Tis all right, is it no'? You will need the horse for the other lady."

"Aye, lad, you are right."

Then everyone began scurrying to prepare for the feast. Liam took charge of it. Dogmael led Baudwin's men to the barracks. Lorne escorted Baudwin and Hamish to the keep.

With the salty sea breeze sweeping his hair back, Quinn hurried down to the shore on his horse, pulling the other with him. One of Baudwin's men had already returned to tell them what was going on. Fenella, Avelina, and Wolf were trudging up the hill with the men, headed for the keep.

Avelina smiled at Quinn, and Wolf raced up to his horse and woofed. Quinn was thrilled to see Avelina's smiling face, and Fenella's too. Wolf was bouncing around like a puppy, wanting him to dismount and play with him. Quinn rode the rest of the way to reach the two women, leaped from his horse and grabbed Avelina up in his arms, swinging her around with jubilation. And then he stopped to kiss her, hugging her tight to his body, her feet still off the ground.

Tears filled her eyes, and she cupped his face in her soft hands. "I love you, Quinn." And that was all that she said.

"As I love you." He loved her for it, not asking any details, not telling him she was sorry it had to be this way. Just that she loved him. He kissed her deeply and then he set her on the ground. "My people are preparing a celebration. I suspect we should be there for it as I doubt anyone will wait on us."

"They wouldna dare."

One of Baudwin's men helped Fenella onto a horse, and Quinn lifted Avelina onto his. "You brought Wolf."

"Of course. He was sitting on the shore, watching your ship sail away. When I prepared to leave, he wouldna be left behind. No' that I planned to leave him there."

"What if I hadna won, Avelina?" he asked, pressing his mouth against her ear as they rode up the hill.

"I knew you would, if I were here."

"And Fenella?"

"She will stay with me until my da can escort her to see Ewen. You and I will go with her, aye?"

"Aye. To ensure this Ewen is the right man for her."

"I'm glad you are the right one for me."

***

The feasting lasted a week and it was decided that two of Baudwin's ships would return home while the men from the first ship would accompany Baudwin and Quinn, who would escort Fenella to see her prospective husband. Quinn would also ally with the clan if he found the man suitable enough to marry Avelina's cousin. Some of his men would also accompany them.

Lorne and Liam would be left in charge of the clan, but Dogmael and Cael also had important roles to play with training the men under Quinn's command.

For now, Quinn and Avelina sat on a piece of driftwood on the shore, looking out to where her island home was. Wolf chased a crab into a hole nearby.

"Your people are as wary of Wolf as mine are," Avelina said.

"Aye. They will come around. They love you though."

She smiled and rested her head against his shoulder. He wrapped his arm around her shoulders. "They love you too, Quinn. Fenella is worried about this Ewen. At least for me, I got to save you from our shore, and got to know you better, first."

"If he isna the one for her, we will look elsewhere for a good man for her."

Avelina sighed. "Thank you."

"I would do anything for you and your cousin, Avelina." He kissed her head.

Wolf raced into the water, snapping at the waves. Then he ran deeper into the water, grabbed a fish, and returned to shore.

"Good boy!" Avelina said.

Before either of them were prepared for what Wolf would do next, he raced to join them, and dropped the flopping fish onto Avelina's lap. She shrieked, and he shook the water from his coat. They both laughed.

"We finally taught him to share his food with us," Avelina said.

"I'm just glad he no longer checks to see if you're okay when we're making love." Quinn tossed the fish to Wolf. "That one's all yours."

Wolf happily scarfed it up and devoured it.

"Should we take him with us?"

"Aye. He is as much your protector as I am. If Ewen and Wolf dinna see eye-to-eye, we'll know he's no' the right man for Fenella."

"I couldna believe that first day you were on the island, and he wasna guarding you, but sleeping with you!"

"We were both cold."

She chuckled.

Just then Wolf came over to curl up next to them.

"Wolf, you are all wet," Avelina said, but her pushing him away wouldn't deter him from snuggling against them.

"Are you ready to take Fenella to see Ewen?" Quinn rose to his feet and helped Avelina up.

"Nay, but we need to go so you can return home and ensure your friends dinna think of taking over the clan in your absence."

Quinn took her hand and led her back up the hill. "They wouldna dare. They think I'm invincible. Only you and I know better."

She wrapped her arm around his waist. "I told Liam you looked like a God when you walked out of the sea."

Quinn laughed. "He told me. And he shared that bit of news with Lorne and more of our friends. Good thing they dinna know the truth."

"That's what made me love you just a little. You were so vulnerable and needed my help. But when I could have perished, you were there for me."

"I couldna let such a bonny lass, who was valiantly attempting to rescue me, drown." Quinn glanced back to see Wolf running to catch up to them, carrying another fish. "You know if we dinna take one of his offerings, he will think we dinna want him to catch fish for us."

"Take it then, but you will have to eat it."

"That one's yours, Wolf," Quinn said. "I wonder if our children will be so easily trained."

She looked up at him and smiled. "Only if you bribe them."

He loved his wife and was looking forward to settling down with her with his clan. He would cherish her always.

Avelina thought the world of Quinn and was amused that so many of his people truly thought he'd walked out of the ocean onto their shores that day, as if he were indestructible. She wasn't about to enlighten anyone. He was her warrior hero who had his vulnerabilities and she loved him for it.

She was glad Fenella had come to her so that she would rescue Quinn, and Fenella hadn't kept him for her own. Quinn was hers, now, and for always.

Wolf darted between them. And Wolf's too.

ABOUT THE AUTHOR

Bestselling and award-winning author Terry Spear has written over sixty paranormal romance novels and four medieval Highland historical romances. Her first werewolf romance, *Heart of the Wolf*, was named a 2008 *Publishers Weekly*'s Best Book of the Year, and her subsequent titles have garnered high praise and hit the *USA Today* bestseller list. A retired officer of the U.S. Army Reserves, Terry lives in Spring, Texas, where she is working on her next wolf, jaguar, cougar, and bear shifter romances, continuing with her Highland medieval romances, and having fun with her young adult novels. When she's not writing, she's photographing everything that catches her eye, making teddy bears, and playing with her Havanese puppies and grand-baby. For more information, please visit www.terryspear.com, or follow her on Twitter,

@TerrySpear. She is also on Facebook at

http://www.facebook.com/terry.spear. And on Wordpress

at: Terry Spear's Shifters http://terryspear.wordpress.com/

Note: I hope that you enjoyed My Highlander and hoped you loved their companion wolf as much as I did. He might not be a shifter, but he was loveable just the same. Thanks for reading my Highland series, The Highlanders!

ALSO BY TERRY SPEAR

Heart of the Cougar Series: Cougar's Mate, Book 1
Call of the Cougar, Book 2
Taming the Wild Cougar, Book 3
Covert Cougar Christmas (Novella)
Double Cougar Trouble, Book 4
Cougar Undercover, Book 5

* * *

Heart of the Bear Series

Loving the White Bear, Book 1

* * *

The Highlanders Series: His Wild Highland Lass (Prequel
Novella), Vexing the Highlander (Prequel Novella),
Winning the Highlander's Heart (Book 1), The
Accidental Highland Hero (Book 2), Highland Rake
(Book 3), Taming the Wild Highlander (Book 4), The
Highlander (Book 5), Her Highland Hero (Book 6), The

Viking's Highland Lass (Book 7), My Highlander (Book 8)

Other historical romances: Lady Caroline & the Egotistical Earl, A Ghost of a Chance at Love

* * *

Heart of the Wolf Series: Heart of the Wolf, Destiny of the Wolf, To Tempt the Wolf, Legend of the White Wolf, Seduced by the Wolf, Wolf Fever, Heart of the Highland Wolf, Dreaming of the Wolf, A SEAL in Wolf's Clothing, A Howl for a Highlander, A Highland Werewolf Wedding, A SEAL Wolf Christmas, Silence of the Wolf, Hero of a Highland Wolf, A Highland Wolf Christmas, A SEAL Wolf Hunting; A Silver Wolf Christmas, A SEAL Wolf in Too Deep, Alpha Wolf Need Not Apply, Billionaire in Wolf's Clothing, Between a Rock and a Hard Place (2017), White Wolf Christmas (2017), SEAL Wolf Undercover (2017)

SEAL Wolves: To Tempt the Wolf, A SEAL in Wolf's Clothing, A SEAL Wolf Christmas, A SEAL Wolf Hunting, A SEAL Wolf in Too Deep, SEAL Wolf Undercover (2017)

Silver Town Wolves: Destiny of the Wolf, Wolf Fever, Dreaming of the Wolf, Silence of the Wolf, A Silver Wolf Christmas, Alpha Wolf Need Not Apply, Between a Rock and a Hard Place (2017), All's Fair in Love and Wolf (2018)

White Wolves: Legend of the White Wolf, White Wolf

Christmas (2017), Flight of the White Wolf (2018)

Billionaire Wolves: Billionaire in Wolf's Clothing, Billionaire Wolf Christmas (2018)

Highland Wolves: Heart of the Highland Wolf, A Howl for a Highlander, A Highland Werewolf Wedding, Hero of a Highland Wolf, A Highland Wolf Christmas

* * *

Heart of the Jaguar Series: Savage Hunger, Jaguar Fever, Jaguar Hunt, Jaguar Pride, A Very Jaguar Christmas

* * *

Romantic Suspense: Deadly Fortunes, In the Dead of the Night, Relative Danger, Bound by Danger

* * *

Vampire romances: Killing the Bloodlust, Deadly Liaisons, Huntress for Hire, Forbidden Love

Vampire Novellas: Vampiric Calling, Siren's Lure, Seducing the Huntress

* * *

Futuristic/Science Fiction Romance: Galaxy Warrior

Other Romance: Exchanging Grooms, Marriage, Las Vegas Style

* * *

Teen/Young Adult/Fantasy Books

The World of Fae:
The Dark Fae, Book 1
The Deadly Fae, Book 2
The Winged Fae, Book 3
The Ancient Fae, Book 4
Dragon Fae, Book 5
Hawk Fae, Book 6
Phantom Fae, Book 7
Golden Fae, Book 8
Falcon Fae, Book 9

The World of Elf:

The Shadow Elf
The Darkland Elf (TBA)

Blood Moon Series:

Kiss of the Vampire
The Vampire...In My Dreams
Demon Guardian Series:

The Trouble with Demons
Demon Trouble, Too
Demon Hunter (TBA)

Non-Series for Now:

Ghostly Liaisons
The Beast Within
Courtly Masquerade
Deidre's Secret

The Magic of Inherian:

The Scepter of Salvation
The Mage of Monrovia
Emerald Isle of Mists (TBA)

    Working on the next Polar Bear shifter book next. More books to come! Terry

Made in the USA
Las Vegas, NV
01 October 2023

78367979R00173